PENGUIN MODERN CLASSICS

1570

VALMOUTH
PRANCING NIGGER
THE ECCENTRICITIES OF CARDINAL PIRELLI

RONALD FIRBANK

Arthur Annesley Ronald Firbank was born in 1886, a grandson of Joseph Firbank, a Durham miner who later amassed a fortune as a railway contractor. His mother, to whom he was greatly attached, was an Irishwoman of considerable beauty and cultivated tastes. Owing to a weak constitution, Firbank was educated mainly at home; in 1906 he went to Trinity Hall, Cambridge, where he was received into the Roman Catholic Church.

Until 1914 Firbank travelled a good deal, but lived mainly in London, habitué of the Café Royal, well-known for his extreme and deliberate aestheticism, his sinuous, loosely-jointed figure, and his morbid nervousness, which issued in hysterical laughter and an elaborately capricious manner. The First World War was spent in retreat in Oxford; then until his death in Rome in 1926 he travelled widely.

Firbank's first work was published in 1905, a volume of two short stories, *Odette d'Antrevernes* and *A Study in Temperament*. Ten years later Grant Richards brought out his first novel, *Vainglory*. The following were published later, all initially at the author's own expense: *Inclinations* (1916); *Caprice* (1917); *Valmouth* (1919); *The Princess Zoubaroff*, a play (1920); *Santal* (1921); *The Flower Beneath the Foot* (1923); *Prancing Nigger* (1924 – published in England 1925 under Firbank's original title, *Sorrow in Sunlight*); *Concerning the Eccentricities of Cardinal Pirelli* (1926). *The Artificial Princess* (1934) appeared posthumously; it had been written before *Vainglory* but put away and forgotten by the author.

RONALD FIRBANK

Valmouth
Prancing Nigger
Concerning the Eccentricities
of Cardinal Pirelli

PENGUIN BOOKS

Penguin Books Ltd, Harmondsworth, Middlesex, England
Penguin Books Pty Ltd, Ringwood,
Victoria, Australia

—

Valmouth first published by Grant Richards 1919

Prancing Nigger (originally *Sorrow in Sunlight*) first published by
Grant Richards 1924

Concerning the Eccentricities of Cardinal Pirelli
first published by Grant Richards 1926

Published in Penguin Books
by arrangement with Gerald Duckworth & Co. Ltd 1961
Reprinted 1964

—

The Complete Ronald Firbank, containing all his
published work in a single volume, with a new introduction
by Anthony Powell, was published by
Duckworth in 1961

Made and printed in Great Britain
by Cox and Wyman Ltd
London, Reading, and Fakenham
Set in Monotype Garamond

66108290

Contents

VALMOUTH

A Romantic Novel

I

DAY was drooping on a fine evening in March as a brown barouche passed through the wrought-iron gates of Hare-Hatch House on to the open highway.

Beneath the crepuscular, tinted sky the countryside stretched away, interspersed with hamlets, meads and woods, towards low, loosely engirdling hills, that rose up against the far horizon with a fine monastic roll.

Although it was but the third month of the year, yet, from a singular softness of the air, already the trees were in full, fresh leaf. Along the hedgerows hawthorns were in bloom, while the many wild flowers by the roadside scented in fitful whiffs an invigorating, caressing breeze.

Seated immediately behind the coachman in the shell-like carriage was a lady no longer young. Her fragile features, long and pointed, were swathed, quasi-biblically, in a striped Damascus shawl that looked Byzantine, at either side of which escaped a wisp of red, crimped hair. Her big, wide eyes, full of innocent, child-like wonder, were set off by arched auburn brows that in the twilight seemed almost to be phosphorescent.

By her side reclined a plump, placidish person, whose face was half concealed beneath a white-lace coalscuttle hat.

'Some *suppose* . . . while *others* – ; again, I'm told . . . And in *any case*, my dear!' The voice came droning in a monotonous, sing-song way.

Facing the ladies a biretta'd priest appeared to be perusing a little, fat, black, greasy book of prayers which he held aslant so as to catch the light. Every now and then he would raise a cold, hypnotic eye above the margin of his page towards the ladies *vis-à-vis*.

'Of whom are you so kindly speaking, Mrs Thoroughfare?' he inquired at length.

The head beneath the coalscuttle-shaped hat drooped confused.

'I? Oh, my dear Father – !'

'Yes? my dear child? . . .'

'I was only telling Mrs Hurstpierpoint how – '

Mrs Hurstpierpoint – the dowager of the gleaming brows – leaned forward all at once in the carriage and pulled the checkstring attached to her footman's arm.

'Benighted idiot!' she exclaimed.

The fellow turned towards his mistress a melancholy, dreamy face that had something of a *quia multum amavit* expression in its wizen whiteness, and raised stiffly to a frayed silk cockade a long, bare hand.

'Didn't I say, blunt-headed booby, to Valmouth?'

'To Valmouth?'

'By way of Fleet. *Pardon*, Thoroughfare,' the dowager murmured, 'you were saying – '

'Evil, evil, evil,' her companion returned. 'Nothing but slander, wickedness and lies. *N'est-ce pas,* Father Colley?'

'What is your book, Father Colley-Mahoney?' Mrs Hurstpierpoint asked.

'St Stanislaus-Kostka, my child.'

'Kostka – ! It sounds like one of those islands, those savage islands, where my big, handsome, strong, – *and* delicate! – darling Dick stopped at once, just to write to his old mother,' Mrs Thoroughfare declared.

'Where is he now, Eliza?'

'Off the coast of Jamaica. His *ship* – ' she broke off as a voice full and flexible rose suddenly from behind a burgeoning quincunx of thorns:

'I heard the voice of Jesus say-y-y! Yahoo, to heel. Bad dog.'

'It's that crazy Corydon,' Mrs Thoroughfare blinked.

'Which, dear, crazy?'

'David Tooke – the brother, you know, of that extraordinarily extraordinary girl.'

'Thoroughfare.'

'Father?'

'That tongue.'

'The last time Dick was at Hare, I thought – '

'*Meet me in glow-ry by the gate o' pearl.* Hi, Douce!' the voice
irrelevantly veered, as, over a near meadow, barking lustily,
sprang a shaggy sheep-dog. 'Hi, Douce boy! ... Doucey!
Douce!'

The Priest pulled the light merino carriage rug higher about
his knees.

'How,' he addressed Mrs Hurstpierpoint, whose chevelure
in the diminishing daylight was taking on almost the appearance of an aureole, 'how if the glorious Virgin required you
to take this young fellow under your wing?'

Mrs Hurstpierpoint bent thoughtfully her eyes to the somewhat 'phallic' passementerie upon her shawl.

'For the sake, I presume,' she queried, 'of his soul?'

'Precisely.'

'But is he ripe?' Mrs Thoroughfare wondered.

'Ripe?'

'I *mean* – '

There was a busy silence.

Descending a narrow tree-lined lane the carriage passed
into a leisurely winding road, bounded by market-gardens
and the River Val. Through a belt of osier and alder Valmouth, with its ancient bridge and great stone church, that
from the open country had the scheming look of an ex-
cathedral, showed a few lit lamps.

Mrs Thoroughfare twittered.

'I did require a ribbon, a roughish ribbon,' she announced,
'and to call as well at the music-shop for those Chopin
sonatas.'

'A "roughish" ribbon?' Father Colley-Mahoney echoed in
searching tones. 'And pray, might I ask, what is that?'

'It's – Oh, Father.'

'Is it silk? Or satin? Or is it velvet? Is it', he conscientiously
pressed, 'something rose-leafy? Something lilac? ... Eh?
Or sky-blue, perhaps? ... Insidious child!'

'Insidious, Father?'

'Prevaricating.'

'Pax, Father,' Mrs Thoroughfare beseeched.

Father Colley-Mahoney gazed moodily above the floppy

fabric of her hat at an electric two-seater that was endeavouring to forge by the barouche from behind.

As it came abreast of it the occupants, a spruce, middle-aged man, and a twinkling negress, who clasped in her arms a something that looked to be an india-rubber coil, respectfully bowed.

'Dr Dee, and la Yajñavalkya!'

'Those appliances of hers – ; that she flaunts!'

'In massaging her "cases,"' Mrs Thoroughfare *sotto-voce* said, 'I'm told she has a trick of – um.'

'Oh?'

'And of – um!'

'Indeed?'

'So poor Marie Wilks' nurse told my maid . . .'

'When', Father Colley-Mahoney murmured, '*was* Miss Wilks a hundred?'

'Only last week.'

'Nowadays', Mrs Hurstpierpoint commented, 'around Valmouth centenarians will be soon as common as peas!'

'The air,' Mrs Thoroughfare sniffed, 'there's no air to compare to it.'

'For the sake of veracity, I should be tempted to qualify that.'

'I fancy I'm not the only one, Father, to swear by Valmouth air!'

'Valmouth air, Valmouth air.'

'At the Strangers' Hotel', Mrs Thoroughfare giddily went on, 'it seems there's not a single vacant bed. No; nor settle either. . . . Victor Vatt, the delicate *paysagiste* – the English Corot – came yesterday, and Lady Parvula de Panzoust was to arrive today.'

'I was her bridesmaid some sixty years ago – and she was no girl then,' Mrs Hurstpierpoint smiled.

'She stands, I fear, poor thing, now, for something younger than she looks.'

'Fie, Thoroughfare!'

'Fie, Father?'

'*La jeunesse – hélas,*' Mrs Hurstpierpoint softly said, '*n'a qu'un temps.*'

Father Colley-Mahoney looked absently away towards the distant hills whose outlines gleamed elusively beneath the rising moon.

Here and there, an orchard, in silhouette, showed all in black blossom against an extravagant sky.

2

TROTTING before his master, the fire-flies singing his tale, ran the watch-dog Douce. From the humid earth beneath his firm white paws the insects clamoured zing-zing-zing. Nuzzling intently the ground, sampling the pliant grasses, he would return from time to time to menace some lawless calf or cow.

Following a broken trackway through the deserted cornland, the herd filed lazily towards the town in a long, close queue. Tookes Farm, or Abbots Farm, as it indifferently was called, whither they now were bent, lay beneath the decayed walls of St Veronica, the oldest church in the town. Prior to the Reformation the farm buildings (since rebuilt and considerably dwindled) had appertained, like much of the glebeland around Valmouth, to the Abbots of St Veronica, when at the confiscation of the monasteries by the Crown one Thierry Monfaulcon Tooke, tennis-master to the Court of King Henry VIII, feinting to injure himself one day while playing with the royal princesses, had been offered by Henry, through their touching entreaties 'in consideration of his mishap,' the Abbey Farm of St Veronica's, then recently vacated by the monks; from which same Thierry (in the space of only six generations) the estate had passed to his descendants of the present time. Now in the bluey twilight as seen from the fields the barns and outhouses appeared really to be more capacious than the farm itself. With its whitewashed walls and small-paned latticed windows it showed poorly enough between the two sumptious wheat-ricks that stood reared on either side. Making their way across the long cobble bridge that spanned the Val, the cattle turned into an elmlined lane that conducted to the farmyard gates, where, pottering expectantly, was a tiny boy.

At a bark from Douce he swung wide a creaking crossbarred gate overspread by a thorn-tree all in flower.

With lethargic feet the animals stumbled through, proceeding in an automatic way to a strip of water at the far end of the yard into which they turned. By the side of it ran an open hangar upheld by a score of rough tarred posts. Against these precocious calves were wont as a rule to rub their crescent horns. Within showed a wagon or two, and a number of roosting doves.

Depositing his scrip in the outhouse the cowherd glanced around.

'Where's Thetis got?' he asked, addressing the small boy, who, brandishing a broken rhubarb-leaf, was flitting functionarily about.

'Thetis? ... She's,' he hopped, 'standing in the river.'

'What's she standing there for?'

'Nothing.'

'... Must I thrash you, Bobby Jolly?'

'Oh, don't David.'

'Then answer me quick.'

'When the tide flows up from Spadder Bay she pretends it binds her to the sea. Where her sweetheart is. Her b-betrothed. ... Away in the glorious tropics.'

' 'Od! You're a simple one; you are!'

'Me?'

'Aye, you.'

'Don't be horrid, David to me. ... You mustn't be. It's bad enough quite without.'

''Od.'

'What with granny – '

'She'll not be here for long.'

'I don't think she'll die just yet.'

'It's a cruel climate,' the young man ruefully said, looking impatiently up through his eyelashes towards the stars.

It was one of the finest nights imaginable. The moon reigned full in the midst of a cloudless sky. From the thorn-tree by the gate the sound of a bird singing floated down exuberantly through the leaves.

'Aye, cruel,' he muttered, shouldering a pitch-fork and going out into the yard. As he did so the church clock rang out loudly in the air above.

'Shall I find 'ee, Thetis?'

'Nay. Maybe I'll go myself.'

Beyond the low yard wall gleamed the river, divided from the farm by a narrow garden parcelled out in vegetables and flowers.

A cindered pathway sloping between spring-lettuces and rows of early tulips whose swollen calyxes, milk-white, purple, and red, probed superbly the moon-mist, led to the water's edge where, clinging to the branches of a pollard-willow, a girl was gently swaying with the tide. On her head, slightly thrown back, and slashed all over with the shadow of the willow leaves, was perched a small sailor's toque adorned with a spread gannet's wing that rose up venturesomely from the ribboned cord. Her light print frock, carelessly caught about her, revealed her bare legs below the knees.

The cowherd paused hesitant.

'Thetis – !' he called.

Self-absorbed, wrapped in enchanting fancies, she turned: 'H'lo?'

'Come in now.'

'I shan't.'

'Come in, Thetis.'

'I won't. I will not.'

'You'll catch your death!'

'What of it?'

'The-tis. ...'

With a laugh, she whisked further out into the stream.

Through her parted fingers, in microscopic wavelets, it swept, all moon-splashed from the sea.

Laughing, she bent her lips to the briny water.

3

In a little back sitting-room overlooking the churchyard
Granny Tooke, in a high rush-chair, was sharing a basin of
milk with the cat.

It was her 'Vibro day', a day when a sound like wild-bees
swarming made ghostly music through the long-familiar
room. Above the good green trees the venerable wood dial
of St Veronica's great clock informed her that, in the normal
course of things, Madam Yajñavalkya and her instruments
should already be on their way.

'Was there ever a cat like ye for milk, Tom?' the old lady
wondered, setting down the half-emptied bowl on the whatnot
beside her, and following with a poulterer's discerning eye
the careless movements of the farm pigeons as they preened
themselves on the long gross gargoyles of the church.

Once, long ago, in that same building she had stood a
round-cheeked bride. Alas for life's little scars! . . . Now, all
wrapped up like a moulting canary, her dun, lean face was
fuller of wrinkles than a withered russet. Nevertheless, it was
good still to be alive! Old Mrs Tooke sighed with self-com-
placency as her glance took in the grave-ground, in whose
dark, doughy soil so many former cronies lay asleep. It was a
rare treat for her to be able, without any effort, to witness
from time to time a neighbour's last impressive pomps; to
watch 'the gentlemen' in their tall town tiles 'bearing up
poor fellows'; to join (unseen in her high-rush-chair, herself
in carpet-slippers) in the long, lugubrious hymn; to respire
through the window chinks of her room the faint exotic
perfume of aromatic flowers from a ground all white with
wreaths.

But today, there were no obsequies to observe at all.

Through the window glass she could see Maudie and
Maidie Comedy, daughters of Q. Comedy, Esq., the local
estate agent and auctioneer, amusing themselves by making

daisy chains by the mortuary door, while within the church some one – evidently not the vicar's sister – was casting the stale contents of an altar-vase through a clerestory window (sere sweet by sweet), quite callous of passers-by.

Mrs Tooke blew pensively the filmy skin forming upon her milk. A long sunbeam lighting up the whatnot caused the great copper clasp of her Bible to emit a thousand playful sparks, bringing to her notice somewhat glaringly a work of fiction that assuredly wasn't hers. . . . Extending a horny hand towards it, she had hardly made out a line when her grand-daughter looked languorously in.

'Your towels are nicely steaming,' she said, resting her prepossessing, well-formed face against the polished wood-work of the door.

Mrs Tooke coughed dryly.

'So far', she murmured, 'Mrs Yaj ha'n't come.'

'It's such a splendid morning.'

'Where's David?'

'He went out early with the barley-mow.'

'Any orders?'

'The hotel only – extra butter.'

'Be sure to say it's risen. Butter and eggs', Mrs Tooke dramatically declared, 'have gone up. And while you're at the Strangers' you might propose a pair of pigeons, or two, to the cook.'

Miss Tooke turned yearningly her head.

'You'd think,' she faltered, 'they were seagulls, poor darlings, up there so white.'

'If only I could get about the place', Mrs Tooke restively pursued, 'as once I did.'

'Maybe with warmer weather here you will. This very night the old sweetbrier tree came out. The old sweetbrier! And none of us thought it could.'

'In heaven's name,' her grandmother peevishly snapped, 'don't let me hear you talk of thinking. A more feather-brained girl there never lived.'

'I often think, at any rate', Miss Tooke replied, 'I was born for something *more brilliant* than waiting on you.'

'Impudent baggage! Here, take it – before I tear it.'

'My library book?'

'Pah to the library. I wish there was none.'

Miss Tooke shrugged slightly her shoulders.

'There's Douce barking,' she said, 'I expect it's Mrs Yaj.'

And in effect a crisp rat-a-tat on the yard-door gate was followed by a majestical footfall on the stair.

'Devil dog, pariah! Let go of me,' a voice came loudly drifting from below; a voice, large, deep, buoyant, of a sonorous persuasiveness, issuing straight from the entrails of the owner.

Mrs Tooke had a passing palpitation.

'Put the chain on Douce, and make ready the thingamies!' she commanded, as Mrs Yajñavalkya, wreathed in smiles, sailed briskly into the room.

She had a sheeny handkerchief rolled round and round her head, a loud-dyed petticoat and a tartan shawl.

'Forgive me I dat late,' she began. 'But I just dropped off to sleep again – like a little chile – after de collation.'

'Howsomever!' Mrs Tooke exclaimed.

'Ah! de clients, Mrs Tooke!' The negress beamed. 'Will you believe it now, but I was on my legs this morning before four! ... Hardly was there a light in the sky when an old gentleman he send for me to de Strangers' Hotel.'

Mrs Tooke professed astonishment.

'I understood you never "took" a gentleman,' she said.

'No more do I, Mrs Tooke. Only', Mrs Yajñavalkya comfortably sighed. 'I like to relieve my own sex.'

'Up at four!' Mrs Tooke archly quavered.

'And how do you find yourself today, Mrs Tooke? How is dat sciatica ob yours?'

'To be open with you, Mrs Yaj, I feel today as if all my joints want oiling!'

'What you complain ob, Mrs Tooke, is nothing but stiffness – due very largely from want ob par. Or (as we Eastern women sometimes say) from want ob vim. Often de libber you know it get sluggish. But it will pass. ... I shall not let – you hear me? – I shall not let you slip through my fingers: oh no: your life wif me is so precious.'

'I can't hope to last very much longer, Mrs Yaj, anyway, I suppose.'

'That is for me to say, Mrs Tooke,' the imperious woman murmured, beginning to remove, by way of preliminary, the numerous glittering rings with which her hands were laden.

'Heysey-ho!' the old lady self-solicitously sighed, 'she's getting on.'

'And so's de time, Mrs Tooke! But have no fear. Waited for as I am by a peeress of distinction, I would never rush my art, especially wif you. No; oh no. You, my dear, are my most beautiful triumph! Have I not seen your precious life fluttering away, spent? Den at a call . . . I . . . wif my science – wif dese two hand have I not restored you to all de world's delights?'

'Delights,' Mrs Tooke murmured, going off into a mournful key. 'Since the day my daughter-in-law – Charlotte Carpster that was – died in child-bed, and my great, bonny wild-oat of a son destroyed himself in a fit of remorse, there's been nothing but trouble for me.'

'And how is your young grandchild's erot-o-maniah, Mrs Tooke? Does it increase?'

'God knows, Mrs Yaj, what it does.'

'We Eastern women', Mrs Yajñavalkya declared, drawing off what perhaps was once her union-ring, 'never take lub serious. And w'y is dis, Mrs Tooke? – Because it is so serious!'

'Love in the East Mrs Yaj, I presume, is *only* feasible indoors?'

'Nobody bothers, Mrs Tooke. Common couples wif no place else often go into de jungle.'

'Those cutting winds of yours must be a bar to courting.'

'Our cutting winds! It is you who have de cutting winds. . . . It is not us. . . . No; oh no. In de East it is joy, heat!'

'Then where do those wicked blasts come from?'

'Never you mind now, Mrs Tooke, but just cross dose two dear knees ob yours, and do wot I bid you. . . . Dis incipient pass', the beneficent woman explained, seating herself in the window-bench facing Mrs Tooke's arm-chair, 'is a daisy. And dat is sure, O Allah la Ilaha', she gurgled, 'but I shall have you soon out in de open air again, I hope, and den you shall visit *me*. . . . De white acacia-tree in my back garden is something so beautiful dis year; at dis season it even eclipse my holly. . . . Ah, Mrs Tooke! Whenebber I look at a holly it put me in mind ob my poor Mustapha again. It has just de same playful prickle as a mastodon's moustache. Husband and wife ought to cling together, Mrs Tooke; if only for de sake ob de maintenance; it's hard often, my dear, for one in de professional-way to make both ends meet; clients don't always pay; you may rub your arms off for some folk (and include all de best specifics), but never a dollar will you see!'

'Howsomever,' Mrs Tooke exclaimed, eyeing mistrustfully her granddaughter, who had re-entered the room unobtrusively with the towels.

She had a sun-hat on, equipped to go out.

'Where are you off so consequential?' the old lady interrogatively said.

'Nowhere in particular.'

'In that big picture-hat – ? Don't tell me!'

'I shall be back again, I dare say, before you're ready,' Miss Tooke replied, withdrawing on tiptoe from the room.

'Dat enlarged heart should be seen to, Mrs Tooke. Do persuade her now to try my sitz-baths. I sell ze twelve tickets ver cheap – von dozen for only five shillings,' the young girl could hear the mulattress murmur as she closed the door.

Taking advantage of her grandame's hour of treatment, it was her habit, whenever this should occur, to sally forth for a stroll. Often she would slip off to Spadder Bay and lie upon the beach there, her pale cheek pressed to the wet sea-shingle; oftener perhaps she would wander towards Hare-Hatch House in the hope of a miraculous return.

This morning her feet were attracted irresistibly towards Hare.

Crossing the churchyard into the Market Square, where, above booths and shops and the flowered façade of the Strangers' Hotel, towered the statue of John Baptist Daleman,

b. 1698, *ob.* 1803, Valmouth's illustrious son, Miss Tooke
sauntered slowly across the old brick bridge that spanned the
Val. Here, beneath a cream canvas sunshade traced at the
borders with narrow lines of blue, sat Victor Vatt, the landscape artist, a colour-box upon his knee. At either side of
him crouched a pupil – young men who, as they watched the
veteran painter's hand, grew quite hot and red and religious-
looking.

Bearing on, Miss Tooke branched off into an unfrequented
path that led along the river-reach, between briers and little
old stunted pollard-willows, towards Hare. Kingfishers
emeralder than the grass passed like dream-birds along the
bank. Wrapped in fancy, walking in no great hurry, she would
pause, from time to time, to stand and droop, and dream and
die. Between the sodden, creaking bark of pollard-willows,
weeping for sins not theirs, the sea, far off, showed pulsating
in the sun.

> 'I loved a man
> And he sailed away,
> Ah hé, ah hé,'

she sang.

From Valmouth to Hare-Hatch House was reckoned a
longish mile. Half buried in cedar woods, it stood on high
ground above the valley of the Val, backed by the bluish hills
of Spadder Tor. Ascending a zigzag track she entered a small
fir plantation that was known by most people thereabouts as
Jackdaw Wood; but, more momentously, for her it was *the*
wood. How sweet he had kissed her in its kindly gloom. . . .
On those dead fir-needles hand in hand, his bright eyes bent
to hers (those dear entrancing eyes that held the glamour of
foreign seaports in them), he had told her of her goddess
namesake of Greece, of the nereid Thetis, the sister of Calypso,
and the mother of Achilles, the most paradoxical of all the
Greeks. On these dead fir-needles he had told her of his ship –
the *Sesostris* – and of his middy-chum, Jack Whorwood, who
was not much over fifteen, and the youngest hand on board.
'That little lad,' he had said, with a peculiar smile that
revealed his regular pointed teeth, 'that little lad, upon a

cruise, is, to me, what Patroclus was to Achilles, and even more.'

Ruminating, she roamed along, brushing the rose-spiked self-heal and and the red-thimbled fox-gloves with her dress. Upon a fitful breeze a wailing repeated cry of a peacock smote like music on her ear and drew her on. Striking the highway beyond the little copse she skirted the dark iron palings enclosing Hare. Through the armorial great gates – open as if expectant – the house lay before her across a stretch of drive.

Halting she stood, lost in amorous conjectures, surveying with hungry eyes the sun-bleached, mute façade.

Oh, which amongst those tiers of empty windows lit his room?

Above each tall window was a carved stone mask. Strange chiselled faces, singularly saturnine ... that laughed and leered and frowned. His room perhaps faced the other way? Her eyes swept the long pseudo-classic pile. Above the gaunt grey slates showed the tops of the giant cryptomerias upon the lawn.

She had never penetrated there.

To one side of it on a wooded hillock rose a garden temple open to the winds, its four white columns uplifting each a bust.

Beneath the aerial cupola three people at present were seated, engaged in tranquil chat.

Transfixed, Miss Tooke considered them. She was there, in spirit, too, 'holding her own', as her grandmother would have said, with those two patrician women and the priest.

4

THEY were ringing the angelus. Across the darkling meadows, from the heights of Hare, the tintinnabulation sounded mournfully, penetrating the curl-wreathed tympanums of Lady Parvula de Panzoust.

'There's the dinner-bell, coachman!' her ladyship impatiently exclaimed, speaking through the ventilator of her cab. 'Please to get on.'

Whipping up his horse with an inventive expletive, the driver started forward at a trot.

Lady Parvula relaxed.

The invitation to dinner at Hare-Hatch House had included her daughter, the Hon. Gilda Vintage, as well; a fair girl whose vast fortune as sole heiress of the late Lord de Panzoust caused her to be considered one of the most tempting present *partis* in the land. Bring Gilda, Mrs Hurstpierpoint had written to Lady Parvula, 'so that, not unlikely', her ladyship blissfully mused, 'Captain Thoroughfare will be there!'

Captain Thoroughfare.

There were rumours, to be sure, he was above Love.

Lady Parvula studied dreamily her hands. (She had long, psychic, pallid, amorous fingers, much puffed at the tips and wrinkled.)

'Oh, how I wish *I* were!' she reflected. 'But that is something I never was. . . . Who was that I saw by the ditch just now? *Quel joli garçon!* Quite – as Byron said of D'Orsay – a "*cupidon déchaîné*." . . . Such a build. And such a voice! Especially, when he called his horrid dog to heel. "*I heard the voice of Jesus say, yahoo – yahoo, bad dog!*"'

Lady Parvula threw a little palpitating smile towards the evening star.

'He must be mine', she murmured, 'in my manner . . . in my way . . . I always told my dear late Lord I could love a shepherd – peace be to his soul!'

A grey-haired manservant, and a couple of under-footmen wearing the violet vestments of the House-basilica (and which for moral reasons they were requested of an evening to retain), were meanwhile awaiting the arrival of the Valmouth cab, while conversing in undertones among themselves as servants sometimes do.

'Dash their wigs!' the elderly man exclaimed.

'What's the thorn, Mr ffines?' his colleague, a lad with a face gemmed lightly over with spots, pertly queried.

'The thorn, George?'

'Tell us.'

'I'd sooner go round my beads.'

'Mrs Hurst cut compline, for a change, tonight.'

'. . . She's making a studied toilet, so I hear.'

'Gloria! Gloria! Gloria!'

'Dissenter.'

'What's wrong with Nit?'

The younger footman flushed.

'Father Mahoney sent for me to his room again,' he answered.

'What, *again*?'

'Catch me twice – '

'*Veni cum me in terra coelabus!*'

'S-s-s-s-s-s-sh.'

'*Et lingua . . . semper.*'

'On the whole', the butler said, 'I preferred Père Ernest.'

'And so did half the maids.'

'Although his brilliance here was as you may say wasted.'

' 'Pon my word! It's a deadly awful place.'

'With the heir-presumptive so much away it's bound to be slow and quiet.'

'Why', George gurgled, 'the Captain should be heir of Hare I never could make out!'

'Mr Dick's dead father', Mr ffines replied, 'was a close relative of Mrs Hurst.'

'The Admiral?'

'And it was as good as a combination . . .' he further explained, 'only he was too poor. And things fell out otherwise.'

'There'd be a different heir, I s'pose, if missis married ag'in?'

''Tisn't likely. Why she'll soon be a centenarian herself.'

'You've only to change her plate', Nit, with acumen, said, 'to feel she's there.'

'So I should hope!'

'And as to Father Colley. My! How he do press!'

The servitors waxed silent, each lost in introspection, until the rattle of the Valmouth cab announced the expected guest.

Alighting like some graceful exotic bird from the captivity of a dingy cage, Lady Parvula de Panzoust hovered a moment before the portal as much to manipulate her draperies, it seemed, as to imbreathe the soft sweet air.

The sky was abloom with stars. . . .

In the faint elusive light flitter-mice were whirling about the mask-capped windows, hurtling the wind-sown wall-flowers embedded in the fissure of each saturnine-hewn face.

'Come back for me again by ten o'clock, remember,' her ladyship commanded her coachman, prior to following the amaranthine skirts of the two footmen into the house.

Passing through the bleak penumbra of the hall and along a corridor bristling with horns of every description, she was shown into a deep, T-shaped, panelled room profusely hung with pictures.

There seemed at present to be no one in it.

'The mistress, I presume, is with the scourge,' the butler announced, peering impassably around.

Lady Parvula placed her fan to her train.

'Let her lash it!' she said. 'In this glorious room one is quite content to wait.'

And indeed there could not be the least doubt that the drawing-room at Hare-Hatch House was sufficiently uplifting to be alone in without becoming dull.

Here were the precious Holbeins – the finest extant – and the Ozias Humphry in its original oval frame, while prominent above the great Jacobean fireplace, with a row of lamps shining footlight-wise beneath it, was the youthful portrait of the present mistress from the hand of Ingres.

Garbed in Greek draperies, she was seen leaning her head against a harpsichord, whose carved support rose perpendicularly from end to end of the canvas like some flower-wreathed capital.

Less redoubtable perhaps were an infinity of Morlands, fresh and fragrant, in their oblong, cross-ribboned frames, a Longhi or two – a Piazza, a Punchinello in a little square, and a brilliant croquis signed *Carmontelle* of a Duchess trifling with a strawberry.

By a jaguar-skin couch far down the room an array of long-back chairs in the splendid upholstery of the seventeenth century suggested to Lady Parvula's mind an occasional 'public' correction. And everywhere ranged fortuitously about were *faïence* flower-tubs bearing large-leaved plants that formed tall canopies to the white, pensive statues grouped patiently beneath.

She was just passing a furtive hand over the promising feet and legs of a Discobolus, broken off, unfortunately, at the height of the loins, as Mrs Thoroughfare entered.

All billowing silks and defenceless embroideries, she was looking tonight like a good-natured sphinx – her rather bulging, etiolated cheeks and vivid scarlet mouth expanded in a smile.

'I know of no joy', she airily began, 'greater than a cool white dress after the sweetness of confession.'

Lady Parvula cast an evasive eye towards the supine form of a bronze hermaphrodite, whose long, tip-tilted, inquisitive nose protruded snugly above a smart Renaissance quilt.

'No! Really! Elizabeth!' she exclaimed.

Mrs Thoroughfare breathed in a way that might have been called a sigh.

'And where is Gilda?' she asked.

'Gilda . . . Gilda's still at school!'

'Oh!'

'And Dick?'

'Dick . . . Dick's still at sea!'

'Wicked fellow.'

'A crate of some wonderful etherized flowers', Mrs

Thoroughfare informed, pivoting with hands outspread, about a tripod surmounted by a small braziero, 'came from him only this afternoon, from Ceylon.'

Lady Parvula plied her fan.

'Even at Oomanton', she murmured, 'certain of the new hybrids this year are quite too perfect.'

'Eulalia and I often speak of the wondrous orchids at Oomanton Towers.'

Lady Parvula expanded.

'We're very proud of a rose-lipped one', she said, 'with a lilac beard.'

'A lilac . . . *what?*' It was Mrs Hurstpierpoint's voice at the door.

'Eulalia!'

'Is it Sodom?' she inquired in her gruff, commanding way, coming forward into the room.

She had a loose, shapeless gown of hectically-contrasted colours – one of Zenobia Zooker's hardiest inspirations – draped from the head à l'Évangile.

Lady Parvula tittered.

'Goodness, no,' she said.

'Because Father Mahoney won't hear of it ever *before* dessert.'

'How right.'

'He seems to think it quite soon enough,' the mistress of Hare murmured, passing an intimate arm about her old friend's waist.

Lady Parvula cooed half-fluttered. In a time-corroded mirror she could see herself very frail, and small, and piquant in its silver-sheeted depth.

'To be continually beautiful, like *you*, dear,' her hostess said. 'How I wish I could. . . .'

'Yet I date my old age,' Lady Parvula replied, 'from the day I took the lift first at the Uffizi!'

'You dear angel.'

'One's envious, almost, of these country clowns, who live, and live, and live, and look so well!'

'Many find the climate here trying to begin with', Mrs

Hurstpierpoint said, 'owing to the amount of cosmic activity there is; but the longevity of the Valmouthers attracts all kinds of visitors to the town.'

'At the Strangers' a Contessa di Torre Nuevas has the room next to me – and *oh!* how she snores!'

'Do they make you comfortable?'

'Most.'

'You must miss the society of your girl.'

'Dear child. She is training under Luboff Baltzer – in Milan.'

'To what end?'

'Music. And she is in such cruel despair. She says Luboff insists on endless counterpoint, and *she* only wants to play valses!'

'She hardly sounds to be ambitious.'

'It depends; measured by Scriabin's *Quasi-Valse*, or the *Valse in A flat major*, she may have quite intricate idylls. . . .'

Mrs Thoroughfare simmered. 'I do so love his *Étrangeté*,' she said.

'Was it you, Betty', Mrs Hurstpierpoint demanded, 'before Office I heard amusing yourself in Our Lady?'

'I am sure, Eulalia, I forget.'

Lady Parvula's hand wandered vaguely towards the laurel-leaf fillet that encompassed irresponsibly her pale, liver-tinted hair.

'After the Sixtine Chapel', she remarked, 'I somehow think your Nuestra Señora de la Pena is the one I prefer.'

'You *dear* you! You should have been with us Easter Day! Our little basilica was a veritable bower of love.'

'Have you any more new relics?'

'Only the tooth of St Automona Meris, for which', Mrs Hurstpierpoint, in confidence, was moved to add, 'I've had my tiara-stones turned into a reliquary.'

'You funny animal!'

'If we go on as we go on', Mrs Thoroughfare commented as dinner was ceremoniously announced, 'we'll be almost *too* ornate!'

It was what they, each in their way, were ready for.

'I adore dining *en petit comité*,' Lady Parvula exclaimed, accepting gaily her hostess's propellent arm.

It was past blue, uncurtained windows to the dining-room, that remained, too, uncurtained to the night.

In the taper-lit, perhaps pre-sixteenth-century room – a piece of *Laughing and Triumphing* needlework in the style of Rubens completely hid the walls – the capacious oval of the dinner-table, crowned by a monteith bowl filled with slipper-orchids, showed agreeably enough.

'Where can Father be?' Mrs Hurstpierpoint wondered, sinking to her chair with a slight grimace. Rumour had it that she wore a bag of holly-leaves pinned to the lining of her every gown; it even asserted that she sometimes assumed spiked garters.

'He went to the carpenter's shop, Eulalia', Mrs Thorough-fare replied, 'to give "a tap or two", as he said, to your new *prie-dieu*.'

'And so you've lost Père Ernest,' Lady Parvula murmured, humbling a mitred napkin with a dreamy hand.

'Alas! our stationariness soon bored him. He preferred flitting about the world like you.'

'I go about', Lady Parvula admitted, 'as other fools in quest of pleasure, and I usually find tedium.'

'If I recollect', Mrs Hurstpierpoint said, 'the Valmouth cattle-show was *our* last gaiety.'

'Your pathetic-eyed, curious oxen . . . it's a breed you don't see everywhere! My husband – my Haree-ee-ee' (either from coquetry or from some slight difficulty she experienced in pronouncing her y's, Lady Parvula pronounced 'Harry' long) 'tried them, in the park down at Oomanton Towers; but they didn't do.'

'No?'

'They got leaner and leaner and leaner and leaner in spite of cakes and cakes and cakes and cakes. . . . Poor Haree-ee-ee, my dearly beloved lord, even allowed them on to the lawn, where they used to look in at the ground-floor windows. One dreadful evening – we were taking tea – a great crimson head and two huge horns tossed the cup I was holding out of my hands, which sent me off – I'm just all over nerves! – into a state of *défaillance*; the last thing you may imagine I wanted, as it was Gilda's last night at home.'

'You should consult local advice.'

'It's what I intend doing.'

'We hear of several of our hidalgos having been immortalized lately, thanks to Victor Vatt.'

Mrs Thoroughfare smiled indulgently.

'Those disciples of his,' she demurely said, 'oh; are they all they seem?'

'Lady Lucy Saunter swears not!'

'Is Lady Lucy at Valmouth?'

'Indeed she is. . . . And *so* poorly and *so* run-down. She says her blood is nothing but rose-water.'

'I suppose the town is full of imaginary invalids *comme toujours*?'

'My dear, one sees nothing else. So many horrid parliament-men come here apparently purely to bask.'

Mrs Thoroughfare's face lit.

'Like our two whips!' she made chucklingly rejoinder. 'Last Epiphany in a fit of contrition we sent a tiny *enfant du chœur* (a dangerous, half-witted child . . . but pious: pious . . .! And with the sweetest face; oh hadn't Charlie a witching face last Epiphany, Eulalia? His hair's good yet, and so are his taper hands, but his voice has gone, and so too have his beautiful roses) into town for a couple of whips. They duly appeared. But two such old vote-hunters. . . . "My God," Eulalia said, "we asked for whips and Thou sendest *scourges*".'

'Well! Quite a harum-scarum, one of the Vile-islands, sits for Oomanton, who pretends, I believe,' Lady Parvula breathed, 'to be an advocate for Gilda; but if *I* ever venture to propose an alliance to my ewe-lamb usually she answers: "I don't want to marry *any*-one, thank you, mama! I prefer to be free." She has no real cognizance, dear lambkin, of anything at all.'

'Sooner or later she'll make her choice!'

'Men, men! . . . "They are always there," dear, aren't they, as the Russians say?'

Mrs Hurstpierpoint repressed a grimace.

'Nowadays,' she murmured, 'a man ... to me ... some-how ... oh! he is something so wildly *strange*.'

'Strange?'

'Unglimpsable.'

'Still, some men are ultra-womanly, and they're the kind I love!' Mrs Thoroughfare chirruped.

'I suppose that none but those whose courage is un-questionable can venture to be effeminate?' Lady Parvula said, plunging a two-pronged fork into a 'made' dish of sugared-violets served in aspic.

'It may be so.'

'It was only in war-time, was it, that the Spartans were accustomed to put on perfumes, or to crimp their beards?'

'My dear, how your mind seems to dwell upon beards.'

'Upon *beards*?'

'It's perfectly disgusting.'

'In the old days do you remember "Twirly" Rogers?'

'Out with the Valmouth Drag,' Mrs Thoroughfare sighed, 'how well he looked in his pink coat!'

Lady Parvula assented.

'Those meets', she said, 'on the wintry cliffs above the world had a charm about them. One could count more alluring faces out with the Valmouth, my husband used to say, than with any other pack. The Baroness Elsassar – I can see her now on her great mauve mount with her profile of royalty in misfortune – never missed. Neither, bustless, hipless, chinless, did "Miss Bligh"! It was she who so sweetly hoisted me to my saddle when I'd slid a-heap after the run of a "fairy" fox. We'd whiffed it – the baying of the dogs is something I shall never forget; dogs always know! – in a swede-field below your house from where it took us by break-neck, rapid stages – (oh! oh!) – to the sands. There, it hurried off along the sea's edge, with the harriers in full cry; all at once, near Pizon Point, it vanished. Mr Rogers, who was a little ahead, drew his horse in with the queerest gape – like a lost huntsman (precisely) in the *Bibliothèque bleue*.'

'It's a wonder he didn't vomit.'

'I and Miss Bligh lay on the beach for hours – !'

'With a *dominus vobiscum*,' Mrs Hurstpierpoint remarked, turning her head at the silken swish of her chaplain's gown.

Flecked with wood shavings, Saint Joseph-wise, it brought with it suggestions of Eastern men in intriguing, long burnooses; of sandalled feet; of shadûf singing boys; of creaking water-wheels and lucerne-laden camels.

Bowing her face before the stiff, proud thumb and crooked forefinger raised to bless, Mrs Hurstpierpoint remained a moment as if in transport, looking, with her figured veils and fuzzed hair-wreathings, like some Byzantine peacock searching for fleas.

'Lulu Veuve? Veaujolais? Clos Voukay? Or Château-Thierry?' the butler broke the silence.

Lady Parvula hesitated.

'If only not to be too like everyone else, *mon ami*,' she murmured, her perfervid, soul-tossed eyes wandering towards the priest, 'you shall give me some of each.'

Father Colley-Mahoney launched a dry, defensive cough, involuntarily starting Nit.

'How incomparable their livery is!' Lady Parvula commented.

'It has a seminary touch about it,' Mrs Hurstpierpoint conceded, 'though at Headquarters it's regarded (I fear!) as inclining to modernism, somewhat.'

'Pray what's that?'

'Modernism? Ask any bishop.'

Lady Parvula rippled.

'I once,' she said (resolutely refusing a stirring salmis of cock's-combs *saignant* with *Béchamel* sauce), 'I once peeped under a bishop's apron!'

'Oh . . . ?'

'And whatever did you see?' Mrs Thoroughfare breathlessly asked.

'Well . . . I saw', Lady Parvula replied (helping herself to a few *pointes d'asperges à la Laura Leslie*), 'I saw . . . the dear Bishop!'

Father Mahoney kindled.

'Apropos,' he said, 'his Eminence writes he is offering an ex-voto to Nuestra Señora of a silver heart.'

'In any particular intention?'

'No. Its consecration he leaves to our discretion.'

'He owes, they say,' Mrs Thoroughfare murmured, consulting the menu with Spanish gravity, 'to women at least the half of his red hat. . . .'

Lady Parvula's glance explored the garden.

A hyacinthine darkness flooded the titanic cedars before the house above whose immemorial crests like a sad opal the moon was rising.

'Parvula,' her hostess evinced concern, 'you're tasting nothing.'

'I shall wait,' Lady Parvula made answer, 'Eulalia, for the *Madeleines en surprise!*'

'An abbess, and one of my earliest penitents,' Father Mahoney said, 'professed to find "delicious" small slips of paper traced thickly across with holy texts.'

'Really? . . . It sounds like parlour games!'

Mrs Hurstpierpoint was moved to sigh.

'No one remembers cribbage now,' she lamented, 'or gleek, or bi-ri-bi.'

'No; or ombre. . . .'

'Or lansquenet. . . .'

'Or spadille. . . .'

'Or brelan. . . .'

'But for cards, country evenings would be too slow!'

'Indeed, when Father reads us Johnny Bunyan after dinner I fall asleep,' Mrs Thoroughfare declared.

'Have you nothing brighter than that?'

'We read here', Father Mahoney interpolated, 'books only of a theological trend. Not that', he disconsolately added, 'the library upstairs doesn't contain a certain amount of Rabelaisian literature, I regret to say.'

'Rabelaisian, Father?' Mrs Hurstpierpoint faintly shrieked.

'I don't choose, my child, to think of some of the "works" we harbour.'

'Those Jacobean dramatists, and the French erotic works

of the eighteenth century, of course, would be free . . . but
Pére Ernest didn't reject them; many a stern metaphor have
I heard him draw from *Dr James's Powders* and *Mr Foote's Tea* –
and all the rest of it.'

Lady Parvula considered with a supercilious air the im-
material green of a lettuce-leaf.

'Oh, well,' she said, 'even at Oomanton, I dare say, there
are some bad books too; in fact, I know there are! Once my
ewe-lamb came to me with what appeared to be a medieval
lutrin. "Oh, mama," she said, "I've found such a funny
word." "What is it, my precious?" I said. " – , mama!" she
answered with the most innocent lips in life . . . which sent
me off – I'm just all over nerves! – into a fainting state; fairly
scaring my lambkin out of her wits.'

Mrs Hurstpierpoint extended towards her guest a hand that
was not (as Lady Parvula confided afterwards to the Lady
Lucy Saunter) too scrupulously clean.

'Those fainting-fits', she said, motioning an order to Nit as
he flitted by with an ingenuity of tartelettes, 'should be taken
in time. For my sake, allow Dr Dee of Valmouth to systematic-
ally overhaul you.'

'Overhaul me! What for?'

But Mrs Thoroughfare uttered a cry.

'Oh poor wee mothlet!' she exclaimed, leaning forward to
extricate a pale-winged moth struggling tragically in one of
the sconces of a candelabra. . . .

'If ffines tonight was not enough to infuriate an archangel!'
Mrs Hurstpierpoint commented, resplendently trailing (the
last toothsome dish having been served) towards the holy-
water stoup of old silver-work behind the door.

Lady Parvula joined her.

'After your superexcellent champagne', she exclaimed, 'I
feel one ought to go with bared feet in pilgrimage to Nuestra
Señora and kindle a wax light or two.'

'My dear, I believe you've latent proclivities!'

'Eulalia!'

'Parvula!'

'Never.'

'Ah, don't say that.'

'Dearest,' Lady Parvula perversely marvelled, 'what a matchless lace berthe!'

'It was part of my corbeille – '

'Like *doubting Thomas*, I must touch with my hands.'

'Touch! Touch!'

Father Mahoney fidgeted.

'Beyond the vigil-lamp', he objected, 'Nuestra Señora will be quite obscure.'

'Then all the more reason, Father, to illumine it!' Lady Parvula reasoned.

'Are you resolved, Parvula?'

'Of course. And I'm agog to see the tooth, too, of St Automona Meris (Do you imagine she ever really ate with it horrid Castilian garlic *olla cocida*? Or purple *pistos insalada*? She, and Teresa together, in some white *posada*, perhaps, journeying South), and your Ghirlandajo and the miracle-working effigy, and afterwards, until the fly comes round, you shall teach me gleek!'

'You dear angel . . . it's very simple!'

'Then let us play for modest points.'

Mrs Hurstpierpoint crossed herself with her fan.

'As if', she horror-struck said, 'I should consent to play for immodest ones! Are you coming Elizabeth, too?' she asked.

'In one moment, Eulalia; I must speak to Father first,' Mrs Thoroughfare replied, folding her arms lightly across the back of her chair.

'Don't, dear, desert us!' Mrs Hurstpierpoint, withdrawing, enjoined.

There was a short pent silence.

'Do you think, Father', Mrs Thoroughfare broke it at last, 'she suspects?'

'Rest assured, my poor child,' Father Mahoney answered, 'your confession to me tonight exceeds belief.'

'Was there ever such a quandary!' Mrs Thoroughfare jabbered.

'They obeyed the surge of their blood – what else?' Father Mahoney dispassionately said.

Mrs Thoroughfare's full cheeks quivered.

'Oh, my darling boy,' she burst out, 'how *could* you!'

'My poor child, try not to fret.'

'It makes one belch, Father – belch.'

'They're joined irremediably, I understand?'

'From what he writes I conclude the worst.'

'Won't you show me what he says?'

'The card,' she murmured, drawing it from her dress, 'is covered, I fear, by the chemicals that were in the crate, gummed to the stem as it was of a nauseating lily.'

'Decipher the thing, then, to me – if you will.'

Mrs Thoroughfare adjusted a lorgnon tearfully to her nose.

' "These are the native wild-flowers," he writes (what, I wonder, Father, must the others be!), "the native wildflowers of my betrothed bride's country. Forgive us, and bless us, mother. Ten thousand loves to you all." '

'O, wretched boy.'

'O, Father.'

'That ever any Black woman should perform the honours at Hare!'

Mrs Thoroughfare smiled mirthlessly.

'Well – if it comes to that – Eulalia, *herself*, tonight, is more than grubby,' she said.

5

THE installation of a negress at the Nook, Mrs Yajñavalkya's old-style dwelling in the Market Square, came to Valmouth, generally, as a surprise.

Almost from the outset of her arrival in the town, soft-
muted music, the strange, heart-rending, mournful music of
the East – suggestive of apes, and pearls, and bhang, and the
colour blue – was to be heard, surging from the Nook in
monotonous improvisation.

Madame Mimosa, the demi-mondaine, the only 'one'
there was thereabouts, hearing it from the Villa Concha, next
door, fancied she detected rivalry, competition – *the younger
generation* – and took to her *bravura* (cerise chiffon, and a long,
thick, black aigrette) before the clock told noon. Nurse Yates,
hard by, heard 'zithers' too, and flattered herself the time was
ripe to oust Mrs Yajñavalkya from the town, 'automatically'
capturing her clients as they dropped away. Mrs Q. Comedy,
née Le Giddy, ever alert to flare an auction, told her Quentin
she supposed Mrs Yajñavalkya would shortly be giving up
her house and going off into Valopolis, or New Valmouth,
where she might conduct a *bagnio* with more facility, perhaps,
than beneath the steeple of the church. While all the time,
shining smiles, Mrs Yajñavalkya herself went about affairs
much in her usual way.

Of a morning early she would leave the Nook followed by
a little whey-faced English maid, to whom she allowed
twelve pounds a year 'because she is so white', to take her
way towards the provision stalls encamped beneath John
Baptist Daleman's virile, but rudimentary, statue in the square,
where flitting from light to shade, she would exchange
perhaps a silver coin against a silver fish, or warm-leafed
cauliflower, half dead on the market stones. Sometimes,
quickly dismissing her little Gretchen, she would toddle off
up Peace Street into Main Street, and enter, without knocking,

38

the house of Dr Dee, but more frequently mistress and maid would return to the Nook together, when almost immediately from her chimneys would be seen to rise a copious torrent of smoke.

From the Strangers' Hotel across the way Lady Parvula de Panzoust, like the local residents themselves, had been a puzzled spectator of the small particular coterie at the Nook, since, to her ever-deepening vexation, her shepherd-with-the-dog was a constant caller there.

Had he anything, then, the matter? His constitution, was it not the mighty thing it seemed? His agile figure (glowing through corduroys and hob-nailed boots; his *style d'amour*), was it nothing but a sham? Or had he an intrigue, perhaps, with one or other of the women of the house?

Now and then a dark face framed in unbound hair would look out through a turret window of the Nook, as if moved to home-sickness at the cries of a beautiful cockatoo that hung all day in the window of Sir Victor Vatt's sitting-room at the hotel.

'Dear Vatt,' the bird would say with sonorous inflections, taking off some artist, or sitter perhaps, 'dear Vatt! He is splendid; so o-ri-gi-nal and exuberant; like an Italian Decorator.' Or, *vivo*: 'Now, Vatt! Do me a Poussin.' Or, the inflection changing *languido dolce*: 'Come, Vatt! Paint me in a greenhouse ... in a st-oove; a little exotic; paint me (my little Victor!) like Madame Cézanne! They say,' *meno languido*, 'they say he gave her one hundred and fifteen sittings! Pretty Poll!'

Loiterers in the Market Square, observing the attentive negress trim the window, smiled and called her a caution, more cautious-like, said they in the local vernacular, than 'Old Mrs Rub-me-down', inferring Mrs Yajñavalkya. Lady Parvula de Panzoust, alone, a sure connoisseur of all amative values, was disposed to allow the negress her dues, divining those ethnologic differences, those uneasy nothings that again and again in the history of the world have tempted mankind to err. She descried, therefore, whenever the parrot's loquaciousness induced the negress to look out, a moon-faced girl with high-set, scornful eyes almost in her forehead and bow-curved pagan lips of the colour of rose-mauve stock. Her anatomy, singularly independent in every way, was, Lady Parvula surmised, that of a little *woman* of twelve. Was it, she asked herself, on this black Venus' account Adonis visited the Nook? Or was it for other reasons, graver, sadder ones ... such as, for instance, dressing the gruesome injury of the boar?

One sunny May-day morning, full of unrest, Lady Parvula de Panzoust left the hotel for a turn on the Promenade. It was a morning of pure delight. Great clouds, breaking into dream, swept slowly across the sky, rolling down from the uplands behind Hare-Hatch House, above whose crumbling pleasances one single sable streak, in the guise of a coal-black negress, prognosticated rain.

'Life would be perfect,' she mused, 'if only I hadn't a corn!' But the Oriental masseuse was the sole proficient of the chiropodist's art at Valmouth, and Lady Parvula de Panzoust felt disinclined to bare her tender foot to the negress's perspicacious gaze. Yet after going a few painful yards this is what she realized she must do. 'After all,' she reflected, 'I may perhaps ascertain her pastoral client's condition, and so free my mind from doubt!'

She was looking charmingly matinal in a simple tweed costume, with a shapely if perhaps *invocative* hat, very curiously indented, and well cocked forward above one ear. She held a long ivory-handled sunshade in the form of a triple-headed serpent, and a book that bore the irreproachable Christian title *Embrassons-Nous*.

'And who knows,' she sighed, lifting Mrs Yajñavalkya's sun-fired knocker with a troubled hand, 'he may even be there himself!'

The little chalk-faced maid that answered the door said her mistress was in, and preceding the evident 'London lady' up a short flight of stairs, ushered her with a smile of triumph into a small but crowded cabinet whose windows faced the Square.

'Is it for a douche, m'm,' she asked, 'or ought I to start the steam?'

'Not on *my* account!' Lady Parvula murmured with dilated retinas, scanning the signed diplomas and framed credentials displayed upon the walls. A coloured 'Insurance' almanac, privately marked with initials and crosses – engagements no doubt of Mrs Yajñavalkya's – gladdened gaily their midst.

'Chance me finding her,' she reflected, moving involuntarily towards a brilliant draped mirror above the chimney-place, where a tall piece of branched coral was stretched up half-forbiddingly against the glass.

Through its pink sticks she could see reflected in the room behind part of a calico-covered couch with the negress's bureau beyond, on which at present stood a half-eaten orange and a jar of white pinks.

A twitter of negro voices was shrilly audible through the wood partition of the wall.

'*Yahya!*'

'*Wazi jahm?*'

'*Ah didadidacti, didadidacti.*'

'*Kataka mukha?*'

'*Ah mawardi, mawardi.*'

'*Jelly.*'

'A breeze about their jelly!' Lady Parvula conjectured, complacently drawing nearer the window.

Before the Villa Concha, a little curtained carriage attached to an undocked colt with a bell at its ear signified that Madame Mimosa was contemplating shortly a drive.

Through what blue glebe or colza-planted plains would her rainbow axles turn?

Mrs Yajñavalkya's ambling step disturbed her speculations.

'Have I not de satisfaction,' she ubiquitously began, 'ob addressing Milady Panzoust?'

Lady Parvula nodded.

'I believe you do chiropody?' she said.

'Dat is a speciality ob de house – de cultivation ob de toes. Vot is dair so important? O wen I consider de foot ... de precious precious foot! For de foot support de body; it bear de burden ob ten thousand treasures! ... *Kra.* And dat's vot I alvays say.'

'Undoubtedly,' Lady Parvula assented, 'whatever there *is*, it bears.'

'It gib gentle rise to ebberything,' Mrs Yajñavalkya pursued.

'Perhaps – sometimes – it carries charms.'

'*Ukka-kukka!*' the negress broke off, dropping darkly to the floor. 'My niece, Niri-Esther, she fill de flower vases so full dat de water do all drip down and *ro-vine* de carpet.'

'Then of course she's in love?'

'Niri-Esther!'

'Now and then an interesting patient must wish to approach you.'

'I alvays', Mrs Yajñavalkya blandly yapped, 'decline a gentleman. Often ze old greybeards zey say, "Oh, Mrs Yaj," zey say, "include our sex." And I laugh and I say, "I've enough to do wif my own"!'

Lady Parvula surrendered smilingly her shoes.

'Still, I sometimes see', she said, 'call here a young tall man with his dog.'

'He call only to fetch de fowls dat flit across to my acacia-tree from de farm.'

'Is that all?'

'Being so near de church, de house is open to ebbery passing ghoul. De incubes and de succubes dat come in, and are so apt to molest . . . ob an evening especially, ven de sun fall and de sky turn all caprice, I will constantly dispatch my little maid to beg, to implore, and to beseech dat Dairyman Tooke will remove his roosters.'

'Dairyman Tooke?'

'Or his prize sow, maybe – a sow! Ah, dat is my abomination!'

'Probably the antipathy springs through the belief in reincarnation.'

''No doubt at all dat is one ob de causes.'

'The doctrine of Transubstantiation must often tell on your nerves.'

'When I die', Mrs Yajñavalkya said, her eyes disappearing

expiringly in their sockets, 'I would not wish to be transubstantiated into a horse or a cow or a sheep or a cat. No; oh no! I will wish to be changed into a little bird, wid white, white feathers; treasuring', she wistfully added, 'meantime de poet's words:

'My mother bore me in the southern wild,
And I am black, but O! my soul is white.'

'Your songsters too', Lady Parvula said, 'have also their poignance.'

'Ah! when Niri-Esther read Tagore,' Mrs Yajñavalkya glowed, 'dat is something beautiful! Dat is something to make de tears descend.'

'To hear her render the love lyrics of her country, just the most typical things, would interest me immensely if it might some day be arranged.'

'But why not?'

'A *séance* in your garden amidst the acacia leaves – Mademoiselle Esther and I! And when the young man came to retrieve his birds, I vow he'd find no turkey!'

'Believe me,' Mrs Yajñavalkya murmured, indrawing succulently her cheeks and circumspectly toying with her file, 'believe me, he's awfully choice.'

'He has youth.'

'He's awfully, awfully choice!' the negress murmured, admiring the intricate nerve-play of her patient's foot.

'It's just a Valmouth type,' Lady Parvula observed.

'Ah! It is more dan dat.'

'How?'

'Much more in ebbery way.' Mrs Yajñavalkya looked insoluble.

'I don't I fear follow . . .' Lady Parvula gasped.

'I have known what love is, I!' the negress heaved. 'Dair are often days ven I can neither eat, nor drink, nor sleep, ven my fingers hab no strength at all (massage den is quite impossible) – I am able only to groan and groan and groan – ah, my darling!'

'A nigger?'

'A nigger! No. He was a little blonde Londoner – all buttoned-and-braided, one ob de *chasseurs* at your hotel.'

'Thank you.' Lady Parvula looked detached.

'De dear toe', the operatress raised a glinting, sooty face, 'is quite inflamed! De skin', with unwitting cynicism she theorized, 'may vary, but de Creator ob de universe has cast us all in de same mould; and dat's vot I alvays say.'

'In what part, tell me, is your home?'

'Here!' the negress lisped.

'Geographically, I mean.'

'Geographically, we're all so scattered. Von ob my brother, Djali, he in Ujiji Land. *Kra*. He a Banana-Inspector. Official. He select de virgin combs from off de tree; dat his Pash-on, dat his Cult. Other brother, Boujaja, he in Taihaiti. He a lady-killer, well-to-do-ish; he three wives, *kra*; and dose three women are my sisters-in-law. . . . De Inspector, he no marry; I don't know why!'

'Then your niece', Lady Parvula pressed, 'is from Taihaiti?'
But Mrs Yajñavalkya was abstruse.

'Do you care to undergo a course ob me?' she asked. 'For de full course – I make you easy terms; and I alvays try', she airily cozened, 'to end off wid a charming sensation.'

'Massage merely as sensation does not appeal to me: – and otherwise, thank you, I'm perfectly well.'

'I gib a massage lately to de widowed Duchess ob Valmouth for less! "Yajñavalkya," she laugh and say after I had applied my court cream (half a crown; five shillings): "Yajñavalkya, your verve, it's infectious." "My what, your grace?" I say. "Your verve," she reply; "it's so *catching*".'

'I always admired her,' Lady Parvula remarked, 'you'd almost say she was a man.'

'Her testimonial is on my bureau dair.'

'You must be proud of your tributes.'

'Zey come from all sides. . . . Queen Quattah, she write again and again for my balsam ob mint, or my elixir ob prunes; but my greatest discovery, milady, my dear, was de use ob tiger-lily pollen for "superfluous hair".'

Lady Parvula moved uncomfortably in her chair. She was

sufficiently alert to feel the animal magnetism from a persistent pair of eyes.

'*Wushi!*' Mrs Yajñavalkya turned too.

'*Kataka?*' a voice came from the door.

'My relative Niri-Esther,' Mrs Yajñavalkya explained, 'she ask me what I do.'

'She seems', Lady Parvula commented, 'to have been crying.'

'She cry for a sting ob a wasp dat settle on her exposed bosom. I tell her – at de window – she shouldn't expose it!'

'Oh?'

'De wasps dis year dey are a plague.'

'*Kataka . . .; kataka mukha?*'

Advancing with undulating hesitation, the young black girl brought with her something of uttermost strangeness into the room.

Incontestably, she was of a superior caste to Mrs Yajñavalkya, albeit her unorthodox values tended, perhaps, to obscure a little her fundamental merit.

She wore a dishabille of mignonette-green silk and a bead-diapered head-dress that added several inches to her height; her finger-slim ankles were stained with lac and there were rings of collyrium about her eyes.

With one hand clasped in the other behind her back, she stood considering Lady Parvula de Panzoust.

'*Chook,*' Mrs Yajñavalkya grumbled.

'*Owesta wan?*'

'*Obaida.*'

'She has the exuberance of an orchid,' Lady Parvula cried. 'Could Sfax – he is my gardener down at Oomanton Towers – behold her now, he'd exclaim,' "A Urania Alexis, your ladyship!" and pop her into a pot.'

'Niri-Esther's clothes, I sometimes venture to tink, are a little too vainglorious! ! ! At her age', Mrs Yajñavalkya retailed, 'and until I was past eighteen, I nebber had more in de course ob a year dan a bit ob cotton loincloth. You may wear it how you please, my poor mother would say, but dat is all you'll get! And so, dear me, I generally used to put it on my head.'

'She eyes one like a cannibal.'

'Are you quite well?' the young black woman waveringly asked.

Lady Parvula answered with a nod.

'Come here and show me,' she said.

'I drop de *mushrabiyas* – ; so nobody den can see in!'

'Why O, why O,' Mrs Yajñavalkya complained, 'will dat *hetoera's* horrid coachman draw up alvays just opposite to my gate?'

'She is later dan usual today,' her relative rejoined.

'Wears her horse', the elder negress demanded, 'a rose?'

'De poor unhappy thing; he wear both a favour and a strap.'

'The looser the mistress . . . the tighter the bearing-rein!' Lady Parvula remarked.

Mrs Yajñavalkya languished.

'She dribe her chestnut for day work, and reserbe a white for evening use. Not dat', she amplified, 'one move more rapidly dan de other; no, oh no; Madame Mimosa refuse to dribe her horses fleet! She seldom elect to aribe betimes; she say it "good" to keep de clients waiting. It's a question ob policy wif her dat "two hours late".'

'I suppose simply to engender suspense.'

'*C'est une femme qui sait enrager. Allez!*'

'You know French?'

'Like ebberything else!'

Lady Parvula expanded.

'I said to my maid this morning: "Oh, Louison!" I said, "what does the prommy place here remind you of?" "Of nothing, your ladyship," replied she. "Oh, *doesn't* it?" I said; "well, it does me! It reminds me of the Promenade des Sept Heures at Spa".'

'Ah, de dear spot!'

'For brio, and for beauty and from the look of the trees, I said to her, it reminds me of the Promenade des Sept Heures at Spa.'

'You may go far before you will find a prettier place dan dis is.'

'True, I never go out but I see someone sketching.'

Mrs Yajñavalkya was convulsed.

'A certain Valmouth widow, living yon side de church, found a Francis Fisher lately lying in her ditch (some small *plein-air* ob his, I suppose, he had thrown away), so she forwarded it to London just to ask what it would fetch, and sold it to a dealer for more dan fifty pounds.'

'Bravo. I must try to pick up a Vatt!'

'Curious how he faber de clodhopper type. Who would want to hang a beggar on his walls? Dair are enough in de world without. Believe me.'

'Indeed there are.'

'An artist I alvays admire, now', the negress murmured, retying with coquetry her patient's shoe-string, 'is Mr FitzGeorge! All his models are ladies . . . daughters ob clergymen, daughters of colonels . . . and even his male sitters are,' she twittered, 'sons ob good houses.'

'Some one should paint your niece!' Lady Parvula rose remarking.

'*Fanoui ah maha?*'

'*Tauroua ta.*'

'*Yahya.*'

'What's that she says?'

'That she will be glad to make music for you at any time.'

'That will be delightful.'

'And I, also,' the dark-skinned woman assumed her silkiest voice, 'will endeavour to have a few fugitive fowls over from de farm. De dogs shall bark, and de birds shall fly (de sky is full ob de whirring ob wings), but de lover and his beloved shall attain Nirvana.'

'Nirvana?'

'Leave it to me and you and he shall come together.'

'Oh, impossible.'

'Leave it to me.'

'I never run *any* risks,' Lady Parvula babbled.

'Risks! Vot risks? Risks! . . . O Allah la Ilaha! Shall I tell you vot de Yajñavalkya device is? Vot it has been dis thousand and thousand ob year? It is *bjopti*. *Bjopti!* And vot does *bjopti* mean? It means *discretion*. *S-s-s-s-s-s-s-s-s-s-s-s-s-s-s-s-s-s-s-s-s-s-s-sh!*'

Lady Parvula toyed reflectively with her rings.

'At balls in a quilted skirt and with diamonds in my hair I've often been hugely admired as a shepherdess,' she said. 'I well remember,' she tittered, 'the success I had one evening – it was at the British Embassy in Paris – as a shepherdess of Lely. I had a lamb (poor, innocent darling, but so heavy and so hot; worse than any child) with me, that sprang from my arms quite suddenly while I was using my powder-puff and darted bleating away beneath the legs of Lord Clanlubber (at that time ambassador) out into the Champs Élysées, where it made off, I afterwards heard, towards the Étoile. And *I* never saw it again! So that you see,' she murmured, depositing her benefactress's fee vaguely upon the couch. 'I've a strong bond with shepherds, having myself, once, lost a lamb. . . .'

'In a like rig-up you would stir de soul ob Krishna, as de milkmaid Rádhá did!'

'I'm quite content to "stir" my neighbour instead.'

'Believe me,' the dark-skinned woman murmured, following her visitor to the stairhead, with a sigh that shook the house, 'he's awfully, awfully choice!'

' – . . .'

'He has a wee mole – on de forehead!'

'Ah, and he has another: yes! in the deep pool above his upper-lip – ; the channel affair. . . .'

'He's *awfully* choice!'

'*C'est un assez beau garçon*,' Lady Parvula answered with a backward aesthetic glance.

Leaning from the hand-rail, like some adoring chimpanzee, Mrs Yajñavalkya watched her recede, the wondrous crown of the vanishing hat suggesting forcibly the peculiar attributes of her own tribal gods.

The shadow upon the forewall of her little English maid descending the staircase with a chamber-pot from above recalled her to herself.

'*Ah, zoubé kareen pbf!* Why weren't you in readiness, Carry, to open de door?' she inquired, returning thoughtfully towards her sanctum with the intent to sterilize her tools.

On a spread kerchief, pitcher-posture, upon the floor her relative was bleaching idly her teeth with a worn bit of bone, while turning round and round like a water-wheel in her henna-smeared fingers the glass hoop-clasp at her abdomen.

Mrs Yajñavalkya gave way to a joyous chuckle.

'Mrs Richard Thoroughfare, Mrs Richard Thoroughfare!' she addressed the prostrate belle.

'*Chakrawaki – wa?*'

'Mrs Dick, Mrs Thorough-dick, Mrs Niri fairy!'

'*Suwhee?*'

With an eloquent listening eye, Mrs Yajñavalkya laid a hand to her ear.

'De bridal litter', she playfully announced, 'from Hare-Hatch House, is already at de far corner ob de adjacent street!'

The water-wheel ceased as the mauve lips parted.

'Ah, Vishnu!' the young black girl yawned. 'Vot den can make it come so slow?'

6

A CAMPAIGN of summer storms of a quasi-tropical nature
was delaying the hay harvest that in Valmouth, as in the
neighbouring Garden Isles, was usually celebrated before the
last week in May.

Not since the year 17—, when milord Castlebrilliant's cur-
ricle was whirled to sea with her ladyship within, had there
been such vehement weather.

At Hare-Hatch House the finest hornbeam upon the lawn
had succumbed, none too silently, while in the park several of
the centennial cedars were fallen, giving to the grounds somehow a tragic, classic look.

And indeed, with her favourite hornbeam, Mrs Hurstpierpoint's nerves had also given way.

One afternoon, just as the bell of Nuestra Señora was
sounding Terce, the lament of the peacocks announced a
return of the storm. Since midday their plangent, disquieting
cries had foretold its approach. Moving rapidly to and fro in
their agitation, their flowing fans sweeping rhythmically the
ground, they traced fevered curves beneath the overarching
trees, orchestrating, with barbarity, as they did so, their
strident screech with the clangour of the chapel bell that
seemed, as it rang, to attract towards it a bank of tawny gold,
cognac-coloured cloud, ominously fusing to sable.

Sauntering up and down in the shadow of the chapel wing,
the mistress of the manor, this afternoon, was also mingling
her voice, intermittently, as though a plaintive, recurring
motif in a slightly trying musical score, with her birds and
her bell. 'Eliza! Eliza!' she called.

Seated upon the fallen hornbeam, Mrs Thoroughfare was
regarding distraitly the sky.

Ever since the windy weather a large pink kite like a six-
humped camel had made above the near wood its extraneous
appearance. To whom, Mrs Thoroughfare asked herself,

bewildered, could such a monstrous toy belong? There was something about it that alarmed her, alarmed her more than all the storm-clouds put together.

'Elizabeth!'

As if cleft by passing lightning the name on the tense hot air writhed lugubriously away amid the trees.

'In, in,' Mrs Thoroughfare beseeched.

But Mrs Hurstpierpoint had already turned towards the house, where an under-footman was busily closing the ground-floor windows against the dark, shining spots of falling rain. And falling too, Mrs Thoroughfare noted, came the bewildering kite, headforemost, as though jerked smartly earthward in the flyer's hand. A burst of near thunder sent her perforce to join her friend, whose finer, more delicate nature was ever apt to be affected by a storm.

She found her in a corner of the vast drawing-room clasping a 'blessed' rosary while listening in a state of compressed hysterics to the storm.

'I'm an old woman now': she was telling her beads: 'and my only wish is to put my life in order – was that another flash?'

'Darling.'

'Is that you, my little Lizzie?'

'Tchut! Eulalia.'

'Oh-h-h-h! ... Betty dear! The *awful* vividness of the lightning!' Mrs Hurstpierpoint wailed.

Through the nine tall windows with their sun-warped, useless shutters, like violet-darting swallows, the lightning forked.

'Let us go,' Mrs Thoroughfare said in a slightly unsteady voice, 'shall we both, and confess?'

'Confess!'

'Father's in Nuestra now.'

'My dear, in my opinion, the lightning's so much more ghastly through the stained-glass windows!'

Mrs Thoroughfare pressed her hands lightly to her admired associate's humid brow.

'Dear mother was the same,' she cooed. 'Whenever it

thundered she'd creep away under her bed and make the servants come and lie down on top ... (it was in the eighteenth century of course ...) so that should the brimstone burst it must vent its pristine powers on them. Poor innocent! It was during a terrific thunderstorm at Brighton, or *Brighthelmstone* as they called it then, that several of the domestics fell above her head. ... And the fruits of that storm, as I believe I've told you before, Eulalia, are in the world today.'

'My dear ... every time the weather breaks you must needs hark back to it.'

Mrs Thoroughfare showed pique.

'Well *I*', she said, ambling undeterred towards the door, 'intend to pray.'

'Who knows but our prayers may meet?' Mrs Hurstpierpoint murmured, returning to her beads, that in the sombre brilliance of the darkened room shed different pale and supernatural lights as they swung from side to side in her nerveless hands.

'Adorable Jesus,' her mouth moved faintly beneath the charcoal shadow of her moustache, 'love me even as I do Thee, and I', she deeply breathed, 'will land Thee a fish! I will hook Thee a heretic; even though,' her tongue passed wistfully over her lips, 'to gain an open sinner I should be impelled to go to London, O Lord; for I will bend to Thy Sovereign Purpose (irrespective of my little kitchenmaid whom I most certainly mean to force) a thoroughgoing infidel; something very putrid ... very lost. And so, O my Saviour Dear,' beatifically she raised her face, 'I will make Thee retribution for the follies of my youth.'

Her lips grew still.

From the adjacent chapel soft, insinuating voices assailed agreeably the ear.

'Victories ...' 'Vanquish ...' 'Virtue ...' 'Virgin ...'

Mrs Hurstpierpoint's veiled glance dropped from her rafters, hovering with a certain troubled diffidence over the ruff and spade-beard of a dashing male portrait, until it dwelt on the face of the time-piece on the commode below, so placed as to exclude as far as possible the noble arch of her kinsman's shapely legs. The slow beat of the flower-wreathed pendulum usually filled the room.

Long ago, it was related, it had been consulted in an hour of most singular stress. And it was as if still some tragic pollen of anguish-staring eyes clung to the large portentous numerals of the Louis Sixteenth dial. Two steel key-holes in the white full face loomed now like beauty patches in the flickering light.

'I feel I'm ready for my tea,' Mrs Hurstpierpoint reflected, taking up an invalidish posture on the jaguar-skin couch.

The inebriating, slightly acrid perfume of a cobra lily, wilting in its vase, awoke solicitous thought within her of her distant heir.

Soon the dear lad would give up his junketings, she mused, and take to himself a wife.

Her eyes absorbed fondly the room.

'Ah! Ingres!' she sighed, 'your portrait of me is still indeed most like ... more like and much more pleasing, I think, than the marble Dalou did. ...' And fearful lest she should fall a victim to her own seductiveness, against the peevish precepts of the church, she averted her eyes towards the young naval officer in the carved Renaissance frame, into whose gold-wrapped, slim-wristed hands, with the long and lissom fingers, swelling towards their tips like big drop pearls, Hare-Hatch House and all its many treasures would one day pass.

A flare of dazzling brightness on the wainscoting caused her to knit her brows, and like a tall reed, wrapped in silk, her maid, wheeling a light chaufferette, advanced towards her.

'Is the worst of the storm over yet, Fowler, do you consider?' Mrs Hurstpierpoint gently groaned.

The maid's sallow face, flame-lit, looked malign as she drooped her trim-coiffed head.

'Now that the wind has deprived the statues of their fig leaves, 'm,' she replied, 'I hardly can bear to look out.'

'Oh? *Has* it? What? Again?'

'All round the courtyard and in the drive you'd think it was October from the way they lie!'

'Sister Ecclesia will be distressed going home, I fear. Even *an altar-cupid* – She's so sensitive,' Mrs Hurstpierpoint remarked.

'It's mostly dark, 'm, before she's done.'

'Unless the summer quickly mends the Hundred Club's fête must be postponed!'

'It's odd, 'm,' the waiting woman answered, adding a pinch of incense to the fire, 'how many a centenarian seems more proof against exposure than others not yet in their prime. Only a short while since my Lady Parvula's maid – she's been spending the day here among us – got caught in the wet while taking a turn with Miss Fencer and Nit; and now there she is, sitting before the kitchen range, in borrowed hose, with a glass of hot toddy.'

'I dare say her licentious stories have brought on this storm!'

'She was very full to be sure at meal-time of a fraudulent marriage, saying how no one or nothing was inviolate or safe.'

'The sole dependable marriage is the Spiritual marriage! On that alone can we implicitly rely.'

'And she was very full, too, of her ladyship's jewelled pyjamas.'

'Holy Virgin!'

'The storm sounds almost above us.'

'Lift the lid of the long casket – and pick me a relic,' Mrs Hurstpierpoint enjoined, surveying apprehensively the dark clumps of wind-flogged trees upon the lawn.

'Any one in particular, 'm?' the maid inquired, slipping, with obedient alacrity, across the floor.

'No; but not a leg-bone, mind! A leg-bone relic somehow –' she broke off, searching with her great dead eye dreaming the sad camphor-hued hills for the crucifix and wayside oratory that surmounted the topmost peak.

'You used to say the toe, 'm, of the married sister of the Madonna, the one that was a restaurant proprietress (Look alive there with those devilled-kidneys, and what is keeping Fritz with that sweet-omelette?), in any fracas was particularly potent.'

'Yes ... bring the toe of the Madonna's married sister, and then come and read to me out of Père Pujol,' her mistress answered, it being one of her chosen modes of penance (as well as a convenient means of paving the way to papalism) to call from time to time on her servants to come and read to her aloud. How often afterwards, in the soundless watches of the night, must the tonic words of a Pujol, or a brother Humphrey Caton, recur to dull procrastinating minds linked, made earthly in souvenir, with her own kind encouraging looks! Indeed, as a certain exalted churchman had excellently expressed it once, Oral-punishment, the mortification of the sparkling ear, was more delightful to heaven inasmuch as frequently it was more far-reaching than a knot in a birch or a nail in a boot.

But with Fowler, one of the earliest converts of the house, there was no need any more to push to extremes.

'*Figlia mia*,' she jarringly began with a great thick 'G' fully equal, her mistress reckoned, to a plenary indulgence alone, '*figlia mia*, examine your conscience, ask your heart, invoke that inner voice which always tells the truth, and never, no, never, betrays us! For the spark will live through the rains, lighting up dead fires: fire which is still fire, but with purer flame. ...'

'Lest your cap-pin kindles, *presto* there. Never', Mrs Hurstpierpoint intervened, 'read of bad weather during storm!'

'One day St Automona di Meris, seeing a young novice yawning, suddenly spat into her mouth, and *that* without malice or thought of mischief. Some ninety hours afterwards the said young novice brought into the world the Blessed St Elizabeth Bathilde, who, by dint of skipping, changed her sex at the age of forty and became a man.'

'A *man* – ! Don't speak to me of *men*. Especially one of that description!' Mrs Hurstpierpoint rapped. 'Inflict something else.'

'Something more poetical perhaps?'

'What is that thick, twine-coloured linen book I see the back of, beneath the young mistress's shawl?'

'Anthropology again, I expect, 'm,' Fowler answered.

'This craze for anthropology with her is something altogether new.'

'It frets her to form no idea of the tribes the Captain's been among.'

'It only makes her dream. She was talking so (being forced to fly to my little rosewood night-stool, I overheard her) in her sleep again.'

'Miss Fencer was saying so too. Only this morning (in calling her) she heard her say: "I will *not* go in beads to the opera." (Or was it "berries" she said?) "Tell King Mbmonbminbon so!" Anyway, Miss Fencer was so completely seized she just emptied the early tea vessel on to the floor.'

Mrs Hurstpierpoint exchanged with her maid a lingering, expressive glance.

'I *know* she's worried! I *know* she's keeping something from me! and I *know* she'll tell me in the end!' so the dependent, who was apt to read her mistress's face with greater accuracy than she did her books, interpreted the glance.

'The volume I find, 'm, beneath the shawl,' she said, 'is the *Tales from Casanova*.'

'Child that my soul's treasure is!' There was a second significant glance.

'Well, well; for St Francis's sake,' Mrs Hurstpierpoint said, steeling herself to listen, 'an Italian story is always permitted at Hare.'

'There was once upon a time two sisters,' Fowler falteringly began, 'named Manette and Marton, who lived with a widowed aunt, a certain Madame Orio, in the city of Venice. The disposition of these fair Venetians was such that – , such – ,' she floundered.

'Their disposition? . . . Yes? It was such?'

'Such –'

'That?'

' . . . Well, I declare!'

'How often, Fowler,' Mrs Hurstpierpoint said with some asperity, 'must I beg you not to employ that ridiculous phrase in my hearing?'

'Very good, 'm, but it's all Portuguese to *me*! ... And wagged his Persian tail.'

'Go on.'

'One evening', she went on, 'while Madame Orio was fast asleep in her little belvedere (it being the good old lady's habit to repair there to rest after a bottle or two of red Padua wine), Manette and Marton left the widow's house noiselessly in the Campo San Zobenigo, and made their way running towards the Piazza of St Mark's. It was a radiant night in early April. All Venice was in the open air. The moon, which –'

Listening with detached attention lest her ears should be seduced and tickled rather than soundly chastened, Mrs Hurstpierpoint's mind turned somewhat sombrely to her future connexion with her heir's fiancée. Some opinionated, wrong-headed creature, *une femme mal pensante*, in the house, she mused, would be indeed tormenting. While on the other hand, of course, Dick's bride *might* add a new interest to the place; in which case Elizabeth's attitude too would be sure to change.

Mrs Hurstpierpoint plied speculatively her beads catching between her *Aves* just enough of the tale to be able to follow its drift.

Music, she heard. Those sisters ✠ a ripe and rich marquesa ✠ strong proclivities ✠ a white starry plant ✠ water ✠ lanterns ✠ little streets ✠ Il Redentore ✠ Pasqualino ✠ behind the Church of ✠ Giudecca ✠ gondola ✠ Lido ✠ Love ✠ lagoon ✠ Santa Orsola ✠ the Adriatic –

With a sigh at the mutability of things, she realized that with a young daughter-in-law of her own Elizabeth would no longer be towards her her same gracious self. With the advent of Dick's wife a potential disturbing force would enter Hare. New joy would bring new sorrow. Whoever he might choose to marry, intrigue, jealousy would seldom be far away. Should Gilda Vintage be the *partie*, then Lady Parvula de Panzoust with her irrelevant souvenirs would be a constant figure at Hare: she would 'come over' probably quite easily – sooner, even than her daughter! 'And her *First* Confession,'

Mrs Hurstpierpoint ruminated with a crucial, fleeting smile, 'if (by some little harmless strategy) I could arrange it, I should dearly love to hear!'

Her cogitations were interrupted by the return of Mrs Thoroughfare, leading by the hand a reluctant Poor Clare for a cup of tea.

Proscribed by her Order to Silence, and having nothing in her physionomy to help her out, Sister Ecclesia's position at present was one of peculiar difficulty and constraint.

In the Convent of Arimathaea, at Sodbury hard by Hare whence she came, her indiscreet talkativeness had impelled a wise, if severe, Mother-Superior to impose upon her the *Torture* of Silence – which supplice had led her inevitably into tricks; Sister Ecclesia had contracted mannerisms therefrom. Though uttering no audible word her lips seldom were still. Strangers sometimes took her to be a saint, in touch with heaven. Bursting to speak she would frequently, when in society, shake clenched hands in the air impotently like a child. Sometimes, in order to find an outlet to her pent emotions, she would go as far as to kick and to pinch, and even to dance (her spirited hornpipes with Captain Thoroughfare were much admired at Hare), while with a broomstick she was invaluable – a very tigress – drawing blood directly. Indeed, as Mrs Hurstpierpoint was wont to say, her arm seemed born for a birch. Thrice a year Sister Ecclesia was allowed the use of her tongue when instead of seeking intercourse among the nuns she would flit off quite alone towards the sea-shore and blend her voice with the errant gulls until her unrestrained cries and screams frequently caused her to faint.

With vacuous, half-closed lids, Mrs Hurstpierpoint accepted her generous shower-bath of Eau Benite.

'Out? Already,' she murmured, simultaneously offering her hand on one side while abandoning her lips on the other.

'And oh! Eulalia,' Mrs Thoroughfare's voice shook with inflections, 'who should one find in Nuestra Señora ... (in the Capella Love of the Salutation) but Lady Violet Logg? Lady Violet! Elegant to tears, and with two such wisps of

58

boys! Boys of about seventeen – or eighteen, Eulalia! Like the mignons of Henry the Third.'

'I suppose . . . no umbrella.'

'And I am sure that Edie's pricked.'

'I know of more than one in the house to be wobbling!' Fowler averred as with rush-like gait at the view of the butler's crane-like legs, harbinger of the tea-board (in the dark of his mind might he not aspire to build with her? Swoop! Fly to church with her: make a nest of her? Snatch at her? Bend her, break her – God knew how! – to his passions' uses?), she flexibly withdrew.

'If anyone calls, ffines,' Mrs Hurstpierpoint said, rousing herself and running a hand to her half-falling hair, 'better simply say I'm out.'

'Les-bia – ah-h . . .!' Mrs Thoroughfare struck a few chords airily on the open piano.

'And, ffines . . . an extra cup.'

'An extra, 'm?'

'Insensate!'

'Hitherto 'm (and I've seen some choice service I am sure) I always gave entire satisfaction.'

'You never saw choicer service (I am quite sure) than with *me*, ffines,' Mrs Hurstpierpoint said, complacently adjusting a pin. 'And I'd have you to remember it!'

'Julia, Duchess of Jutland thought the world of me.'

'And so do I, ffines. I think the world of you too – *this* world! . . .'

'White Mit-y-lene . . .' Mrs Thoroughfare broke melodiously in, 'where the gir –'

'What was that song about lilacs, Lizzie?' Mrs Hurstpierpoint, turning to her, asked.

'*Lilacs*, Eulalia?'

'Something to do with lilacs: *lilacs en fleur*; an old air of France.'

> 'Le temps des lilas et le temps des roses,
> Ne reviendra plus à ce printemps ci.
> Le temps des lilas et le temps des roses.
> Est passé, le temps des œillets aussi.

Le vent a changé, les cieux sont moroses,
Et nous n'irons plus courir et cueillir
Les lilas en fleur et les belles roses;
Le printemps est triste et ne peut fleurir.

Oh, joyeux et doux printemps de l'année
Qui vint, l'an passé, nous ensoleiller,
Notre fleur d'amour est si bien fanée.
Las! que ton baiser ne peut l'eveiller.

Et toi, que fais-tu? pas de fleurs écloses,
Point de gai soleil ni d'ombrages frais;
Le temps des lilas et le temps des roses
Avec notre amour est mort à jamais.'

Mrs Thoroughfare's voice ebbed.

'May a woman know, dear,' Mrs Hurstpierpoint softly said, 'when she may receive her drubbing?'

'Oh I've no strength left in me today, Eulalia, I fear, for anything,' Mrs Thoroughfare answered.

'Positively?'

'Ask Ecclesia!'

But with the French song over Sister Ecclesia had edged with much wild grace, from the room.

'She's returned to her prayers, I suppose.'

'Or to Father.'

'Happily, quite in vain!'

'*Che volete?*'

'I miss Père Ernest,' Mrs Hurstpierpoint sighed, leisurely sipping her tea.

'Yes, dear, but he had too many ultramontane habits. ... There was really no joy in pouring out one's sins while he sat assiduously picking his nose.'

'Which reminds me', Mrs Hurstpierpoint serenely said, 'to gather my nectarines. ...'

'Your nectarines ...?'

'Sir Victor begs me for a few nectarine models. Nectarines meet to sit to him. Not *too* ripe.'

'I should think he only wanted them for himself,' Mrs

Thoroughfare cooed, opening wide a window that commanded an outlook of the lawns.

The atmosphere was clearer now. Before the house the mutilated statues and widowed urns showed palely white against a sky palely blue through which a rainbow was fast forming. By the little garden pergola open to the winds some fluttered peacocks were blotted nervelessly amid the dripping trees, their heads sunk back beneath their wings: while in the pergola itself, like a fallen storm-cloud, lolled a negress, her levelled, polecat eyes semi-veiled by the nebulous alchemy of the rainbow.

'What are you doing fiddle-faddling over there, Elizabeth?' Mrs Hurstpierpoint asked.

'Look, Eulalia,' Mrs Thoroughfare said, catching her breath; 'someone with a kite is on our lawn!'

Mrs Hurstpierpoint was impelled to smile.

'In the old days', she murmured, brushing a few crumbs from her gown, 'sailing a kite heavenward was my utmost felicity. No ball of string, I remember, was ever long enough!'

'This is no christian and her kite, Eulalia, or I'm much mistaken. . . .'

'No christian, Elizabeth?'

'It's a savage.'

Mrs Hurstpierpoint sank humbly to her knees.

'*Gloria in Excelsis tibi Deo!*' she solemnly exclaimed.

7

THE the plaintive pizzicato of Madame Mimosa's Pom pup 'Plum-Bun' aroused Mrs Yajñavalkya one triumphal summer morning while lying in the voluminous feather-bed that since lately she shared with her niece.

'*Zbaffa pbf!*' she complained, addressing an ape-like image, cut in jade, that stood at the bed-end, its incensed arms and elongated eyes defensively alert. Beside her Niri-Esther, indiscreetly *enceinte*, was still asleep.

'O de worries!' the negress murmured, leaving indolently her bed and hitching higher the blind.

It was a Market morning. . . . Beneath a mottled sky some score or so little carts covered in frail tarpaulins of unnamable sun-scorched colours were mustered before the Daleman Memorial where already a certain amount of petty chicanery had begun.

'Dat is a scene now which somehow make me smile,' Mrs Yajñavalkya commented. 'Ya Allah, but whenever I see a Market I no longer feel Abroad. . . . And w'y, I wonder, is de reason ob dis? . . . Because human nature is de same ebbery-where.'

'Any old flint glass or broken bottles for a poor woman today?' a barrow-hawker smote into her reflections from below.

Mrs Yajñavalkya indrew her head.

It was one of her fullest mornings, being the eve of Mrs Hurstpierpoint's reunion in honour of the centenarians of the place, who together with their progeny assembled yearly in the closed drawing-rooms, or beneath the titanic cedars, of Hare.

And for these annual resuscitations Mrs Yajñavalkya's invigorating touch was deemed almost indispensable.

Consulting her tablets, she found Tooke's Farm to be first on her list, when it might be that the dairyman himself would be about. Disheartening contretemps had followed hitherto her every intriguing effort. He had responded to her summons to 'take a look at the Vine' in the small grape-house at the extremity of the garden, politely, if unorthodoxly enough, bringing with him, with Mrs Tooke's 'compliments', a sumptuous barrowful of well-seasoned offal, whereat Lady Parvula de Panzoust, poised like a Bacchante amid the drooping grapes, had taken to fastidious heels in alarm.

'If I cannot throw dem both together,' she brooded, 'be it only out ob doors … I will be obliged to quench lub's fever wif a sedative.'

The venerable dial of St Veronica's wood clock, and a glimpse of Nurse Yates' under-sized form crossing the Square, advised her not to dawdle, and soon she too, was threading her way amid the arguing yokels and the little carts.

Beneath a strip of awning that shook slightly in the soft sea air a sailor with eyes like sad sapphires was showing a whale caught in the bay, to view which he asked a penny. Partially hid within a fishing creel it brought back to Mrs Yajñavalkya the unfaithful wives of her own native land who were cast as a rule to the sharks.

Refusing payment only to revive poignant memories of aunts and cousins, sisters and sisters-in-law, as well as a close escape of her own, Mrs Yajñavalkya disdainfully moved away.

In a cottage garden at the corner of the market-place she could distinguish the sexton of St Veronica's meandering round his beehives in a white paper mask. From his shuffling step and obvious air of preoccupation, it was as though in some instinctive way he was aware that the consequences of the Hare-Hatch rout would shortly drive him to 'resume' his spade.

Flitting fleetly by, Mrs Yajñavalkya attained the weather-beaten farmyard gate where, grinning as he watched her approach, stood Bobby Jolly.

'Is your master in, you little giggling Valmouth goose?' she inquired.

'David? He won't be back till evenfall.'

'Oho?'

'He's felling trees in Wingley Woo,' the child replied, looking up quizzically into the negress's face.

Between his long curly lashes were blue eyes – not very deep: a slight down, nearly white, sprouted below a dainty little nose, just above the lip at the two corners.

'No matter. So long as the dear dowager has not gone with him,' Mrs Yajñavalkya replied, jauntily entering the yard. On the dung-hill that rose against the church to the sill of the clerestory windows lay Douce – treacherously asleep, his muzzle couched on a loose forepaw.

'He leave behind him de dog?'

''Cos of pheasants.'

Mrs Yajñavalkya shaded her brow from the sun with her hand.

Through an open barn she could trace the River Val winding leisurely coastward through cornfields white with glory. A hum of bees from the flower plot by the garden wall filled the air with a ceaseless sound and raised the mind up to Allah.

She chanced on Mrs Tooke essaying the effect of a youthful little cap before the glass.

'Charming,' the negress cried. 'Delicious!'

Decked with silk bandstrings and laces, the old lady's long bluish profile, calcined on the grave-ground without, recalled to Mrs Yajñavalkya one of the incomparable Dutch paintings assigned to Franz Hals, in Evadne, Duchess of Valmouth's boudoir.

'Faith, my dear,' Mrs Tooke exclaimed, 'but you frightened me.'

'And how do you find yourself, Mrs Tooke, today?' the negress archly asked.

Troubled at being surprised in an act of vanity, a thing she professed to abhor, Mrs Tooke was inclined to be captious.

'Today I feel only passably well, Mrs Yaj,' she replied.

'I've seen you worse, Mrs Tooke.'

'I fear I shall soon become now a portion for foxes.'

'Dat is for me to say, Mrs Tooke.'

'I ha'n't the constitution at all that I had.'

'De prospect ob a function may have occasioned a touch ob fever; nothing but a little cerebral excitement, de outcome ob neurasthenia, which my methods, I hope, will remove.'

'I wish I hadn't a wen, Mrs Yaj! A sad hash your methods made of it.'

'De more you cauterise a wen, Mrs Tooke ... Besides, wot's de good ob worry? Not poppy, nor mandragora, nor all the drowsy syrups of the world, shall ever soothe it or medicine it away. Remember.'

Mrs Tooke sighed submissively.

'Where did I put my Bible?' she plaintively asked, peering around the long-familiar room.

'I wonder you're not tired ob your Bible, Mrs Tooke.'

'Fie! Mrs Yaj. You shouldn't speak so.'

'You should read de Talmud for a change.'

'It sounds a poor exchange.'

'Do you really believe now, Mrs Tooke my dear, in de Apostolic Succession? Can you look me in de eyes and say you do?'

'I ha'n't paid any heed lately to those chaps, Mrs Yaj; I'm going on to Habakkuk.'

'Was not he de companion ob de Prodigal son?'

'Maybe he was, my dear. He seems to have known a good many people.'

'Dat is not de name now ob a man, Mrs Tooke, to observe a single wife, nor even a single sex. ... No! Oh no; a man wif a name like dat would have his needs!'

'Heysey-ho! We most of us have our wants.'

'From all one hears, Mrs Tooke, your grandson hasn't many.'

'Yoiks Mrs Yaj! He was at me just now for a Bull.'

'And do you tell me so, Mrs Tooke?'

'A farm's no farm without a Bull, says he; and t'other day 'twas a shorthorn milcher he'd have had me buy.'

'He seems insensitive to women, Mrs Tooke! I think, my dear, he never was truly enmeshed.'

'He's unimpressionable, I'm thankful to say.'

'I know ob one now, Mrs Tooke, who would be glad to

be on his two legs again tomorrow night – and who *will* be, my dear, I dare say, although I did refuse him.'

Mrs Tooke evinced detachment.

'They tell me Doris Country's dress is being edged with ermine,' she observed, fastening her eye on a piece of old Valmouth ware representing a dog with a hen in its mouth, that occupied the dresser.

'You'll need your *boa* as de nights are chilly.'

'Od: I've no ermine skin myself!'

'Dair are furs beside ermine, Mrs Tooke. Wot is dair smarter dan a monkey's tail trimmed in black lace? – wid no stint mind to de strings; dat is a combination dat always succeed.'

'Belike.'

'In my land ermine, you know, is exclusive to de khan or, as you would say, de king.'

'His Majesty, the Can!' the old lady shyly marvelled.

'He my beloved sovereign.'

'And your Queens (I presume) are Pitchers?'

'Never you mind now, Mrs Tooke, never you mind! but just let me rub a little ob dis on de seat ob your ovaries; de same as I did once to a Muscovite princess. . . . "Your magic hand, my dear," she say, "it bring such joy and release. . . ."'

'I wish I had your brawn, Mrs Yaj!'

'Noble, or ignoble, Mrs Tooke, I treat my clients just de same!'

'You old black bogey, what should I do without you?'

'*Inshallah!*' The negress shrugged, glancing over her shoulder at a sudden sneeze from Miss Tooke behind her.

Bearing in her arms the sacrificial linen, she waded forward in a ray of dusty sunlight, as if fording in fancy the turbid Val that should transport her to Love's transcendent delights, in illimitable, jewelly seas.

'It's a hard thing, Mrs Yaj,' Mrs Tooke observed, 'to be dependent on a wench who spends half her life in the river! If *I* was a fish I'd snap at her legs.'

'I've no doubt you would, Mrs Tooke, but joking, my dear, apart, unless as a finish to a douche cold water I always discommend. Dair (in moderation no doubt) it is good;

otherwise in my opinion it is injurious to de circulation, impeding and clogging de natural channels and so hampering de course ob de blood, and often even gibbing excuse to de body's worst enemy ob all – I mean de gastric juices.'

Mrs Tooke's brows knit together. She scowled.

'Let her keep her distance,' she exclaimed, 'with her contagious heavy cold!'

'I am sure I've no will to come near you,' Miss Tooke replied with a desolating sigh as she fell to earth.

She was looking restless and pale and strangely avid for love.

'You'll not die in an old skin if you fret it so, Thetis girl, ah, that ye won't.'

'What's the use of living then? Life is only acceptable on the condition that it is enjoyed.'

Mrs Tooke blinked, eluded.

'Belike,' she said, 'by God's grace tomorrow night we'll both have a bit of a fling. Oh-ay, I do mind the nestful of field-mice we had in the spring-cart last year. I had been out all day among the clover, but, Lord! I never knew 'twas full of they mice, till a satire, in livery, shoved his hand (like a sauce-box) into the cart, under pretext of helping me down, when pouf! out they all hopped from under my train, furnishing the tag-rag and bobtail there was standing about with all manner of *immund* remarks. . . .'

'And where was this, Mrs Tooke?' the negress aloofly asked.

'Why at Hare, Mrs Yaj, last year.'

Miss Tooke sighed again, and drawing a cut citron from her apron pocket she applied it gently (as directed by 'Susuva' in *The Woman's Friend*) to the roots of her nails.

> 'When I am dead
>   Ah bring me flow-ers,
>   Spread roses and forget-me-nots,'

she somewhat hectically hummed.

'You bits of raw shoots seldom hark to any sense, though 'twere better often to be a primrose in the wilderness than a polyanthus in a frame. And you'll remember, maybe, I said so, when I'm grassed down in the earth and gone,' Mrs Tooke declared, riveting her attention on the tombstones below.

Several of the nearer epitaphs were distinctly legible through the farmstead windows, such as '*Josephine – first wife of Q. Comedy Esqre dies of Jealousy, March 31st 1898: Remember her*,' while the rest, monotonously identical, for the most part betokened 'inconsolable widows' and were nothing, according to Mrs Tooke (who had eyes for a wedding as well as for a funeral), but 'a " — " tangle of lies!' One gaunt, tall cross, however, half hidden by conifers, a little apart, almost isolated, solitary, alone, was, to the excellent Englishwoman, in its provocativeness, as a chalk egg is to a sensitive hen. Here lay Balty Vincent Wise, having lived and died – *unmarried*. Oh what a funny fellow! Oh what a curious man! . . . What did he mean by going off like that? Was no woman good enough for him then? Oh what a queer reflection to be sure; what a slur on all her sex! Oh but he should have settled; ranged himself as every bachelor should! Improper naughty thing! He should be exorcized and whipped: or had he loved? Loved perchance *elsewhere* . . . ? The subject of many a fluttered reverie he gave, by his eccentric manes, just that touch of mystery, that piquant interest to the churchyard that inwardly she loved – Balty!

'There are times, Mrs Yaj, when I find the look-out cheerless.'

'Still! Radder dan see "Marsh-lights" . . .'

'Ah . . . I shall never forget how Mr Comedy (when he lost his first wife) passed the night in the graveyard, crying and singing and howling, with a magnum of Mumm. . . .'

With a wry little laugh Miss Tooke turned and moved away.

'Since you've all, then, you need,' she said, 'I'll take a pail of clams and yams, I think, to feed the pigs.'

'Let 'em farrow if they choose, and keep clear of the river, mind; don't let me hear of you in the Val again today.'

'The Val! You ought to see the Ganges, Mrs Tooke! Ah, dat is some river indeed.'

'In what way, Mrs Yaj?'

'A girl may loiter there with her amphora and show her ankles to de fleets of sailing sampans often to her advantage. ... Many a match-making mother have I known, my dear, to send her daughter to stand below some eligible Villa with instructions to toy for an hour with her crock.'

'As I'm a decent widow, Mrs Yaj, you negresses are a bad lot, I'm afraid.'

'O w'y?'

'I expect it's something to do with your climate.'

'We Eastern women love the sun ...! When de thermo-meter rise to some two hundred or so, ah dat is de time to lie among de bees and canes.'

'I could never stand the stew – , it would take all *my* stamina.'

'My little maid, Carry, is de same as you. De least spell ob warmth prostrate her wid de vertigoes.'

'You've had her some time now, Mrs Yaj.'

'So I have, Mrs Tooke, so I have; dô I say often I've a mind to take a page; but a growing boy in de house, my dear – you *know* what dey are! However, Carry I soon shall have to dis-miss. ... She dat otiose! She dat idle! She will read by de hour from my medical dictionary, dô I defend her eber to open it, because dair are tings she is perhaps better without de knowledge ob! *Kra*. And how she wreck my china! Before I came to dis place I had no stylish services; but I would go out and pick myself a plate ob a fresh green leaf, and den wèn it had served its purpose, after each course, I would just throw it away; and like dat dair was no expense and none ob dese breakages at all.'

'Well, there are plenty of pleasant trees round Valmouth, Mrs Yaj, I'm sure; and you're welcome to flower-leaf or vegetable from these acres, my dear, at any time; you shall sup off Dock a-Monday, and Cabbage Tuesday, Violet-hearts on Wednesday, Ivy Thursday, Nettle Friday, King Solomon's seal Saturday, and Sunday, you old black caterpillar, you can range as you please through the grass.'

'I have my own little garden, Mrs Tooke, my dear, you

forget: but dat white calf now out yonder . . . my niece beg me to say she'd buy it, as she desire to sacrifice it to a certain goddess for private family reasons.'

'For shame, Mrs Yaj. It makes me sad to hear you talk like a heathen.'

'Such narrow prejudice; for I suppose it will only go to de butcher in de end?'

'Disgusting.'

'Butchers are so brutal, Mrs Tooke . . .! Dair hearts must be so unkind . . . men without mercy! And dat's wot I alvays say.'

'Ts!'

'And remember dis, my dear. It is for her deity and not for herself she seek the calf.'

'Be quiet.'

'Niri-Esther only relish roots, a dish ob white roots and fruits – unless dis last few days, when she express a fancy for water-melon jam! But where I say in Valmouth can you find water-melon jam? O de worries, Mrs Tooke!'

'I ha'n't seen her kite so much lately, Mrs Yaj.'

'Babies are so tender. . . . Little children are so frail . . .' the negress said to herself aloud.

'What's that my dear?'

'I miss a mosque, Mrs Tooke, and de consolation ob de church; but when I turn to Allah, I suppose de Holy Mihrab near to me and den,' the negress murmured, bestowing a parting pinch upon the aged dame, 'all is well.'

Her day indeed was but begun. In many a cloudswept village bespattering the hills her presence was due anon.

Issuing from the farm-house she hovered to consider the itinerary ahead – culminating picturesquely (towards sunset) in a ruined stomach – some six miles from the town. Deliberatingly traversing the yard, where, here and there, fowl were pecking negligently at their shadows, she recognized in the penumbra of a cart-shed the arrowy form of Lady Parvula de Panzoust.

She wore a dress of becoming corduroy and a hat all rose-pink feathers, the little basket upon her arm signifying, evidently – *eggs*.

Following her (with more perhaps than his habitual suspicion) was churlish Douce.

'Poor, dear, beautiful, patient beast!' the negress could hear her say in tones of vivacious interest as she fondled the dog's supple back and long, soft, nervelessly drooping ears. Then suddenly stooping, she exclaimed vehemently, as if transported: 'Kiss me, Bushy!'

8

It was the auspicious night when as to a Sabbat the centenarians of Valmouth, escorted by twittering troops of expectant heirs, and toad-eating relatives, foregathered together, like so many warlocks and witches, in the generously loaned drawing-rooms and corridors of Hare.

Originating in the past with the corporation, as a subtle advertisement to the salubrity of the climate, these reunions were now in such high favour that the Valmouth Town Hall, a poor poky place, was no longer capable of holding so numerous an attendance, obliging the municipality to seek a more convenient rendezvous elsewhere; hence the cordial offer of the Hare ladies to 'throw open' their doors annually had been accepted officially with a thousand pleasant thanks; and by degrees, by dint of some acted *Mystery*, played to perfection by the Nuns of Sodbury and the Oblates of Up-More, these reunions had afforded full scope for the diplomatic furtherance of Rome.

Something of Limbo, perhaps, was felt by those at present gathered in the long salon, bafflingly lit by an old-fashioned chain-chandelier that threw all the light upwards, towards the ceiling, leaving the room below (to the untold relief of some) in semi-obscurity; but the night being fine, many preferred to wander out attracted by the silken streamers of a vast marquee.

Leaning on the arm of a swathed tangerine figure, Mrs Hurstpierpoint, decked in wonderful pearls like Titian's Queen of Cyprus, trailed about beneath the mounting moon, greeting here and there a contemporary with vague cognition. She seemed in charming spirits.

'Your ladyship dribbles!' she complacently commented, shaking from the curling folds of her dress a pious leaflet, *The — of Mary*, audaciously scouting the Augustinian theory 'that the Blessed Virgin conceived our Lord through the Ears.'

Looking demurely up she saw wide azure spaces stabbed with stars like many Indian pinks.

The chimeric beauty of the night was exhilarating.

In the heavy blooming air the rolling, moon-lit lawns and great old toppling trees stretched away, interfusing far off into soft deeps of velvet, dark blue violet, void.

'The last time I went to the play', the tangerine figure fluted, 'was with Charles the Second and Louise de Querouaille, to see Betterton play Shylock in *The Merchant of Venice*.'

'Was he so fine?' Mrs Hurstpierpoint asked, her query drowned in a dramatic dissonance from the pergola – climax to a blood-stirring waltz.

On the lawn-sward couples were revolving beneath the festooned trees that twinkled convivially with fairy-lamps, but the centre of attraction, perhaps, at present was the Mayor.

'Congratulations', his voice pealed out, 'to Peggy Laugher, Ann and Zillah Bottom, Almeria Goatpath, Thisbe Brownjohn, Teresa Twistleton, Rebecca Bramblebrook, Junie Jones, Susannah Sneep, Peter Palafox, Flo Flook, Simon Toole, Molly Ark, Nellie Knight, Fanny Beard, May Thatcher, May Heaven, George Kissington, Tircis Tree, Gerry Bosboom, Gilbert Soham, Lily Quickstep, Doris Country, Anna Clootz, Mary Teeworthy, Dorothy Tooke, Patrick Flynn, Rosa Sweet, Laurette Venum, Violet Ebbing, Horace Hardly, Mary Wilks – '

'*In saeculum saeculi*, apparently!' Mrs Hurstpierpoint shrugged.

On the fringe of the throng, by a marble shape of Priapus green with moss, Lady Parvula de Panzoust was listening, as if petrified at her thoughts, to the Mayor.

'I shall never forget her,' the tangerine bundle breathed, 'one evening at Salsomaggiore –!'

'For a fogy, she's not half bad, is she, still?'

'I consider her a charming, persuasive, still beautiful, and *always* licentious woman. . . .'

'And with the art . . . not of returning thistles for figs?'

'There are rumours – I dare say you know – of an affair here in the town.'

'Poor Parvula . . . ! a scandal, more or less, it will make no difference to her whatever,' Mrs Hurstpierpoint answered lucidly, turning apprehensively at the sound of a jocose laugh from Mrs Yajñavalkya.

Très affairée, equipped in silk of Broussa, she was figurable perhaps to nothing so much as something from below.

'That little black niece of hers, my dear, is extremely exciting. . . .'

'Divinely voluptuous.'

Mrs Hurstpierpoint tossed a troubled leaflet.

'She is ravishing,' she declared, wafting a butterfly kiss to the Abbess of Sodbury – Mère Marie de Cœurbrisé. *Née* a Begby of 'Bloxworth', Mère Marie's taste for society was innate, and her *petits goûters* in the convent parlour were amazing institutions, if Sister Ecclesia, before her lips were bound, was to be believed.

'It puts me in mind of Vauxhall when I was a girl,' she chuckled.

'Oh – oh!'

'*Wunderschön! Bella, bella.*'

Her old orchidized face, less spiritualized than orchidized by the convent walls, in the moonlight seemed quite blue.

'And my birch, the blessed broom. . . . Is it in Italy? Has His Holiness complied with the almond-twigs?' Mrs Hurstpierpoint inquired, drawing her away just as Mrs Yajñavalkya, believing the leaflet to be as fraught with meaning as a Sultan's handkerchief, dispatched her niece to pick it up.

Such an unorthodox mode of introduction could not but cause the heart a tremor.

'In de case ob future advance,' Mrs Yajñavalkya enjoined her niece (smiling impenetrably at her thoughts), 'be sure to say de dear billet shall receive your prompt attention.'

'*Paia!*' Niri-Esther assented.

She was looking vanquishing in a transparent sleeveless tunic, over a pair of rose-mauve knickers of an extraordinary intensity of hue. In her arms she held a sheaf of long-stemmed, pearl-white roses – *Soif de Tendresse.*

'We shall enter de palace by de garden gate . . . by de gate ob de garden . . .' Mrs Yajñavalkya reflected, her eyes embracing the long, semi-Grecian outline of the house.

Before the mask-capped windows, Lady Parvula de Panzoust pointed sharply the dusk with a shimmering fan.

'Your Diana', the negress, approaching, coughed, 'we speak ob as Hina. But she is de same; she is de moon.'

'Ah?'

'She is de moon. . . .'

'Soon again, she'll be dwindling.'

'May you enjoy ambrosia: a lover's tigerish kisses, ere she disappears.'

Lady Parvula braced nervously her shoulders.

'Who is the woman in the cerements?' she inconsequently wondered.

'Dat dair she some stranger.'

'It amuses one to watch their dying flutters. . . .'

'You should take notice ob de wife ob de Mayor. Dô she be a hundred and forty, and more, yet she hardly look de age ob "consent"!'

'Have you nothing else – more interesting – to tell me?' Lady Parvula asked, motioning to the shade of the nearest tree.

'Assuredly,' the negress answered, following towards the dark-spreading Spina-Christi over against the house.

I, I, I, I! A night-bird fled on startled wings.

'Like the cry of an injured man!' Lady Parvula murmured, sinking composedly to a garden chair.

'Like de cry ob a djinn!'

'Well; is one any nearer? does he seem in a coming-on stage?' her ladyship blithely asked.

The oriental woman swelled.

'De way he questioned me concerning you, milady,' she unctuously made reply, 'was enough to make a swan bury its head beneath de water.'

'Silly fellow and is he crazy about me, you say? Dear boy. Well.'

'He say he ready to eat you.'

'To – what?'

'Ah de rogue!'

'Eat me . . . and when does he wish to devour me?' Lady Parvula touched nervously the white plumes and emeralds in the edifice of her hair.

'Ah de wretch!'

'Doesn't he say?'

'Al-ways he is hungry, de ogre!'

'The great, big, endless fellow!'

'Al-ways he is clamouring for a meal.'

'Let him guard as he can those ambered freckles!'

'Dey would draw de mazy bees.'

'I so feared he was going to be shy.' With pensive psychic fingers the enamoured Englishwoman toyed with a talismanic bagatelle in New Zealand jade.

'Believe me, he only play de part ob de timid youth de better to surprise you.'

'Simple angel!'

'He resist.'

'I once made a grand resistance – and oh! don't I regret it now . . . the poor dear was of low birth: humble origin: no condition: my husband's amanuensis! But oh! oh! !'

'Dose villain valets. Dey are de very men wif dair fair hard hair and dair chiselled faces. . . .'

'This was a paid secretary. . . . But oh, oh! Even my Lord. He could hardly spell. . . .'

'His face was his fortune?'

'Possibly. But I never was careless of appearances, as I told you I think once before. To my good name I cling. Mine, I congratulate myself, is entirely proof. No one has ever really been able to make a heroine out of me! The bordomette of circumlocution one submits to meekly perforce. In the Happy East you live untrammelled by the ghouls of our insular convention.'

Mrs Yajñavalkya shook a stiff forefinger.

'Sho,' she muttered, allowing soft, discarnate voices to articulate and move on.

'Her great regret you know . . .' the murmur came, 'she is . . . God forgive her . . . the former Favourite of a king; although, as she herself declares, *only* for a few minutes. Poor darling! ... Yes! My poor Love! She gave herself to an *earthly* crown. ...'

'An ex-mistress of a king: she has the air.'

'It is Eulalia's *constant torment!*' The voices ebbed.

Lady Parvula looked down at the blue winter-violets in the front of her dress.

'Her sway was short!' she wondered.

She was all herself in a gown of pale brocade with a banana pattern in gold fibre breaking all over it.

'In an affair ob kismet – for it is kismet; what (I ask you to tell me) is reputation? What is it, reputation, in a case ob dis discription? Dis Smara. Dis Mektoub. Dis Destiny!'

'Sound him again. Put out final feelers,' Lady Parvula murmured, waving dismissal with a tap of her fan.

With a wise expressive nod the negress turned away.

Picking her way over the contorted roots of the trees she shaped her course towards the house, pausing to admire a universe of stars in a marble basin drip drop dripping, drip drip dropping, over with the clearest water.

'Vaea, vaea,' she mused, 'satufa lu-lu fiss.'

Looking up she perceived David Tooke, as if in ambush behind a statue of Meleager that resembled himself.

'Vot do you dair so unsocial?' she demanded in her softest gavroche speaking voice.

The young yeoman smiled slowly.

'Is it true', he abstrusely answered, 'that in your country bulls consort with mares, and rams seek after cows, and the males of partridges do curious things among themselves?'

'Whoebber told you so told lies.'

'Told lies?'

'Dey told you only ob de few exceptions.'

'Ah.'

He seemed a trifle moonstruck.

'But ob vot importance is it? ... Suppose *dey do?* Come on now, and hitch your wagon to a star.'

'I'll hitch my wagon where I choose.'

'Up wid dose dear shafts.'

'Tiddy-diddy-doll!' ungraciously he hummed.

'You marry her – and be a Lord!'

'Be off! Don't pester me.'

'Come on now.'

'Heart and belly: not I!'

'Must I *pull* you?'

'Pull me?'

'Drag you to milady.'

'Don't make me a scene, because my nerves can't stand it!'

'Vas dair ebber a eunuch like you?'

'Why does she want to come bothering me?'

'I have nebber heard of such contempt ob de peerage', Mrs Yajñavalkya fairly snorted.

'Here's Granny,' he breathed.

And indeed rounding a garden path on her grand-daughter's arm Mrs Tooke was making a spirited progress of the grounds.

'Glad am I, my dear,' the negress cried, 'to see you're still so able . . .'

'Isht! My legs gae all tapsalteerie!'

'Dat is nothing but Nature's causes. What is wobblyness ever but de outcome simply ob disuse?'

'Just hark to my joints! I'm positively tumbling to bits!'

'And where are you off to, Mrs Tooke?'

'To make a beau-pot, Mrs Yaj.'

'What do you call a *beau-pot*, Mrs Tooke?'

'A posy, Mrs Yaj.'

'And vot's a posy, Mrs Tooke?'

'A bunch of flowers, my dear.'

'In de East dair is a rose, deep and red, dat when she open go off, pop, pop, pop – like de crack ob a gun!' and relinquishing her quarry, with a meaning glance, the negress strolled away.

'He is frigid. Dat I will admit: and bearish a little, too. But de boy is not such a fool,' she philosophized, gazing around her for a sign of her niece.

Through a yew-hedge, thinner at the bottom than at the top, she could see the feet of the dancers as they came and went.

A drowsy Tzigane air, intricate, caressing, vibrated sensuously to the night.

'May I have the pleasure . . . ?' a mild-faced youth, one of the Oblates of Up-More, addressed her.

'Delighted,' she answered, with equanimity, accepting his arm.

'Your countrywoman doesn't dance,' he observed, signalizing Niri-Esther astride the seat-board of a garden swing, attached to the aerial branches of a silver fir.

She was clinging mysteriously to the ropes as though her instinct told her they had known the pressure of the palms of someone not altogether indifferent to her heart.

'Just at present . . .' the negress shrugged, submitting to be borne off by the will of a man.

'Ga – ga,' Niri-Esther gurgled, rubbing her cheek languorously against the cord.

'A push is it?' Mrs Hurstpierpoint aborded her with a smile. 'Is it a push you wish for, dear child? Is that', she dismantlingly ogled, 'what you're after?' and taking silence for assent, she resolutely clasped the black girl from behind below the middle.

Niri-Esther fetched a shout.

'Oh! Eulalia! ! !' Mrs Thoroughfare approached *à pas de loup*. 'What are you up to, Eulalia? What are you doing?'

'Go away, Thoroughfare. Now go away.'

'Oh, Eulalia.' Mrs Thoroughfare shrank.

'Is not that *heavenly*, dear child?' the formidable woman queried, depositing a rich muff of Carrick-macross lace, bulging with propaganda upon the ground.

'Stop!'

'Was not that divine, my dear? Didn't you like it?' The hieratic woman pressed, passing her tongue with quiet but evident relish along her upper lip.

Niri-Esther turned aside her head.

The constipated whiteness of a peacock in the penumbra of the tree was disquieting to her somewhat.

'Bird!!' Mrs Hurstpierpoint chuckled.

'Ours at home are much bigger.'

'Are they, dear child?'

'Much.'

'I want us to be friends. Will you?'

'Why?'

'Ah, my dear ... "why"? Because,' Mrs Hurstpierpoint quavered, leaning forward to inhale the singularly pungent perfume proceeding from the negress's person, 'because you're very lovable.'

'Eulalia!' Mrs Thoroughfare reimportunated.

'Yes, Elizabeth!'

'I'm anxious to speak to you for a moment privately, Eulalia.'

'Well –'

'Oh, Eulalia!' Mrs Thoroughfare faltered. 'Madame Mimosa is here ... exercising her calling ...'

'What?'

'Oh, Eulalia. ...'

'ffines! And turn her out.'

'At least, darling, she was arm-in-arm ... entwined, Eulalia.'

'Prude Elizabeth. Was that all you had to say?'

Mrs Thoroughfare cast a grim glance towards Niri-Esther.

'Oh, she's a monstrous kid, Eulalia! ... Isn't she just?'

'I don't agree with you there, Elizabeth, at all.'

'Oh, she's a nutty girl; she's a bit of all right.'

'Why are you so down on her, Eliza?'

'I, Eulalia? I'm not down. I think her charming.'

'I'm glad you do.'

'She has her immaturity. I divine this and that.'

'Pho.'

'I guess a great deal.'

'How dear Richard would have admired her.'

'Dick would? How?'

Mrs Hurstpierpoint lifted her shoulders slightly.

'Your son has a many-sided nature to him, Elizabeth,' she observed; 'which I suppose is not surprising when one thinks of you!'

'What do you mean, Eulalia?'

'What I say, darling. Dick's a man of several facets – no specialist! Thank the Lord!'

'Her habit of covering up her mouth with her hand when not speaking isn't exactly pretty.'

'She needs debarbarizing, of course.'

'She'd still be black, Eulalia!'

'Black or no, she's certainly perfectly beautiful.'

'She may appeal to your epicurism, dear, although she mayn't to mine.'

'She was telling me – only fancy, Lizzie – that the peacocks in her land are much bigger –!'

'I should think they were, Eulalia. I should imagine they would be.'

'I found her so interesting.'

'I've no doubt of that, Eulalia.'

'But where is she?'

Apparently, like the majority of persons present, she had sauntered over to where a wordless passional play performed by mixed religions seemed to be scoring a hit.

On an overt stage ranged beneath the walls of Nuestra Señora de la Pena brilliantly lit within, two pretty probationers, Mystylia and Milka Morris, protégées of the ladies of the house, were revealing themselves to be decidedly promising artists, while gathered in a semicircle about the stage the audience was finding occasion to exchange a thousand casuistries relative to itself or to the crops.

There uprose a jargon of voices:

'Heroin.'

'Adorable simplicity.'

'What could anyone find to admire in such a shelving profile?'

'We reckon a duck here of two or three and twenty not so old. And a spring chicken *anything to fourteen.*'

'My husband had no amorous energy whatsoever; which just suited me, of course.'

'I suppose when there's no more room for another crow's-foot, one attains a sort of peace?'

'I once said to Doctor Fothergill, a clergyman of Oxford and a great friend of mine, "Doctor," I said, "oh, if only you could see my –"'

'*Elle était jolie! Mais jolie! . . . C'était une si belle brune . . .!*'

'Cruelly lonely.'

'Leery. . . .'

'Vulpine.'

'Calumny.'

'People look like pearls, dear, beneath your wonderful trees.'

'. . . Milka, tonight – she is like a beautiful Cosway.'

'Above social littleness. . . .'

'Woman as I am!'

'Philanthropy.'

'. . . A Jewess in Lewisham who buys old clothes, old teeth, old plate, old paste, old lace. And gives very good prices indeed.'

' 'Er 'ealth I'm please to say is totally established.'

'If she pays her creditors *sixpence* in the *pound* it's the utmost they can expect.'

'Wonderful the Duchess of Valmouth's golden red hair, is it not?'

' "You lie to me," he said. "I'm not lying, and I *never* lie," I said. "It's *you* who tell the lies." Oh! I reproached him.'

'I'm tired, dear, but I'm *not* bored! . . .'

'What is a boy of twenty to me?'

'It's a little pain-racked face – not that she really suffers.'

Sister Ecclesia chafing at her Vows, martyred to find some outlet to expression, was like to have died, had not Nature inspired her to seek relief in her sweetest, most inconsequent way.

'I give her leave', Mère Marie de Cœurbrisé said, 'to demand "the Assembly's pardon."'

Drawn by this little incident together, Lady Parvula de Panzoust and Mrs Q. Comedy, a lady with white locks and face – the only creature present in a hat – had fallen into an animated colloquy.

'These big show seats', Lady Parvula sighed, 'are all alike: insanitary death-traps!'

The local land-agent's wife sent up her brows a little.

'Were you ever over Nosely?' she interjected.

'The Lauraguays'? Never!' Lady Parvula fluttered a painted fan of a bouquet of flowers by Diaz.

'My husband has the letting of it, you know.'

'Ah, hah –? Well, I always admire Richard the Third, who leased his house in Chelsea to the Duchess of Norfolk for the yearly rental of one red rose.'

Mrs Comedy's mouth dropped.

'But that was hardly business!' she remarked.

'Who knows though? Perhaps it was,' Lady Parvula answered, appraising her Corydon through the eyelets of her fan.

'I've a sure flair for a figure,' she mused, 'and this one is prodigious.'

'Some say they find the country "warping".'

'Oh, but I feel I want to kiss you!' Lady Parvula ecstatically breathed.

'Madam?' Mrs Comedy recoiled.

Just at this juncture, over the lawn-party, appeared the truant poll-parrot of Sir Victor Vatt. Wheeling round and round the chapel cross in crazy convolutions, the bird was like something demented.

'Dear Vatt,' it cried, 'he is splendid: so o-ri-gi-nal: and exuberant; like an Italian Decorator. Come, Vatt! Paint me in a greenhouse ... in a st-oove; a little exotic! ... Where's my bloody brush?'

'I forget', the Abbot of Up-More (a man like a sorrowful colossus) said, fingering fancifully the ring of red beard that draped his large ingenious face, 'if Vatt is for us or no.'

'He is to be had,' Mrs Hurstpierpoint answered. 'In my private-list I have entered him as "Shakeable": Very: he will come for a touch ...' she added, wincing at some shooting stars that slipped suddenly down behind the house.

'As Othniel prevailed over Chushanrishathaim so ought likewise we, by self-mortification and by abstinence, to proselytize all those who themselves perhaps uncertain, vacillate ingloriously upon the brink,' the Abbot cogently commented.

With angelic humour Mrs Hurstpierpoint swept skyward her heavy-lidded eyes.

'I thought last night, in my sleep', she murmured, 'that Christ was my new gardener. I thought I saw Him in the Long Walk there, by the bed of Nelly Roche, tending a fallen flower with a wisp of bast. . . . "Oh, Seth," I said to Him . . . "remember the fresh lilies for the altar-vases. . . . Cut all the myosotis there is," I said, "and grub plenty of fine, feathery moss. . . ." And then, as He turned, I saw of course it was not Seth at all.'

'Is Seth leaving you?'

'He leaves us, yes, to be married,' Mrs Hurstpierpoint replied, acknowledging a friendly little grimace from Niri-Esther, who appeared to be comporting herself altogether unceremoniously towards Thetis Tooke over the matter of a chair.

'Nowadays, the young people sit while their elders stand!' the Abbott succinctly said, riveting a curly-pated *enfant de cœur* lolling coxcombically beneath the nose of a doating Statilia.

Mrs Hurstpierpoint kicked out the fatigued silver folds of her Court train with some annoyance.

'Charlie,' she beckoned.

'Here 'm,' the child chirped, coming up.

'Where's your chivalry, Charlie? Your respect to the ladies?' The lad looked down abashed.

'Come nearer, Charlie. (Quite close, Little-Voice!) Is that ink on your head, I see?'

'Probably. . . . Father often wipes his pen in my hair,' the boy replied, darting off down a gravel path, where, having strayed away from the rest, Mrs Tooke was dropping curtsies to the statues.

'She's loose.'

'Oh! At her time?'

'Very, very loose.'

The Abbot caressed his beard.

'Indeed, she looks a squilleon,' he raptly conjectured.

'She's *shakeable*, Abbot, I mean: in other words one could have her . . .' Mrs Hurstpierpoint explained.

'Ah: I see.'

'My tongue is over-prone perhaps to metaphor. My cherished friend sometimes scolds me for it; only a fellow-mystic – some saint, would ever know, she says, what I'm driving at often. . . . Dear Lizzie. . . . If I could but influence her to make a Retreat; a change from Hare seems highly expedient for her; and at Arimathaea she would have still her Confessor! For something, I fear, is weighing on her mind; some sorrow she tells me nothing of; and it makes her so difficult. Just now we almost quarrelled. Yes. She grew jealous. And of a negress. Not the old one. "Dina-dina-do". I mean the girl in drawers. So I feel somehow Sodbury is the place for my poor angel. Just for a time. They have there, I believe, at present, Julie Bellojoso, and her sister, Lady Jane Trajane – also little Mrs Lositer; Grouse Dubelly that was; she, of course, a fixture! . . . Thus my excellent, exquisite friend would have comradeship: and she would return here, I trust, softened, chastened, and with a less dingy outlook on life. For her talk, lately, Abbot, has been anything but bright. Indeed, she frightens me at times with her morose fits of gloom. *Entre nous* I lay the blame on the excellence of the garden as much as anything else! Our wall-fruit this year has been so very delicious; were not those dark Alphonsos perfection? Dear Father Notshort, though, forgets my wicker basket! But he was always a favourite of mine; and one hears he has great authority with the Duchess. I hope she will decide to make the plunge from Hare. Her little starveling flower-face almost makes me want to cry. I feel as if I wanted to give her straight to Jesus. She is here somewhere tonight. With her *triste* far look. I often say she has the instinct for dress. Even a skirt of wool with her feels to shimmer. . . . Lady Violet Logg also is somewhere about: my Poor Heart found her the other day – the day, it was, of the appalling storm – in Nuestra Señora, practically on her knees . . . and with *both* her boys.' Mrs Hurstpierpoint diffusely broke off, directing her glance towards the municipal marquee.

Emerging from it amid a volley of laughter, came a puny, little old, osseous man of uncertain age, brandishing wildly to the night an empty bottle of Napoleon brandy.

'Ho! broder Teague,' his voice flew forth, 'dost hear de decree?

'Lilli burlero, bullen a-la.
Dat we shall have a new deputie,
Lilli burlero, bullen a-la.
Lero lero, lilli burlero, lero lero, bullen a-la,
Lero lero, lilli burlero, lero lero, bullen a-la.

Ara! but why does he stay behind?
Lilli burlero, bullen a-la.
Ho! by my shoul 'tis a protestant wind.
Lilli burlero, bullen a-la.
Lero lero, lilli burlero, lero lero, bullen a-la,
Lero lero, lilli burlero, lero lero, bullen a-la.

Now, now de heretics all go down,
Lilli burlero, bullen a-la.
By Chrish' and Shaint Patrick, de nation's our own – '

But with quick insight the *maître d'orchestre* had struck up a capricious concert waltz, an enigmatic, *au delà* laden air; Lord Berners? Scriabin? Tschaikovski? On the wings of whose troubled beat were borne some recent arrivals.

Entering the garden from the park, they would have reached the house, perhaps, unheeded, but for a watchman upon his rounds.

'A fine night, Captain!' The armed protector Mrs Hurstpierpoint saw fit to employ against itinerant ravishers or thieves addressed his master.

'A delicious night indeed!'

'A little rain before morning maybe . . .'

For Captain Thoroughfare had found his way home again, anxious yet diffident enough to introduce his bride to her new relations: while to lend a conciliatory hand Lieutenant Whorwood himself had submitted to pass a few days at Hare, his cajoling ways and prepossessing face having quite melted Mrs Hurstpierpoint upon a previous visit.

And, indeed, as he lagged along in the faint boreal light

behind his friend he resembled singularly some girl masquerading as a boy for reasons of romance.

He had a suit of summer mufti, and a broad-brimmed blue beaver hat looped with leaves broken from the hedgerows in the lanes, and a Leander scarf tucked full of flowers: loosestrife, meadowrue, orchis, ragged-robin.

But it was due to Thetis Tooke that their advent was first made known.

'Oh! Is it y-you, Dick?' she crooned, catching sight of her lover: 'dear, is it you? Oh, Dick, Dick, Dick, my life!' She fell forward with a shattering cry.

9

It was in the deserted precincts of a sort of Moorish palace in the purlieus of the town that Lady Parvula de Panzoust and David Tooke were to come together one afternoon some few days subsequent to the Hare-Hatch fête.

In the crazy sunlight the white embattled Kasbahs of the vast rambling villa (erected by a defunct director of the Valbay Oyster beds, as a summer resort, towards the close of the eighteenth century) showed forcefully, albeit, perhaps, a little sullenly, above the frail giraffe-like trunks of the birch-trees, and the argent trembling leaves of the aspens, that periodically shaded the route.

'I know I should despise myself, but I don't!' Lady Parvula told herself, unrolling a bruised-blue, sick-turquoise, silk sunshade very small like a doll's. 'Such perfect cant, though, with four "honeymoons" in the hotel, to be forced oneself to take to the fields ...! Oh Haree-ee-ee,' she flashed an *œillade* up into the electric-blue dome of her parasol, 'why did you leave me? Why did you leave your tender "Cowslip" by the wayside all alone? Do you hear me, Haree-ee-ee? Why did you ever leave me? And Gilda too, my girl. Oh, my darling child ... do you know the temptation your mother is passing through? Pray for her ... excuse her if you can. ... We shall be like the little birds tonight. Just hark to that one: *tiara, tiara, tiara*. It wants a tiara!'

Her aphrodisiac emotions nicely titillated, Lady Parvula de Panzoust was in her element.

'The Roman bridge in Rimini, the *Long* bridge in Mantua ...' she murmured to herself erotically, dreamily, as she crossed the Val.

She wore a dress of filmy white stuff, embroidered with bunches of pale mauve thistles, a full fichu, and a large mauve hat with wide mauve ribbons, tied in front in a large knot where the fichu was crossed on her bosom.

'Such red poppies, such blue hills and sea, I never saw!'
she reflected, entering a luxurious lime alley leading to the
house.

A sign-board bearing the words 'commodious residence',
with the name of Mr Comedy subjoined, struck a passing chill.

Evidently he was not yet come.

'I shall scream if he turns up in a dreadful billy-cock, or
plays stupid pranks,' she murmured, pursing forward her
lips that showed like a ripe strawberry in a face as whitened
as a mask of snow.

Beneath the high trees there was a charming freshness.

'*Kennst du das Land, wo die Citronen blühen?*' she vociferated
lightly, glancing up at the sun-fired windows of the house.

'It might suit me, perhaps,' she sighed, sinking down on
an old green garden-seat with the paint peeling off in scales.

But to one of her impatient character expectance usually
makes substantial demands upon the vitality.

' "*Oui, prince, je languis, je* brûle *pour Thésée – Je l'aime*,"' she
lyrically declaimed.

Mightn't he be, perhaps, lurking close somewhere out of
sight?

' "*Laissez-moi ma main . . .*"' she languidly hummed (affecting Carré in Manon).

After all there was no need, it seemed, to have put herself
in quite such a hurry.

'I begin now to wish I'd worn my little bombasine,' she
mused, 'notwithstanding the infernal quantities of hooks. It's
too late to turn back for it, I suppose? I feel all of a-twitter.
. . . These accidental affairs . . . I said I know I never would.
I can't forget the *caïquejee* on the Golden Horn; since that
escapade my nerve has gone completely. How quiet the rooks
are today. I don't hear any. Why aren't they chanting their
unkydoodleums? Swing high, swing low, swing to, swing
fro, swing lal-lal-lal-la. What keeps him ever? Some horrid
cow? I can't bear to think of the man I love under some cow's
chidderkins. Oh, Haree-ee-ee, Haree-ee-ee! Why did you
leave me, Henry, to this sort of thing?'

She peered about her.

In the shade of a tree, a book, forgotten, doubtless, by some potential tenant, was lying face downwards, open upon the grass.

With a belief in lovers' lightest omens, Lady Parvula de Panzoust was tempted to rise.

'*Un Document sur l'Impuissance d'Aimer*,' she pouted, pricking the brochure of Jean de Tinan with the point of her parasol.

'I seem to receive a special warning to take steps. . . . He may require inciting,' she deliberated, dropping very daintily to a grassy slope.

The turquoise tenderness of the sky drew from her heart a happy coo.

Overhead a wind-blown branch, upheld in its fall by another branch below, flecked precociously, with hectic tints, the heavy midsummer greenery.

Half sitting, half reclining, she settled herself reposefully against the tree-bole – limp, undefensive, expectant.

'I shall be down tomorrow with lumbago I dare say,' the latent thought flashed through her.

Nevertheless, the easy eloquence of the pose was worth while, perhaps, preserving.

A weasel, 'with a face like a little lion', she told herself skipped from behind a garden dial – paused, puzzled at the diaphanous whiteness of her gown – turned tail, and disappeared briskly beneath a fissure in the plinth.

The words, '*Donec eris felix, multos numerabis amicos, Tempora si fuerint nubila, solus eris!*' traced thereon, irritated her somehow.

Pulling out a letter from her dorothy bag she beguiled the tediousness of waiting by perusing distraitly its contents.

' "The *première* of Paphos," she read. "Castruccio . . . Delmé. The choruses made me weep. The Carmen Nuptiale was wholly divinely given. I fear these few months in Milan have been all in vain. My glory my voice. An old diva, a pupil of Tiejens . . . *Ah, fors' è lui!* Purity of my . . . No Patti, or Pasta . . . Signor Carsetti . . . thrilling shake . . . *Caro nome*. Lessons. Liras. One of the pensionnaires. . . . From Warsaw . . . worship . . . Mademoiselle Lucie de Cleremont Chatte. Lucie . . . Lucie . . . Lucie".'

Her head flopped forward beneath her heavy hat, her apathetic eyelids closed.

When at length she looked up, the fretted shadow of the house had sloped far toward the south.

Something broke the stillness.

An object that to her perplexity resolved itself into a large pink kite was being dragged slowly past her over the grass. Preceding it, the forms of Captain Thoroughfare and Niri-Esther were to be descried retreating together into the dusk. Catching itself in the garden weeds like a great maimed bird, the kite tore its way along in the wake of the insouciant pair, followed discreetly a few yards to the rear by the sorrowing figure of Thetis Tooke.

Lady Parvula was still meditating on what she had seen, when Mrs Yajñavalkya presented herself from beneath the shade of the boskage.

Her downcast eyes and rapid respiration prepared Lady Parvula to expect the worst.

'What brings you?' she faintly asked.

'Milady P.!' the negress clasped perfervidly beneath her chin her white-gloved hands. 'It is a case ob *unrequited love* . . . but dat does not mean to say you shall not be satisfied. No; oh no. On my honour.'

'The affair then' – Lady Parvula de Panzoust broke a pale-veined leaf, and bit it – 'proves abortive?'

'He will offer no opposition. . . . But on de other hand, he pretend he cannot guarantee to make any advance!'

Her ladyship's lip curled.

'I fear he must be cold, or else he's decadent? . . .' she said, 'for I have known men, Mrs Yajñavalkya – yes, and *many men* too! – who have found us little women the most engrossing thing in life '

'He has abjured, he says, de female sex.'

'Abjured us? Oh impossible!'

'However! he will content your caprice on one condition.'

'Let me hear it.'

'Marriage.'

'Marriage! ! ! ! !'

Lady Parvula wrapped herself in her dignity.

'He seems to *me* to be an unpublished type,' she said severely.

'De great, sweet slighter.'

'I try to follow his train of feeling – but I can't.'

'He is inhuman, milady, and dat is sure.'

Lady Parvula followed absently with her glance a huge clock-beetle, exploring restively the handle to her parasol.

'At once. Where is he?' she demanded.

'I left him yonder at de gate.'

'You got him to the gate!'

'And dair we just parted. "Come along, now," I said, "for wif-out you I refuse to budge".'

'Well, what made you leave him then?'

'*Kra.*'

'As he is a shy, mistrustful misanthrope ... an inverted flower...'

'"Why won't you come?" I say to him. "Do I ask de impossible?" *Kra!*'

'Oh ... I want to spank the white-walls of his cottage!'

'Vot is von misadventure?'

'Do you really believe candidly there's *any* chance?'

'Dis but a hitch!'

'A disappointment, Mrs Yajñavalkya –'

'Take what you can get, milady ... Half a loaf is better dan no bread! Remember; and dat's vot I alvays say.'

'Nonsense – ; he must trot out – ; I want more than crumbs.'

'I get you both de crust *and* de crumb. I obtain you all you desire: only give me de time,' the negress wheezed.

Lady Parvula looked malicious.

'Of course he's *stable*,' she remarked.

'*Inshallah!*'

'Since seeing him in his shirt-sleeves with the peak of his cap turned over his neck, and redolent, upon the whole, of anything but *flowers* ... he no longer thrills me', she alleged, 'to the former extent.'

'I could get you de cousin.'

'What cousin?'

'De Bobby Jolly boy.'

'. . . Too young!'

'He twelve.'

'Go on! He's not eight.'

'Dat child is a king's morsel.'

Lady Parvula had a headshake.

'In the depths of the wilds you'd think young folk were bound to be more or less pent up,' she reflected, in tearful tones.

Mrs Yajñavalkya smiled beneficently.

'It is not right, my dear,' she declared, 'you should be bilked. . . . Vot do you say to de captain ob a ketch? Beyond de Point out dair I have in mind de very goods.'

'As a rule that class is much too Esau. You understand what I mean.'

'Or; have you ever looked attentively at de local schoolmaster?'

'No; I can't say I have.'

'Den you certainly should!'

'A schoolmaster – there's something so very *dredged* –'

'I sometimes say to Doctor Dee he put me in mind ob Dai-Cok.'

'Dai-Cok?'

'De Japanese God ob Wealth.'

'Well – ; I dare say he would do as a poor *pis aller*,' Lady Parvula tittered, retouching her cheeks lightly with a powder-ball.

Not a breath of wind was stirring the trees. High up in the incandescent blue the whitest of moons was riding.

'Hina has lit her lamp. Hina here.'

'Damnation! ! ! !'

'Come with me now my beautiful darling. Come. Come. Be brave. Be patient,' the negress begged.

Lady Parvula rose stiffly to her feet.

'I'll come perhaps a short way with you,' she said, regarding speculatively the interchanging fires of the lighthouse, that revealed, far off, their illusive radiance round the Point.

'How I wish, my dear, I could bow to your wishes!'

'You?'

'Supply de need.'

'I have reconsidered –' Lady Parvula breathed. 'Tell me ... This captain of a ketch ... Has he ... (There are one or two petty questions I would like to put to you quietly as we go along ... !)'

10

THE sky was empurpled towards the west, and the long, desolate road, winding seaward, was wrapped in shadow; and desolate, equally, was her heart.

'I loved you, Dick – : I asked for nothing better, Dear, than to be the wool of your vest . . .' Thetis softly wailed.

Her pale lips quivered.

'I would have done it yesterday,' she moaned, 'only the sea was as smooth as a plate!'

Yet now that it was slashed with little phantom horses it affrighted her. To be enveloped utterly by that cold stampede! Recalling the foolishness they had talked of her naiad namesake, she spat.

A fleet white pony and a little basket-wagon, with Maudie and Maidie, the charming children of Mrs Q. Comedy, rattled by, returning from a picnic on the beach.

'I'd have blacked myself, Dick, for you. All over every day. There would have been such delight, Dear, in my aversion. . . . But you never told me your tastes. You concealed what you cared for from me. And I never guessed. . . . No; you never trusted me, Dick. . . . Besides! Everything's useless now,' she soliloquized, inclining to decipher the torn particles of a letter, littering the high road beneath her feet.

Willows near Pavia –

Weeping-willows near Pavia –

Pavia University –

Pavia –

Her bruised mind sought comfort . . . (vainly) . . . amid the bits –

'Yes. Everything's useless now. For very soon, Dick, I'll be dead!'

From a bank of yellowing bracken, a beautiful cock-pheasant flew over her with a plaintive shriek.

'Dead. . . . I suppose they'll put out the Stella Maris and

dredge the Bay. But the tide will bear me beyond the Point; fortunately; I'm so lightsome! Seven stone. If that . . . oh dear, oh dear. When Nellie Nackman did the same she never left the rocks. It's a matter of build purely.'

Two bare-footed men – Up-Moreites – passed her with a 'famished' stare.

'I have a lovely figure. Totally superior to hers. He doesn't know what I am. . . . Poor Dear. How should he? My honey-angel. . . . Oh, Dick, Dick, Dick, Dick. . . . I ought to curse you, my darling.'

A labourer striding fugitively along in front of her, a young spruce-fir on his back (its bobbing boughs brushing the ground), perplexed her briefly.

'But I can't, I can't curse you, Dick. . . . Dear one, I can't. Neither, I find, can I forgive you. . . . I hope your brats may resemble their mother – that's all.'

As in a stupor, forging headlong forward she was over-taken in the vicinity of Valopolis by the evening *voiture* of Madame Mimosa, the lady's monogram, 'Kiki', wreathed in true-love-knots, emblazoning triply the doors and rear. Pre-sumably the enchantress was returning from the parsonage there – her penchant for Canon Wertnose being well known.

Canon Wertnose, Thetis's thoughts ran on, would bury her were she to be cast ashore. The beach was considered as his 'domain'. . . . Canon Wertnose would call at the Farm. Her grandmother would put on her cap to receive his visit with the whiskerage appended. Canon Wertnose would caress the cat. There would be talk of Habakkuk. . . .

She started.

Seated on a mileage-stone near the road's end was Carry, the little slavey of Mrs Yajñavalkya, her head sunk low over a book.

She had in her hands a huge bright bouquet of Chinese asters, sunflowers, chrysanthemums, and dahlias, which she inhaled, or twisted with fabulous nonchalance in the air as she read. . . . She appeared to be very much amused.

'What are you laughing for, Carry Smith?' Thetis made question.

'Me?' the negress's little apprentice tittered. . . . 'Oh, miss!
. . . I know at last. . . .'

'What futility have you discovered now?'

'I know *at last* – about the gentlemen.'

'About what gentlemen?'

'I know all about them.'

'So do I – traitors.'

'Oh, miss!'

'Don't be a fool, Carry Smith.'

'I know, miss, about them.'

'You may think you do.'

'Ah, but *I know*.' The child kissed her two frail hands to the
first white star.

'Pick up your flowers, Carry Smith, and don't be a dilly,'
Thetis advised, turning from her.

Day was waning.

The retreating tide exposed to view the low long rocks,
encrusting sombrely the shore. Towards the horizon a flotilla
of fishing-boats showed immutable, pink-lacquered by the
evening sun.

'I shall remove my hat I think,' she cogitated. 'It would be
a sin indeed to spoil such expensive plumes. . . . It's not perhaps a headpiece that would become every one; – and I can't
say I'm sorry!'

Her gaze swept glassily the deserted strand.

'It exasperates me though to think of the trouble I gave
myself over maquillage. Blanching my face and fingers (and
often my neck and arms . . .) surreptitiously in the cream-
cans, before their consignment to Market, when all the while',
she mumbled, fumbling convulsively amid the intricacies of
her veil, 'he'd sooner have had me black!'

A little sob escaped her.

'Yes, he'd sooner I'd have been black,' she pursued,
approaching determinedly the water's brink, when, from
the shade of a cruciform stone, stepped Ecclesia, the
Nun.

It was her 'Day'.

Mingling her voice with the planing gulls, winding her

way dolorously amid the harsh bare rocks, she approached Thetis Tooke as if divinely impelled.

*

From the grey headland, where the stone Pharos cast through the gloom its range of shimmering light, a coastguard was surprised to see two women wrestling on the beach below, their outlines dim against the western sky.

II

CLAD in a Persian-Renaissance gown and a widow's tiara of white batiste, Mrs Thoroughfare, in all the ferment of a *Marriage-Christening*, left her chamber one vapoury autumn day and descending a few stairs, and climbing a few others, knocked a trifle brusquely at her son's wife's door.

Through the open passage windows scent-exhaling Peruvian roses filled the long corridors with unutterable unrest, their live oppressive odour quickening oddly the polished assagais and spears upon the walls.

'Yahya?'

'It's me, dear.'

'Safi?'

'May Mother come in?'

'N . . . o.'

'Hurry up, then, Esther – won't you?' Mrs Thoroughfare made reply, continuing resourcefully her course towards the lower regions of the house.

A tapestry curtain depicting *The Birth of Tact*, in which *Taste* was seen lying on a flower-decked couch amid ultra-classic surroundings, divided the stairway from the hall.

'His eye was again at the keyhole,' Mrs Thoroughfare reflected, pausing to glare at ffines, who was imparting technicalities relative to the Bridal-breakfast to his subordinates.

All was hurry and verve, making the habitual meditation in Nuestra Señora a particular effort today.

Yet, *oremus* – there being, indeed, the need.

Beyond a perpetual vigil-lamp or two the Basilica was unlit.

Glancing nervously at the unostentatious (essentially unostentatious) font, Mrs Thoroughfare swept softly over a milky-blue porcelain floor (slightly slithery to the feet) to where her pet *prie-dieu*, laden with pious provender like some good mountain mule, stood waiting, ready for her to mount, which with a short sigh she did.

'Teach me to know myself, O Lord. Show me my heart. Help me to endure,' she prayed, addressing a figurine in purple and white faience by Maurice Denis below the *quête*.

Through the interstices of the be-pillared nave (brilliant with a series of Gothic banners) the sunlight teemed, illuminating the numerous *ex-votos*, and an esoteric little altar-piece of the 'School' of Sodoma.

'O grant me force!' she murmured, unbending a shade at sight of the gala altar-cloth where, crumpled up amid paschal lilies and *fleurs-de-luce*, basked an elaborate frizzed lamb of her own devoted working, the smart sophisticated crown displayed by the creature ablaze with Mrs Hurstpierpoint's unset precious stones.

'Our nuptial bouquets (hers and mine) I like to think are conserved below,' she mused, laying her cheek to her hands and smiling a little wistfully towards a statue of the Virgin – Nuestra Señora de la Pena – standing solitary under the canopy of the apse, her heart a very pin-cushion of silver darts.

'Hail, Mary ...!' she breathed, ignoring a decanter of sherry and a plate of herring sandwiches – a contrivance akin to genius in drawing attention to an offertory-box near by.

From the sacristy the refined *roulades* of a footman (these 'satanic' matches!) reached her faintly:

> 'Oh I'm his gala-gairle ...
> I'm his gala child,
> Yes,' etc.

Useless, under the circumstances, to attempt a *station*! 'Besides,' Mrs Thoroughfare speculated, trailing her Ispahanish flounces over to the dapper, flower-filled chapel of the Salute, 'I bear my own cross, God knows. ...'

The mystic windows, revealing the astonishing Life of St Automona Meris, smouldered brightly.

Automona by way of prelude lolling at a mirror *plein de chic*, her toes on a hassock, reading a billet-doux. Automona with a purple heartsease, pursuing a nail-pink youth. Automona with four male rakes (like the little brown men of Egypt) – her hair down holding an ostrich-fan. Automona, in marvellous mourning and with Nile-green hair, seated like a mummy bolt upright. Automona meeting Queen Maud of Cassiopia: – 'You look like some rare plant, dear!' Her growing mysticism. She meets Mother Maïa: 'I'm not the woman I was!' Her moods. Her austerities. Her increasing dowdiness. Her indifference to dress. She repulses her couturier: 'Send her away!' Her founding of Sodbury. Her end.

'Dear ardent soul!' Mrs Thoroughfare commented, her spirit rejoicing in the soft neurotic light.

Seldom had the Basilica shown itself as seductive.

From a pulpit festooned fancifully in prelatial purple the benediction of Cardinal Doppio-Mignoni would shortly fall.

The last time the cardinal had preached at Hare had been for the harvest festival, when a pyre of wondrous 'wurzels' had been heaped so high on the pulpit-ledge that he had been almost hidden from sight. Whereupon, dislodging a layer, His Eminence had deplaced the lot – the entire structure, Mrs Thoroughfare remembered well, rattling down like cannon-balls on to the heads of those below.

Glancing round, her eyes encountered a taper-lighting acolyte – Charlie, revolving with an air of half-cynical inquiry before a *Madeleine Lisant*, attributed to the 'Master of the Passion', usually kept veiled, but today exposed to view.

Dipping a grimly sardonic finger in the vase of holy water by the door, Mrs Thoroughfare withdrew, halting mechanically just outside to lend a listening ear to a confused discursive sound – the eternal *she she she* of servants' voices.

'. . . She . . . she . . .'

Through a service hatch ajar the chatter came.

'She . . .'

'There's the Blue-Room bell!'

'Confound it.'

'. . . Well, dear . . . as I was saying . . . Never before was I so insulted or outraged! Just catch me taking any more topsy freedoms from her.'

'I should keep my breath to cool my porridge. In your shoes, Sweetie.'

'Sweetie? Who's your sweetie? . . . I'm not your sweetie.'

'No? I shouldn't think you was.'

'In your shoes ... I'd put-myself-out to school, I would, and be taught some grammar!'

'Hurry up, please. .... Come on now with the samovar – and make haste sorting the letter-bag.'

'His Eminence. His Eminence: didn't someone say Cardinal Mignoni's correspondence passed first through Monsignor Girling? ... Lord Laggard ... Lady Laggard. Her ladyship. Her ladyship. ... Mademoiselle Carmen Colonnade – ; *do, re, mi, fa*. ... Signora Pinpipi. The Mrs. The Mrs ...'

'I always know instinctive when the Mrs has on her spiked garters.'

'Do you, dear? ... And *so* do I.'

'You could hear her a-tanning herself before cock-crow this morning in her room. Frtt! but she can swipe.'

'Those holly-bags, too, must tickle one's hams.'

'Now her sister's visiting Valmouth, you'd have thought it was Penance enough!'

'Who are the sponsors beside Lady Laggard?'

'What's that, my dear, to you?'

'There's the Blue-Room bell again! ....'

> 'I'll be your little blue-bell
> If you'll be my little bee.'

'And *don't* forget Mrs Thoroughfare."

'... What Mrs Thoroughfare? Which Mrs Thoroughfare? ... the white Mrs Thoroughfare? The black Mrs Thoroughfare?'

'I've seen a mort o' queer things in my day' (the voice was ffines's), 'but a *negress*; oh deary me!'

'Give me strength, my God, to bear this cross. Uphold me, Holy Mary, or I fail,' Mrs Thoroughfare inwardly breathed, retreating softly towards the drawing-room door.

The renowned room was completely bathed in sun, revealing equally the qualities and defects of the numerous baptismal or bridal gifts set out to be admired.

Bending over a charming little mirror of composite

precious woods, Mrs Thoroughfare detected Lieutenant Whorwood grooming assiduously his romantical curls.

Embarrassed at being taken thus unawares, the young man blushed up to the *rose-mauve* of his lips.

'I realize', said he, 'I'm one of those who, at the last Trump, would run their hand across their hair!'

'Ah? Really – ; would you? Why?'

'Probably', he replied, 'because I'm naturally vain.'

'I adore your hair: – and so does Dick.'

'Did he say so?'

'My boy is very fond of you.'

'And I'm very attached to him.'

'I know you are – and that *is why* I can talk to you about my son,' Mrs Thoroughfare said, keeping the lieutenant's hand captive in her own a moment longer, perhaps, than was actually required.

'After the ceremony, I trust you'll all at length be easy.'

'Their re-union in my opinion', Mrs Thoroughfare declared, 'is nothing but nonsense, but Eulalia seemed so fidgety and nervous – oh! she's so particular now about the least flaw or hitch – ! And we thought it best, perhaps, to humour her.'

'Those black weddings are rarely *en règle*.'

'I would give the whole world willingly for the poor fellow to repudiate the affair altogether – ; *get out of it!* Such a marvellous opportunity ... But no; he's utterly infatuated by his wife, it seems; – too much, alas, I fear ...'

'Dear Mrs Thoroughfare,' the lieutenant sympathetically said, 'don't think I can't understand. I do ... absolutely.'

Mrs Thoroughfare looked appreciative.

'I wish I was more stoic, Lieutenant Whorwood,' she replied, 'I wish I had less heart. ... But I'm super-sensitive. So I suffer like a fool!'

'It isn't my business of course,' he said, 'to meddle in souls. But Father Colley-Mahoney should be skilled to advise.'

'I've an inkling that Father very soon may be resigning his post,' Mrs Thoroughfare returned. 'Such a pity! None of the chaplains ever stay long. ... They seem to dislike Eulalia hauling them out of bed o' nights to say Midnight Masses for her.'

'But *does* she?' the lieutenant murmured, ensconcing himself in an easy-chair.

'Oh, my dear, she's merciless. . . . Eulalia's inexorable. . . . Dom Jonquil, Père Ernest des Martells, she wore them *out*. You're aware of course about THE KING?'

'The old story?'

'For Eulalia with her glowing artist mind – she is a born artist – she reminds me often of Delysia – it is anything but "Old". Her poor spirit, I fear, is everlastingly in the back of the Royal Box that ghastly evening of Pastor Fido: or was it in a corner of it she was? She was so liable to get mixed.'

'I understand at any rate she projects presenting Mrs Richard herself at one of the coming courts.'

'Oh, she's very full of plans – although she tells *me* none of them now.'

'She has been consulting me instead!'

'You remind her of a pet *cicisbeo* she had on her wedding tour – so she pretends.'

'She designs a trip to Paris, and to Vienna too, and Rome; and she has a wild delicious scheme even of visiting *Taormina*.'

'She'll be all over the place now I suppose. I shouldn't wonder if she didn't marry again.'

'It's for little Mrs Richard presumably that she goes.'

'It's ridiculous how she spoils her. But it's useless to remonstrate. One would have thought she'd have shaved her head and put on mourning. One would have thought she would have received her death-blow. I've known her to take to her bed for a mere black-beetle. Yes, oh, I have . . . blubbering and lamenting like a great frightened silly. But for a hulking *black* savage! not a bit of it! She enjoys all the kudos of a heathen's conversion (a "double conversion", as she says, on account of the child) and forgets altogether the discreditable connection.'

'It's really not such a discreditable one after all.'

'I'll refuse to believe this little madcap negress was ever born a Tahaitian princess. No, Lieutenant Whorwood, or that Mrs Yajñavalkya of Valmouth is only her nurse.'

'At Tarooa we knew quite well the brother – the banana man . . . employed on King Jotifa's estate.'

'Beuh!'

'The bride's credentials anyway will probably be examined; as Mrs Hurstpierpoint declares she shall know "no rest" until she has secured for her *the precedence of the daughter of an earl.*'

'Through the Laggards' wire pulling, I wonder.'

'He's vastly struck by her.'

'She provokes him. . . . He finds her piquant.'

'If only she wouldn't run at one quite so much and rumple one's hair!'

'Last night after dinner when *we* all withdrew she amused herself by smacking the hermaphrodite. . . . So Eulalia's full of hopes, she says, that she will sometimes take a hand with the broom. . . .'

'She made a sudden dash for my b-t-m. Greatly to my amazement.'

'Oh, she's a regular puss; my word she is! A regular *civet* if ever there was,' Mrs Thoroughfare wickedly commented.

'She's perhaps a little too playful.'

'Having torn to piecemeal Eulalia's copy of *Les Chansons de Bilitis* and "mis-used" my set of dear Dumas the Elder, one might say in truth – she was destructive.'

'A book is anathema to her.'

'Even a *papier poudré* one; for when I gave her my little precious volume, my little inseparable of *blanc de perle* in order to rub her nose, she started grating her teeth at me – to my utter terror! Rolling her eyes; lolling out her tongue – '

'One has to feel one's way with her.'

'I'm sure I meant it kindly!'

'A negress never powders.'

'Why not?'

'Because she *knows* it's useless,' the lieutenant lucidly explained.

'Her chief pleasure she seems to find in digging about

among the coconut fibre in the conservatory with her hands.'

'She's very fond of gardening.'

'And she is also very fond, I fear, of betel. Yes, I fear my boy is married to a betel-chewer. But of course *that* is nothing. . . . "De worst ob dis place," she said to us last night, "is dat dair is no betel! No betel at all; – not ob any discription!" "Are you a betel-chewer, then, my dear?" I asked, *aghast*. "Oh yes," she answered without winking. "How I do crave for some".'

'It's likely to be injurious to her babe at present.'

'*Which?* She's expecting a second *enfantement*, you know, immediately . . . . Oh she's such a quick puss.'

'A prettier, more *câline* mite than Marigold I never saw.'

Mrs Thoroughfare exchanged a quick glance with heaven.

'It's a pity the servants don't think so,' she said, 'for none of them will go near her! Baby has had three nurses in one fortnight; not that she perhaps is altogether to blame. The new woman, Mrs Kent, that came only yesterday (I got her too through the columns of "Femina") Eulalia seems all against. She can't "abide" her, in fact, as they say in Papiete.'

'So soon?'

'Oh Eulalia's so difficult. And she goes far too much to the Nursery . . . . ! And unfortunately she isn't *mealy-mouthed*. . . . Eulalia says what she thinks,' Mrs Thoroughfare murmured, her voice discreetly sinking as an old maid-servant of the house peered into the room – ostensibly only to sneeze twice – and out again.

'It disturbs her,' the young man ventured, 'that you don't get on better with Mrs Dick!'

Mrs Thoroughfare's eyes wandered ruefully to a superlatively sensitive miniature – one of the numerous wedding-gifts – portraying Niri-Esther, radiant with wax-white cheeks, as seen through the temperament of a great artist.

'There'd be more affection, perhaps, between us,' she returned sadly, 'if she resembled that.'

'It's rather a gem – Who did it?'

'Sir Victor ...'

'It's quite inspired!'

With pensive precision Mrs Thoroughfare drew on a pair of long, primrose-tinted gloves.

'To surprise Eulalia,' she murmured, 'I've commissioned him – only don't let it go further – to compose a Temptation of St Anthony for Nuestra Señora, a subject she has ever been fond of, it being so full of scope. He proposes inducing the local Laïs, Madame Mimosa, to pose as the Temptation: but I say, she isn't seductive enough. . . . No "Temptation": at least, I shouldn't find her one.'

'But why be dull and conventional; why be banal; why should you have a female model?'

'Why, what else, Lieutenant,' Mrs Thoroughfare shifted a camoe bangle dubiously from one of her arms to the other, 'could you suggest?'

'Oh! A thousand things ...' the lieutenant was unprecise.

'No; if he can't find a real temptation, a proper temptation, an irresistible temptation – I shall put him "off" with a little flower-piece, some arrangement, perhaps, of *flame-coloured roses* and tell Eulalia it's the "Burning Bush".'

'The Nation should prevent his old Mother from leaving the country.'

'Oh . . . why? What has she done?'

'Nothing – his masterpiece I meant.'

'I understood him, once, I think, to say that *that* was the *Madame Georges Goujon with Arlette and Ary*. . . ."

'Oh he has so many. His drawing of a Valmouther getting over a stile is something I could covet.'

'They say his study of the drawer of the Bawd's Head Hostelry here is worthy of Franz Hals,' Mrs Thoroughfare related.

But the entry of Mrs Hurstpierpoint bearing a long-clothes baby put an end to the colloquy.

Out of courtesy to the bride, and perhaps from some motive of private thanksgiving, her face was completely covered by a jet-black visard. Big beaded wings rose from her back with a certain moth-like effect.

'Tell me, Elizabeth,' she asked, 'will I do?'

'Do! ! Eulalia – I never saw anything like you.'

'I hope the dear Cardinal won't tell me I'm unorthodox; or do you think he will?'

'Take it off, Eulalia,' Mrs Thoroughfare begged.

'I shall not, Elizabeth!'

'Take it off!'

'No.'

'But why should you conceal yourself behind that odious mask?'

'I wear it, dear, only because a white face seems to frighten baby,' Mrs Hurstpierpoint explained.

'Eulalia, Eulalia.'

'Mind, Elizabeth. . . . Be careful of my wings.'

'You're beyond anything, Eulalia.'

Mrs Hurstpierpoint sat down.

'Sister Ecclesia had just been giving me an account, in dumb show, of the young woman whom she saved from drowning. . . . But for her the sea would have absorbed her. . . . However, she is now comfortably installed in the Convent of Arimathaea, and already shows, it seems, signs of a budding vocation! So peradventure she will become a Bride of the Church.'

'Let us hope so, anyway. But talking of "brides," Eulalia, *where's Esther*?'

'She was outside, dear, a moment ago. . . .'

'In *toilette de noce*?'

'And so excited! She's just floating in happiness – floating, swimming, sailing, soaring, flying. The darling! She is happy. So hap-py! Oh – '

'Really, dear, it's you that seem elated.'

'Your boy has my condemnation, Bessy; but he has also my forgiveness,' Mrs Hurstpierpoint blandly declared.

'Oh, Eulalia, you're too subtle for me.'

'Call her in, darling, do, or she may perhaps take cold, and a bride ought not to do that. I had such a cold on *my* honeymoon I remember, I never really ceased sneezing.'

'Oh, she'll come in I dare say when she wants to, Eulalia.'

'You amuse me, Eliza. . . . What makes you so unaccommodating?'

'It's odd you should ask, Eulalia!'

'Our friendship is unalterable, my little Lizzie, nothing has changed, or come between.'

'Mind Marigold, Eulalia.'

'What is it she wants? I expect it's her bobo!'

'No she doesn't, Eulalia. She doesn't want it at all.'

'Esther has no notion yet of managing a child. . . . Although she appears to have any number of quixoticisms.'

'I expect we shall find she has her own little black ideas about everything, Eulalia.'

'Well, well; if she has, she must drop them.'

'Naturally,' the lieutenant interposed, 'her intellectual baggage is nil – simply nil,' he added, lighting complacently a cigarette.

'Father wouldn't agree with you there at all; and he has had her, remember, daily, for pious Instruction.'

'I fear, Eulalia, she was won as much as anything by our wardrobe of stoles.'

'Father seems half in awe of her. . . . "Is an *egregious* sin a *mortal* sin?" she asked him quite suddenly the other day.'

'Oh! Eulalia!'

'She's devoted, though disrespectful, he tells me,' Mrs Hurstpierpoint murmured, blowing a kiss to the bride who was passing the windows just then.

'Rain fell steadily in the night; the grass must be drenched.'

'Oh, Esther – your feet.'

'When the Spina-Christi sheds its leaves my God what sorrow and stagnance,' Mrs Thoroughfare sighed oppressed.

'Shall you want the horses, do you think, this evening, Elizabeth?'

'I don't want them, Eulalia.'

'Are you sure, Elizabeth?'

'Perfectly, Eulalia.'

'The evening drive is almost an institution of the past. . . .' Mrs Thoroughfare assented.

'Here we are too with winter upon us,' she observed.

'Yes; and this is not the Tropics, my *mignonne* Niri!' Mrs Hurstpierpoint reminded her convert as she came forward into the room.

'In de winter,' the negress lisped, 'our trees are green wif parrots.'

'Are they, my dear?'

'Green!'

'Think of that now, dear child.'

'Green wif dem.'

'Did you hear, Elizabeth, what she said?'

'No, Eulalia.'

'It appears their trees are never bare. Always something.'

'Her salvation, in my estimate, Eulalia, should be equivalent quite to a Plenary-perpetual-Indulgence.'

'And so *I* think too.'

'Had she been more accomplished: wives should second their husbands; if not, perhaps, actually lead them. . . .'

'She does not want abilities, I can assure you, Eliza. She knows how to weave grasses. She can make little mats. She's going to teach me some day; aren't you, Esther? She and I are going to make a mat together. And when we've made it, we'll spread it out, and kneel down on it, *side by side*; won't we, Esther?'

'Yaas!' the negress answered, fondling playfully the Hare hermaphrodite.

'You may look, dear, but don't touch. Esther! Pho pet. My *dear*, what next?'

'There's a mean in all things . . . really.'

'Giddy.'

'Incorrigible.'

'You must learn to recollect yourself, dear child, or else I shall return the Lord Chamberlain our Cards.' Mrs Hurstpierpoint made show of rising.

'Oh, she'd better be presented in Ireland, Eulalia. Dublin Castle to *begin* with – afterwards we'll see – !!'

'Ireland?'

'What do you say, Lieutenant Whorwood?'

The lieutenant laid whimsically his face to a long cylindrical pillow of cloth of silver garnished with beaded-flowers.

'What do *I* say?' he echoed, half closing his eyes and flicking the cigarette-end from his knees, when a discharge of bells from Nuestra Señora, and the arrival of the vanguard of the bridal guests, prevented further discussion.

'Her Grace, the Duchess of Valmouth; the Honourable Mrs Manborough of Castle Malling' – ffines' voice filled the room.

'You shall hold Baby, Lieutenant, while I – ' Mrs Hurst-pierpoint flapped expressively her loose-winged sleeves.

'Sir William West-Wind, Mr Peter Caroon, Mrs Trotter-Stormer, Sir Wroth and Lady Cleobulina Summer-Leyton, Sir Victor Vatt, Master Xavier Tanoski, Lady Lucy Saunter, Miss à Duarté, Miss Roxall, Lady Jane Congress, Lady Constance Cadence-Stewart, Mrs Q. Comedy, Lady Laura-guay, Lady Lukin de Lukin, Mrs Lumlum, Mr Argrove, Mrs Lositer, General George Obliveon, Lady Parvula de Pan-zoust.'

Exhaling indescribably the esoteric *gentillezze* of Love, she was looking almost girlish beneath a white beret de Picador, enwreathed with multifarious clusters of silken balls, falling behind her far below the waist. Wearing a light décolleté day-dress, her figure since her previous visit to Hare had perceptibly grown stouter.

She was eyeing her hostess with wonder unrestrained when a dowager with a fine film of rouge wrapped in many shawls sailing up to her said:

'Persuade my sister do to take off her mask. Can't you persuade her to doff it?'

Lady Parvula dimpled.

'If you, Arabella, can't – why how', she returned, 'should I?'

Lady Laggard shook censoriously her shawls.

'I fear,' she observed, 'my poor sister will be soon a *déclassée*. She has been a sore grief to us – a sad trial! But when she begged me to be a godmother to the little Aida, I could hardly say no.'

'*Cela va sans dire.*'

'Her escapade with King Edred was perfectly disgraceful! She got nothing out of him, you know, for anyone – like the fool that she was. And to see her today going about be-winged, be-masked . . .'

'Sad, isn't it, how the old Hare days seem completely gone: vanished.'

'She conceals her upper-lip, one must allow,' Lady Laggard commented. 'But there was no – or *next* to no – was there – to *speak* of – about the eyes? . . . And nothing, nothing to excuse all that long fall of dreary lace.'

'Really she looks so quaint I can hardly help laughing,' Lady Parvula declared.

'She must be bitterly mortified, I imagine, by this marriage.'

'It shows though, I think, her *savoir faire,* to put the best construction on it.'

'The old Noblesse – where is it now?'

'Ah! I wonder.'

'With a woman like that his career is closed.'

'You may be sure they'll soon be separated!'

Lady Laggard removed an eyelash.

'They're not really married yet, you know,' she alleged.

'N . . . o?'

'The ceremony before I gather was quite null and void.'

'In . . . deed?'

'Their own rites, so it seems, are far far simpler. All they do is *simply* to place each a hand to the torso of the Beloved. And that's as far – will you *believe it,* dear? – as we are at present!'

'Your sister spoke of "special licence".'

'She would; she has the tongue of a Jesuit.'

'I didn't of course realize . . .'

'We were pumping the bride, Lord Laggard and I, and she told us, poor innocent, she was not married yet,' Lady Laggard averred, shaking long tremulous earrings of the time of Seti II of Egypt.

'I notice she likes lights and commotion, which goes to show she has social instincts!'

'Well, it's some time I suppose since there's been a negress.'

'All the fair men – the blondes, she will take from us. . . .'

'I wish I'd a tithe of your charms, dear.'

'But I don't really mind! . . . So long as *I* get the gypsies. . . .'

'They should forbid her from repeating a horrid equivocal epigram of old Dr Dee's – on the Masseuse, La Yajñavalkya.'

'What was it, Arabella?'

'*Her brains are in her arms.*'

'And are they?'

'I don't know, dear, where they are. Such a pity *hers* aren't anywhere. Her incessant "Wot for dis?" gets so on my nerves.'

'I don't wonder. It would on mine. I'm such a nervous woman! Now I've no Haree-ee-ee to look after me I get so fluttered. . . .'

'All these priests in the house I find myself a strain. The old Cardinal, with his monstrous triple-mitre, one goes in terrors of. He was in the passage just now as I came through waiting for someone. And last night – there's only a panel door between our rooms – I heard him try the handle.'

'Their last chaplain – Père Ernest – I remember was a danger. A perfect danger! He could have done anything with me, Arabella, had he willed. I was plastic wax with him.'

'With their faggots of candles (and their incense) they seek to render imbecile our poor sex. Coming by Nuestra, I assure you, I was almost *poisoned*. Or, to use a juster metaphor, perhaps,' Lady Laggard corrected herself, 'suffocated', she added, 'by the fumes.'

'Monsignor Vanhove, Father O'Donoghue, Frater Galfrith, Brother Drithelm, Père Porfirio' – ffines insistently continued in his office until, in sweeping purple and scarlet biretta, Cardinal Doppio-Mignoni himself passed valedictionally through the rooms.

In the extravagant hush, following on his transit, a prolonged peacock's wail sounded electrifying from the park:

Nijny-Novgorod, Nijny-Novgorod – creating among the younger bridesmaids an impression of 'foreboding'.

Only Mrs. Hurstpierpoint, to judge by her rich enveloping laugh, seemed really happy or serene.

'I always intended to visit *Walt Whitman*, didn't I, Lizzie? Poor old Walt! ... I wrote: "Expect me and my maid ... I'm coming!" I said. ... It was the very spring he died.'

Involving some interesting, intellectual trips, she was descanting lightly to right and left.

'I remember you intended once to visit me,' the Bolshevik member for Valmouth, Sir William West-Wind, softly remarked.

'You, Sir William? And when did I ever intend to visit you, I wonder?'

'There was a time', Sir William murmured, 'when I confess I expected you.'

'Have you any intention, Eulalia,' a *douairière* inquired, 'of visiting the present châtelaine of Nosely?'

'You dear angel – I wasn't aware even it was let.'

'To a field-marshal's widow.'

'My brother', one of the bridesmaids giggled, 'was his favourite *aide-de-camp*.'

'And what is *she* like?'

'He describes her as lissom as a glove, lively as a kid, and as fond of tippling as a Grenadier-Guard.'

'She sounds a treasure,' Mrs Hurstpierpoint declared, with a glance backward over her wings.

'Go to Vivi Vanderstart – and say I sent you!' the Duchess of Valmouth was saying.

'Very well, dear, I will.'

'Her boast is, she makes only "Hats for Happy Women".'

'I always pin my faith in Pauline Virot. . . .'

'One should pin one's faith only in God,' Mrs Hurstpierpoint commented blithely.

'Only where, Eulalia?'

'Only with Him.'

'I remember', Mrs Thoroughfare dryly laughed, 'when Eulalia's God was *Gambetta*.'

'Gambetta, Betty – what next will you say, naughty, naughty angel?'

But what Mrs Thoroughfare subsequently would have said was lost amid Church canticles.

It was the call to the altar.

Oscillating freely a long chain incense swinger, a youthful server, magnificent in white silk stockings and Neapolitan-violet maroquin shoes, presented himself on the threshold in a fragrant veil of smoke.

Venite.

Followed by Charlie with the Holy Pyx and by Father Colley-Mahoney and various officiating priests, he traversed from end to end, amid much show of reverence (crossing and crouching), the vast salon.

'Grant she shall find,'

(Pinpipi with her great male voice from 'Nuestra' was waking the echoes beyond)

'On Yniswitrins altars pale,
The gleaming vision of the Holy Grail.'

'Yes; grant Lord her *soul* shall find,' Mademoiselle Carmen Colonnade, the beloved of the Orpheum, Scala, San Carlo, Costanzi, simultaneously (more, or less) struck in, her soft vocal flourishes and pimpant variations soaring, baby-like, high above the strong soprano voice of the severe Pinpipi.

''Es, gwant 'Ord 'er 'oul –
Grant it shall find –
On Ynis-wi-trins walters –
Altarɜ –
WALTERS PALER!
The gleaming vision –
– dazzling –
Of –
The Holy Grail-a!'

'Come, Esther,' Mrs Hurstpierpoint murmured, dashing a tear from her mask.

'Yield the *pas* to a negress! *Never!*' Lady Laggard looked determined.

'Oh, Eulalia!' Mrs Thoroughfare touched her arm.

'You dear queen.'

'Have you seen my boy, Eulalia?'

'No, Elizabeth – ; not today.'

'No one can find him.'

'*Ah les oiseaux amoureux,*' Mrs Hurstpierpoint began a series of seraphic giggles, '*chers oiseaux* ... paradise *uccellinis* ... delicious *Vogels.* ...'

'I feel half-worn-out.'

'Come, Esther child, to church!'

But Niri-Esther had run out of the house (old, grey, grim, satanic Hare) into the garden, where, with her bride's bouquet of malmaisons and vanessa-violets, she was waywardly in pursuit of – a butterfly.

FAREWELL

PRANCING NIGGER

*

I

Looking gloriously bored, Miss Miami Mouth gaped up into the boughs of a giant silk-cotton-tree. In the lethargic noontide nothing stirred: all was so still, indeed, that the sound of someone snoring was clearly audible among the cane-fields far away.

'After dose yams an' pods an' de white falernum, I dats way sleepy too,' she murmured, fixing heavy, somnolent eyes upon the prospect that lay before her.

Through the sun-tinged greenery shone the sea, like a floor of silver glass strewn with white sails.

Somewhere out there, fishing, must be her boy, Bamboo!

And, inconsequently, her thoughts wandered from the numerous shark-casualties of late to the mundane proclivities of her mother; for to quit the little village of Mediavilla for the capital was that dame's fixed obsession.

Leave Mediavilla, leave Bamboo! The young negress fetched a sigh.

In what way, she reflected, would the family gain by *entering Society,* and how did one enter it at all? There would be a gathering, doubtless, of the elect (probably armed), since the best Society is exclusive and difficult to enter. And then? Did one burrow? Or charge? She had sometimes heard it said that people 'pushed' . . . and closing her eyes, Miss Miami Mouth sought to picture her parents, assisted by her small sister, Edna, and her brother, Charlie, forcing their way, perspiring but triumphant, into the highest social circles of the city of Cuna-Cuna.

Across the dark savannah country the city lay, one of the chief alluring cities of the world: the Celestial city of Cuna-Cuna, Cuna, city of Mimosa, Cuna, city of Arches, Queen of the Tropics, Paradise – almost invariably travellers referred to it like that.

Oh, everything must be fantastic there, where even the

very pickneys put on clothes! And Miss Miami Mouth glanced
fondly down at her own plump little person, nude but for a
girdle of creepers that she would gather freshly twice a day.

'It would be a shame, sh'o, to cover it,' she murmured
drowsily, caressing her body; and moved to a sudden spasm
of laughter, she tittered: 'No! really. De ideah!'

2

'SILVER bean-stalks, silver bean-stalks, oh hé, oh hé,' down the long village street from door to door the cry repeatedly came, until the vendor's voice was lost on the evening air.

In a rocking-chair, before the threshold of a palm-thatched cabin, a matron with broad, bland features and a big, untidy figure surveyed the scene with a nonchalant eye.

Beneath some tall trees, bearing flowers like flaming bells, a few staid villagers sat enjoying the rosy dusk, while, strolling towards the sea, two young men passed by with fingers intermingled.

With a slight shrug, the lady plied her fan.

As the Mother of a pair of oncoming girls, the number of ineligible young men or confirmed bachelors around the neighbourhood was a constant source of irritation to her.

'Sh'o, dis remoteness bore an' weary me to death,' she exclaimed, addressing someone through the window behind; and receiving no audible answer, she presently rose and went within.

It was the hour when, fortified by a siesta, Mrs Ahmadou Mouth was wont to approach her husband on general household affairs, and to discuss, in particular, the question of their removal to the town; for, with the celebration of their pearl wedding close at hand, the opportunity to make the announcement of a change of residence to their guests ought not, she believed, to be missed.

'We leave Mediavilla for de education ob my daughters,' she would say; or perhaps: 'We go to Cuna-Cuna for de finishing ob *mes filles!*'

But, unfortunately, the reluctance of Mr Mouth to forsake his Home seemed to increase from day to day.

She found him asleep, bolt upright, his head gently nodding, beneath a straw hat beautifully browned.

'Say, nigger, lub,' she murmured, brushing her hand featheringly along his knee, 'say, nigger, lub, I gotta go!'

It was the tender prelude to the storm.

Evasive (and but half awake), he warned her. 'Let me alone; Ah'm thinkin'.'

'Prancing Nigger, now come on!'

'Ah'm thinkin'.'

'Tell me what for dis procrastination?' Exasperated, she gripped his arm.

But for all reply Mr Mouth drew a volume of revival hymns towards him, and turned on his wife his back.

'You ought to shame o' you-self, sh'o,' she caustically commented, crossing to the window.

The wafted odours of the cotton-trees without oppressed the air. In the deepening twilight the rising moonmist already obscured the street.

'Dis place not healthy. Dat damp! Should my daughters go off into a decline . . .' she apprehensively murmured, as her husband started softly to sing.

> 'For ebber wid de Lord!
> Amen; so let it be;
> Life from de dead is in dat word,
> 'Tis immortality.'

'If it's de meeting-house dats de obstruction, dair are odders, too, in Cuna-Cuna,' she observed.

'How often hab I bid you nebba to mention dat modern Sodom in de hearing ob my presence!'

'De Debil frequent de village, fo' dat matter, besides de town.'

'Sh'o nuff.'

'But yestiddy, dat po' silly negress Ottalie was seduced again in a Mango track –; an' dats de third time!'

> 'Heah in de body pent,
> Absent from Him I roam,
> Yet nightly pitch my movin' tent
> A day's march nearer home.'

'Prancing Nigger, from dis indifference to your fambly, be careful lest you do arouse de vials ob de Lord's wrath!'

'Yet nightly pitch —' he was beginning again, in a more subdued key, but the tones of his wife arrested him.

'Prancing Nigger, lemme say sumptin' more!' Mrs Mouth took a long sighing breath. 'In dis dark jungle my lil jewel Edna, I feah, will wilt away. . . .'

'Wha' gib you cause to speak like dat?'

'I was tellin' my fortune lately wid de cards,' she reticently made reply, insinuating, by her half-turned eyes, that more disclosures of an ominous nature concerning others besides her daughter had been revealed to her as well.

'Lordey Lord; what is it den you want?'

'I want a Villa with a watercloset —' Flinging wiles to the winds, it was a cry from the heart.

'De Lord hab pity on dese vanities an' innovations!'

'In town, you must rememba, often de houses are far away from de parks; — de city, in dat respect, not like heah.'

'Say nothin' more! De widow ob my po' brudder Willie, across de glen, she warn me I ought nebba to listen to you.'

'Who care for a common woman, dat only read de *Negro World*, an' nebba see anyt'ing else!' she swelled.

Mr Mouth turned conciliatingly.

'Tomorrow me arrange for de victuals for our ebenin' at Home!'

'Good, bery fine,' she murmured, acknowledging through the window the cordial 'good night' of a few late labourers, returning from the fields, each with a bundle of sugar-cane poised upon the head.

'As soon as marnin' dawn me take dis bizniz in hand.'

'Only pramas, nigger darlin'', she cajoled, 'dat durin' de course of de reception you make a lil speech to inform de neighbours ob our gwine away bery soon, for de sake of de education ob our girls.'

'Ah sha'n' pramas nothin'.'

'I could do wid a change too, honey, after my last miscarriage.'

'Change come wid our dissolution', he assured her, 'quite soon enuff!'

'Bah,' she murmured, rubbing her cheek to his: 'we set out on our journey sh'o in de season ob Novemba.'

To which with asperity he replied: '*Not for two Revolutions!*' and rising brusquely, strode solemnly from the room.

'Hey-ho-day,' she yawned, starting a wheezy gramophone, and sinking down upon his empty chair; and she was lost in ballroom fancies (whirling in the arms of some blonde young foreigner) when she caught sight of her daughter's reflection in the glass.

Having broken or discarded her girdle of leaves, Miss Miami Mouth, attracted by the gramophone, appeared to be teaching a hectic two-step to the cat.

'Fie, fie, my lass. Why you be so *Indian*?' her mother exclaimed, bestowing, with the full force of a carpet slipper a well-aimed spank from behind.

'*Aïe, aïe!*'

'Sh'o: you nohow select!'

'*Aïe. . . .*'

'De low exhibition!'

'I had to take off my apron, 'cos it seemed to draw de bees,' Miami tearfully explained, catching up the cat in her arms.

'Ob course, if you choose to wear roses. . . .'

'It was but ivy!'

'De berries ob de ivy entice de same,' Mrs Mouth replied, nodding graciously, from the window, to Papy Paul, the next-door neighbour, who appeared to be taking a lonely stroll with a lanthorn and a pineapple.

'I dats way wondering why Bamboo no pass dis evenin', too; as a rule, it is seldom he stop so late out upon de sea,' the young girl ventured.

'After I shall introduce you to de world (de advantage ob a good marriage; when I t'ink ob mine!), you will be ashamed, sh'o, to recall dis infatuation.'

'De young men ob Cuna-Cuna (tell me, Mammee), are dey den so nice?'

'Ah, Chile! If I was your age again . . .'

'Sh'o, dair's nothin' so much in dat.'

'As a young girl of eight (Tee-hee!), I was distracting to all the gentlemen,' Mrs Mouth asserted, confiding a smile to a small, long-billed bird, in a cage, of the variety known as Bequia-Sweet.

'How I wish I'd been born, like you, in August-Town, across de Isthmus!'

'It gib me dis taste fo' S'ciety, Chile.'

'In S'ciety, don' dey dress wid clothes on eberyday?'

'Sh'o; surtainly.'

'An' don't dey nebba tickle?'

'In August-Town, de aristocracy conceal de best part ob deir bodies; not like heah!'

'An' tell me, Mammee . . .? De first lover you eber had . . . was he half as handsome as Bamboo?'

'De first dude, Chile, I eber had, was a lil, lil buoy . . . wid no hair (whatsoeber at all), bal' like a calabash!' Mrs Mouth replied, as her daughter Edna entered with the lamp.

'Frtt!' the wild thing tittered, setting it down with a bang: with her cincture of leaves and flowers, she had the éclat of a butterfly.

'Better fetch de shade,' Mrs Mouth exclaimed, staring squeamishly at Miami's shadow on the wall.

'Already it grow dark; no one about now at dis hour ob night at all.'

'Except thieves an' ghouls,' Mrs Mouth replied, her glance straying towards the window.

But only the little blue-winged bats were passing beneath a fairyland of stars.

'When I do dis, or dis, my shadow appear as formed as Mimi's!'

'Sh'o, Edna, she dat provocative today.'

'Be off at once, Chile, an' lay de table for de ebenin' meal; an' be careful not to knock de shine off de new tin teacups,' Mrs Mouth commanded, taking up an Estate-Agent's catalogue and seating herself comfortably beneath the lamp.

' "City of Cuna-Cuna",' she read, ' "*in the Heart of a Brainy*

District (within easy reach of University, shops, etc.). A charming Freehold Villa. Main drainage. Extensive views. Electric light. Every convenience.'"

'Dat sound just de sort ob lil shack for me.'

3

THE strange sadness of evening, the *détresse* of the Evening
Sky! Cry, cry, white Rain Birds out of the West, cry . . . !

'An' so, Miami, you no come back no more?'

'No, no come back.'

Flaunting her boredom by the edge of the sea one close of
day, she had chanced to fall in with Bamboo, who, stretched
at length upon the beach, was engaged in mending a broken
net.

'An' I dats way glad,' she half resentfully pouted, jealous a
little of his toil.

But, presuming deafness, the young man laboured on,
since, to support an aged mother, and to attain one's desires,
perforce necessitates work; and his fondest wish, by dint of
saving, was to wear on his wedding-day a pink, starched,
cotton shirt – a starched, pink cotton shirt, stiff as a boat's-sail
when the North winds caught it! But a pink shirt would mean
trousers . . . and trousers would lead to shoes . . . 'Extravagant
nigger, don't you dare!' he would exclaim, in dizzy panic,
from time to time, aloud.

'Forgib me, honey,' he begged, 'but me obliged to finish
while de daylight last.'

'Sh'o,' she sulked, following the amazing strategy of the
sunset-clouds.

'Miami angel, you look so sweet: I dat amorous ob you,
Mimi!'

A light laugh tripped over her lips.

'Say, buoy, how you getting on?' she queried, sinking
down on her knees beside him.

'I dat amorous ob you!'

'Oh, ki,' she tittered, with a swift mocking glance at
his crimson loincloth. She had often longed to snatch it
away.

'Say you lub me, just a lil, too, deah?'

'Sh'o,' she answered softly, sliding over on to her stomach, and laying her cheek to the flats of her hands.

Boats with crimson spouts, to wit, steamers dotted the skyline far away, and barques, with sails like the wings of butterflies, borne by an idle breeze, were bringing more than one ineligible young mariner back to the prose of shore.

'Ob wha' you t'inking?'

'Nothin',' she sighed, contemplating laconically a little transparent shell of violet pearl, full of sea-water and grains of sand, that the wind ruffled as it blew.

'Not ob *any* sort ob lil t'ing?' he caressingly insisted, breaking an open dark flower from her belt of wild Pansy.

'I should be gwine home,' she breathed, recollecting the undoing of the negress Ottalie.

'Oh, I dat amorous ob you, Mimi.'

'If you want to finish dat net while de daylight last.'

For oceanward, in a glowing ball, the sun had dropped already.

'Sho', nigger, I only wish to be kind,' she murmured, getting up and sauntering a few paces along the strand.

Lured, perhaps, by the nocturnal phosphorescence from its lair, a water-scorpion, disquieted at her approach, turned and vanished amid the sheltering cover of the rocks. 'Isht, isht,' she squealed, wading after it into the surf; but to find it, look as she would, was impossible. Dark, curious, and anxious, in the fast failing light, the sea disquieted her too, and it was consoling to hear close behind her the solicitous voice of Bamboo.

'Us had best soon be movin', befo' de murk ob night.'

The few thatched cabins that comprised the village of Mediavilla lay not half a mile from the shore. Situated between the savannah and the sea, on the southern side of the sand known as Tacarigua (the 'burning Tacarigua' of the Poets), its inhabitants were obliged, from lack of communication with the larger island centres, to rely to a considerable extent for a livelihood among themselves. Local Market days, held, alternatively, at Valley Village or Broken Hill (the nearest approach to industrial towns in the district around Media-

villa), were the chief source of rural trade, when such mer-
chandize as fish, coral, beads, bananas, and loincloths would
exchange hands amid much animation, social gossip, and
pleasant fun.

'Wha' you say to dis?' she queried as they turned inland
through the cane-fields, holding up a fetish known as a
'luck-ball', attached to her throat by a chain.

'Who gib it you?' he shortly demanded, with a quick
suspicious glance.

'Mammee, she bring it from Valley Village, an' she bring
another for my lil sister, too.'

'Folks say she attend de Market only to meet de Obi man,
who cast a spell so dat your Dada move to Cuna-Cuna.'

'Dat so!'

'Your Mammee no seek ebber de influence ob Obeah?'

'Not dat I know ob!' she replied; nevertheless, she could
not but recall her mother's peculiar behaviour of late, especially upon Market days, when, instead of conversing with her
friends, she would take herself off with a mysterious air,
saying she was going to the Baptist Chapel.

'Mammee, she hab no faith in de Witch-Doctor at all,' she
murmured, halting to lend an ear to the liquid note of a
peadove among the canes.

'I no care; me follow after wherebber you go,' he said,
stealing an arm about her.

'True?' she breathed, looking up languidly towards the
white mounting moon.

'I dat amorous ob you, Mimi.'

4

It was the Feast night. In the grey spleen of evening, through the dusty lanes towards Mediavilla county society flocked.

Peering round a cow-shed door, Primrose and Phoebe, procured as waitresses for the occasion, felt their valour ooze as they surveyed the arriving guests, and dropping prostrate amid the straw, declared, in each other's arms, that never, never would they find the courage to appear.

In the road, before a tall tamarind-tree, a well-spread supper board exhaled a pungent odour of fried cascadura fish, exciting the plaintive ravings of the wan pariah dogs, and the cries of a few little stark naked children engaged as guardians to keep them away. Defying an ancient and inelegant custom by which the hosts welcomed their guests by the side of the road, Mrs Mouth had elected to remain within the precincts of the house, where, according to tradition, the bridal trophies – cowrie-shells, feathers, and a bouquet of faded orange blossom – were being displayed.

'It seem no more dan yestidday,' she was holding forth gaily over a goblet of Sangaree wine, 'it seem no more dan yestidday dat I put on me maiden wreath ob arange blastams to walk wid me nigger to church.'

Clad in rich-hued creepers, she was both looking and feeling her best.

'Sh'o,' a woman with blonde-dyed hair and Buddery eyes exclaimed, 'it seem no more dan just like yestidday; dat not so, Papy Paul?' she queried, turning to an old man in a raspberry-pink kerchief, who displayed (as he sat) more of his person than he seemed to be aware of.

But Papy Paul was confiding a receipt for pickling yuccas to Mamma Luna, the mother of Bamboo, and made as if not to hear.

Offering a light, lilac wine, sweet and heady, Miami circled here and there. She had a cincture of white rose-oleanders, and a bandeau of blue convolvuli. She held a fan.

'Or do you care for anyt'ing else?' she was inquiring, automatically, of Mr Musket (the Father of three very common girls), as a melodious tinkle of strings announced the advent of the minstrels from Broken Hill.

Following the exodus roadward, it was agreeable to reach the outer air.

Under the high trees by the yard-door gate, the array of vehicles and browsing quadrupeds was almost as numerous as upon a market day. The quiet village road was agog, with bustling folk as perhaps never before, coming and going between the little Café of the 'Forty Parrots', with its Bar, spelled *Biar* in twinkling lights. All iris in the dusk, a few loosely-loinclothed young men had commenced dancing aloofly among themselves, bringing down some light (if bitter) banter from the belles.

Pirouetting with these, Miami recognized the twinkling feet of her brother Charlie, a lad who preferred roaming the wide savannah country after butterflies with his net to the ever-increasing etiquette of his home.

'Sh'o, S'ciety no longer what it wa',' the mother of two spare lean girls, like young giraffes, was lamenting, when a clamorous gong summoned the assembly to the festal board.

In the glow of blazing palm logs, stoked by capering pickneys, the company, with some considerable jostling, became seated by degrees.

'Fo' what we gwine to recebe de Lord make us to be truly t'ankful.' Mr Mouth's low voice was lost amid the din. Bending to the decree of Providence, and trusting in God for the welfare of his house, he was resigned to follow the call of duty, by allowing his offspring such educational advantages and worldly polish that only a city can give.

'An' so I heah you gwine to leab us!' the lady at his elbow exclaimed, helping herself to a claw of a crab.

'Fo' de sake ob de chillen's schoolin',' Mr Mouth made reply, blinking at the brisk lightning play through the foliage of the trees.

'Dey tell me de amount of licence dat go on ober dah –'
she murmured, indicating with her claw the chequered
horizon; 'but de whole world needs revising, as de Missionary
truly say!'

'Indeed, an' dat's de trute.'

'It made me cry', a plump little woman declared, 'when
de Minister speak so serious on de scandal ob close dancing.
. . .'

'Fo' one t'ing lead sh'o to de nex'!' Mr Mouth obstrusely
assented, turning his attention upon an old negress answering
to the name of Mamma May, who was retailing how she had
obtained the sunshade beneath which, since noon, she had
walked all the way to the party.

'Ah could not afford a parasol, so Ah just cut miself a lil
green bush, an' held it up ober my head,' she was crooning
in gleeful triumph.

'It's a wonder, indeed, no one gib you a lif'!' several voices
observed, but the discussion was drowned by an esoteric
song of remote tribal times from the lips of Papy Paul:

> 'I am King Elephant-bag,
> Ob de rose-pink Mountains!
> Tatou, tatouay, tatou . . .'

provoking from Miss Stella Spooner, the marvellous daughter
of an elderly father, a giggle in which she was joined by the
youngest Miss Mouth.

Incontestably a budding Princess, the playful mite was
enjoying, with airy nonchalance, her initial experience of
Society.

'Ob course she is very *jeune*,' Mrs Mouth murmured archly,
behind her hand, into the ear of Mr Musket.

'It's de Lord's will,' he cautiously replied, rolling a mystified
eye towards his wife (a sable negress out of Africa), continually vaunting her foreign extraction. 'I'm Irish,' she would
say: 'I'm Irish, deah. . . .'

'Sh'o she de born image ob her elder sister!'

'De world all say she to marry de son ob ole Mamma Luna,
dat keep de lil shop.'

'Suz! Wha' nex'?' Mrs Mouth returned, breaking off to focus Papy Paul, apparently, already, far from sober. 'I hav' saw God, an' I hav' spoke wid de President, too!' he was announcing impressively to Mamma Luna, a little old woman in whose veins ran the blood of many races.

'Dair's no trute at all in *dat* report,' Mrs Mouth quietly added, signalling directions to a sturdy, round-bottomed little lad, who had undertaken to fill the gap caused by Primrose and Phoebe.

Bearing a pannier piled with fruit, he had not got far before the minstrels called forth several couples to their feet.

The latest jazz, bewildering, glittering, exuberant as the soil, a jazz throbbing, pulsating, with a zim, zim, zim, a jazz all abandon and verve that had drifted over the glowing savannah and the waving cane-fields from Cuna-Cuna by the Violet Sea, invited, irresistibly, to motion every boy and girl.

'Prancing Nigger, hab a dance?' his wife, transported, shrilled: but Mr Mouth was predicting a banana slump to Mrs Walker, the local midwife, and paid no heed.

Torso-to-torso, the youngsters twirled, while even a pair of majestic matrons, Mrs Friendship and Mrs Mother, went whirling away (together) into the brave summer dusk. Accepting the invitation of Bamboo, Miami rose, but before dancing long complained of the heat.

'Sh'o, it cooler in de Plantation,' he suggested, pointing along the road.

'Oh, I too much afraid!'

'What for you afraid?'

But Miami only laughed, and tossed her hand as if she were scattering dewdrops.

Following the roving fireflies and adventurous flittermice, they strolled along in silence. By the roadside, two young men, friends, walking with fingers intermingled, saluted them softly. An admirable evening for a promenade! Indescribably sweet, the floating field-scents enticed them witchingly on.

'Shi!' she exclaimed as a bird skimmed swiftly past with a chattering cry.

'It noddin', deah, but a lil wee owl!'

'An' it to make my heart go so,' she murmured, with a sidelong smiling glance.

He had a new crimson loincloth, and a blood-pink carnation at his ear.

'What for you afraid?' he tenderly pressed.

'It much cooler heah, doh it still very hot,' she inconsequently answered, pausing to listen to the fretting of the hammer tree-frogs in the dusk.

'Dey hold a concert, honey lub, all for us.'

Rig a jig jig, rig a jig jig. . . .

'Just hark to de noise!' she murmured, starting a little at the silver lightning behind the palms.

'Just hark,' he repeated, troubled.

Rig a jig jig, rig a jig jig. . . .

5

LITTLE jingley trot-trot-trot, over the Savannah, hey –!

Joggling along towards Cuna-Cuna the creaking caravan shaped its course. Seated in a hooded chariot, berced by mule-bells, and nibbling a shoot of ripe cane, Mrs Mouth appeared to have attained the heights of bliss. Disregarding or insensitive to the incessant groans of her husband (wedged in between a case of pineapples and a box marked 'lingerie'), she abandoned herself voluptuously to her thoughts. It was droll to contemplate meeting an old acquaintance, Nini Snagg, who had gone to reside in Cuna-Cuna long ago. 'Fancy seein' you!' she would say, and how they both would laugh.

Replying tersely to the innumerable 'what would you do ifs' of her sister, supposing attacks from masked bandits or ferocious wild animals, Miami moped.

All her whole heart yearned back behind her, and never had she loved Bamboo so much as now.

' – if a big, shaggy buffalo, wid two sharp horns, dat long, were to rush right at you?' Edna was plaguing her, when a sudden jolt of the van set up a loud cackling from a dozen scared cocks and hens.

'Drat dose fowl; as if dair were none in Cuna-Cuna!' Mrs Mouth addressed her husband.

'Not birds ob dat brood,' he retorted, plaintively starting to sing.

'I t'ink when I read dat sweet story ob old,
    When Jesus was here among men,
How He called lil chillens as lambs to His fold,
    I should like to hab been wid dem den!
I wish dat His hands had been placed ahn my head,
    Dat His arms had been thrown aroun' me,
An' dat I might hab seen His kind look when He said,
    "Let de lil ones come unto Me!"'

'Mind de dress-basket don't drop down, deah, an' spoil our clo',' Mrs Mouth exclaimed, indicating a cowskin trunk that seemed to be in peril of falling; for, from motives of economy and ease, it had been decided that not before Cuna-Cuna should rear her queenly towers above them would they change their floral garlands for the more artificial fabrics of the town, and Edna, vastly to her importance, go into a pair of frilled 'invisibles' and a petticoat for the first amazing time; nor, indeed, would Mr Mouth himself 'take to de pants' until his wife and daughters should have assumed their skirts. But this, from the languid pace at which their vehicle proceeded, was unlikely to be just yet. In the torrid tropic noontime, haste, however, was quite out of the question. Bordered by hills, long, yellow and low, the wooded savannah rolled away beneath a blaze of trembling heat.

'I don't t'ink much ob dis part of de country,' Mrs Mouth commented. 'All dese common palms ... de cedar-wood tree, dat my tree. Dat is de timber I prefer.'

'An' some', Edna pertly smiled, 'dey like best de bamboo. ...'

A remark that was rewarded by a blow on the ear.

'Now she set up a hullabaloo like de time de scorpion bit her botty,' Mrs Mouth lamented, and indeed the uproar made alarmed from the boskage a cloud of winsome soldier-birds and inquisitive paroquets.

'Oh my God,' Mr Mouth exclaimed. 'What for you make all dat dere noise?' But his daughter paid no attention, and soon sobbed herself to sleep.

Advancing through tracks of acacia-scrub or groves of nutmeg-trees, they jolted along in the gay, exalting sunlight. Flowers brighter than love, wafting the odour of spices, strewed in profusion the long guinea-grass on either side of the way.

'All dose sweet aprons, if it weren't fo' de flies!' Mrs Mouth murmured, regarding some heavy, ambered, Trumpet flowers with a covetous eye.

'I trust Charlie get bit by no snake!'

'Prancing Nigger! It a lil too late now to t'ink ob dat.'

Since, to avoid overcrowding the family party, Charlie was to follow with his butterfly net and arrive as he could. And never were butterflies (seen in nigger-boy's dreams) as brilliant or frolicsome as were those of mid-savannah. Azure Soledads, and radiant Conquistadors with frail flamboyant wings, wove about the labouring mules perpetual fresh rosettes.

'De Lord protect de lad,' Mr Mouth remarked, relapsing into silence.

Onward through the cloudless noontide, beneath the ardent sun, the caravan drowsily crawled. As the afternoon advanced Mrs Mouth produced a pack of well-thumbed cards, and cutting, casually, twice, began interrogating Destiny with these. Reposing as best she might, Miami gave herself up to her reflections. The familiar aspect of the wayside palms, the tattered pennons of the bananas, the big silk-cottons (known, to children, as 'Mammee-trees'), all brought to her mind Bamboo.

'Dair's somet'in' dat look like a death dah, dat's troublin' me,' Mrs Mouth remarked, moodily fingering a greasy ace.

'De Almighty forgib dese foolish games!' Mr Mouth protestingly said.

'An from de lie ob de cards . . . it seem as ef de corpse were ob de masculine species.'

'Wha' gib you de notion ob dat?'

'Sh'o, a sheep puts his wool on his favourite places,' Mrs Mouth returned, reshuffling slowly her pack.

Awakened by her Father's psalms, Edna's 'What would you do's' had commenced with volubility anew, growing more eerie with the gathering night.

'. . . if a Wood-Spirit wid two heads an' six arms were to take hold ob you, Mimi from behind?'

'I do nothin' at all,' Miami answered briefly.

'Talk not so much ob de jumbies, Chile, as de chickens go to roost!' Mrs Mouth admonished.

'Or, if de debil himself should?' Edna insisted, allowing Snowball, the cat, to climb on to her knee.

'Nothin', sh'o,' Miami murmured, regarding dreamily the

sun's sinking disk, that was illuminating all the Western sky with incarnadine and flamingo-rose. Ominous in the falling dusk, the savannah rolled away, its radiant hues effaced beneath a rapid tide of deepening shadow.

'Start de gramophone gwine, girls, an' gib us somet'in' bright!' Mrs Mouth exclaimed, depressed by the forlorn note of the Twa-oo-Twa-oo bird, that mingled its lament with a thousand night cries from the grass.

'When de saucy female sing "My Ice Cream Girl", fo' sh'o she scare de elves.'

And as though by force of magic the nasal soprano of an invisible songstress rattled forth with tinkling gusto a music-hall air with a sparkling refrain.

> 'And the boys shout Girlie, hi!
> Bring me soda, soda, soda,
> (Aside, spoken) (Stop your fooling there and let me alone!)
> For I'm an Ice Cream Soda Girl.'

'It put me in mind ob de last sugar-factory explosion. It was de same day dat Snowball crack de Tezzrazine record. Drat de cat!'

'O Lordey Lord! Wha' for you make dat din?' Mr Mouth complained, knotting a cotton handkerchief over his head.

'I hope you not gwine to be billeous, honey, afore we get to Lucia?'

'Lemme alone. Ah'm thinkin'.'

Pressing on by the light of a large clear moon, the hamlet of Lucia, the halting-place proposed for the night, lay still far ahead.

Stars, like many Indian pinks, flecked with pale brightness the sky above; towards the horizon shone the Southern Cross, while the Pole Star, through the palm-fronds, came and went.

> 'And the men cry Girlie, hi!
> Bring me –'

'Silence, dah! Ah'm thinkin'. . . .'

6

CUNA, full of charming roses, full of violet shadows, full of music, full of Love, Cuna . . . !

Leaning from a balcony of the Grand Savannah hotel, their instincts all aroused, Miami and Edna gazed out across the Alemeda, a place all foliage, lamplight, and flowers. It was the hour when Society in slowly parading carriages, would congregate to take the air beneath the pale mimosas that adorned the favourite promenade. All but recumbent, as though agreeably fatigued by their recent emotions (what wild follies were not committed in shuttered-villas during the throbbing hours of noon?), the Cunans, in their elegant equipages, made, for anyone fresh from the provinces, an interesting and absorbing sight. The liquid-eyed loveliness of the women, and the handsomeness of the men, with their black moustaches and their treacherous smiles – these, indeed, were things to gaze on.

'Oh ki!' Miami laughed delightedly, indicating a foppish, pretty youth, holding in a restive little horse dancing away with him.

Rubbing herself repeatedly, as yet embarrassed by the novelty of her clothes, Edna could only gasp.

'. . .' she jabbered, pointing at some flaunting belles in great evening hats and falling hair.

'All dat fine,' Miami murmured, staring in wonderment around.

Dominating the city soared the Opera House, uplifting a big, naked man, all gilt, who was being bitten, or mauled, so it seemed by a pack of wild animals carved of stone; while near by were the University, and the Cathedral with its low white dome crowned by moss-green tiles.

Making towards it, encouraged by the Vesper bell, some young girls, in muslin masks, followed by a retinue of bustling nuns, were running the gauntlet of the profligates that clustered on the curb.

'Oh, Jesus honey!' Edna cooed, scratching herself in an ecstasy of delight.

'Fo' shame, Chile, to act so unladylike; if any gen'leman look up he t'ink you make a wicked sign,' Mrs Mouth cautioned, stepping out upon the balcony from the sitting-room behind.

Inhaling a bottle of sal volatile, to dispel *de megrims*, she was looking dignified in a *décolleté* of smoke-blue tulle.

'Nebba do *dat* in S'ciety,' she added, placing a protecting arm around each of her girls.

Seduced, not less than they, by the animation of the town, the fatigue of the journey seemed to her amply rewarded. It was amusing to watch the crowd before the Ciné Lara, across the way, where many were flocking attracted by the hectic posters of 'A Wife's Revenge.'

'I keep t'inking I see Nini Snagg,' Mrs Mouth observed, regarding a negress in emerald-tinted silk, seated on a public bench beneath the glittering greenery.

'Cunan folk dat fine,' Edna twittered, turning about at her Father's voice:

> 'W'en de day ob toil is done,
> W'en de race ob life is run,
> Heaven send thy weary one
> Rest for evermore!'

'Prancing Nigger! Is it worth while to wear dose grimaces?'

'Sh'o, dis no good place to be.'

'Why, what dair wrong wid it?'

'Ah set out to look fo' de Meetin'-House, but no sooner am Ah in de street dan a female wid her har droopin' loose down ober her back an' into her eyes, she tell me to Come along.'

'Some of dose bold women, dey ought to be shot through dair bottoms!' Mrs Mouth indignantly said.

'But I nebba answer nothin'.'

'May our daughters respect dair virtue same as you!' Mrs

Mouth returned, focusing wistfully the vast flowery parterre of the Café McDhu'l.

Little city of cocktails, Cuna! The surpassing excellence of thy Barmen, who shall sing?

'See how dey spell "Biar", Mammee,' Miami tittered: 'dey forget de *i!*'

'Sh'o, Chile, an' so dey do. . . .'

'Honey Jesus!' Edna broadly grinned: 'imagine de ignorance ob dat.'

7

Now, beyond the Alemeda, in the modish faubourg of Far-ananka, there lived a lady of both influence and wealth – the widow of the Inventor of Sunflower Piquant. The *veto* of Madame Ruiz, arbitress absolute of Cunan society, and owner, moreover, of a considerable portion of the town, had caused the suicide indeed of more than one social climber. Unhappy nostalgic, disdainful, selfish, ever about to abandon Cuna-Cuna to return to it no more, yet never budging, adoring her fairy villa far too well, Madame Ruiz, while craving for the International-world, consoled herself by watching from afar European Society going speedily to the dogs. Art-loving, and considerably musical (many a dizzy venture at the Opera-house had owed its audition to her), she had, despite the self-centredness of her nature, done not a little to render more brilliant the charming city it amused her with such vehemence to abuse.

One softly gloomy morning, preceding Madame Ruiz's first *cotillon* of the Season, the lodge-keeper of the Villa Alba, a negress, like some great, violet bug, was surprised, while tending the brightly hanging grape-fruit in the drive, by an imperative knocking on the gate. At such a matutinal hour only trashy errand-boys shouldering baskets might be expected to call, and giving the summons no heed the mulatress continued her work.

The Villa Alba, half buried in spreading awnings, and surrounded by many noble trees, stood but a short distance off the main road, its pleasaunces enclosed by flower-enshrouded walls, all a-zig-zag, like the folds of a screen. Beloved of lizards and velvet-backed humming-birds, the shaded gardens led on one side to the sea.

'To make such a noise at dis hour,' the negress murmured, going grumblingly at length to the gate, disclosing, upon opening, a gentleman in middle life, with a tooth-brush moustache and a sapphire ring.

'De mist'ess still in bed, sah.'

'In bed?'

'She out bery late, sah, but you find Miss Edwards up.'

With a nod of thanks the visitor directed his footsteps discreetly towards the house.

Although not, precisely, *in* her bed when the caller, shortly afterwards, was announced, Madame Ruiz was nevertheless as yet in dishabille.

'Tiresome man, what does he want to see me about?' she exclaimed, gathering around her a brocaded wrap formed of a priestly cope.

'He referred to a lease, ma'am,' the maid replied.

'A lease!' Madame Ruiz raised eyes dark with spleen.

The visit of her agent, or man of affairs, was apt to ruffle her composure for the day. 'Tell him to leave it and go,' she commanded, selecting a nectarine from a basket of iced fruits beside her.

Removing reflectively the sensitive skin, her mind evoked, in ironic review, the chief salient events of society, scheduled to take place on the face of the map in the course of the day.

The marriage of the Count de Nozhel, in Touraine, to Mrs Exelmans of Cincinnati, the divorce of poor Lady Luckcock in London (it seemed quite certain that one of the five co-respondents was the little carrot-haired Lord Dubelly again), the last 'pomps', at Vienna, of Princess de Seeyohl *née* Mitchening-Meyong (Peace to her soul! She had led her life). . . . The christening in Madrid of the girl-twins of the Queen of Spain. . . .

'At her time, I really *don't* understand it,' Madame Ruiz murmured to herself aloud, glancing, as though for an explanation about the room.

Through the flowing folds of the mosquito curtains of the bed, that swept a cool, flagged floor spread with skins, showed the oratory, with its waxen flowers, and pendent flickering lights, that burned, night and day, before a Leonardo saint with a treacherous smile. Beyond the little recess came a lacquer commode, bearing a masterly marble group, depicting a pair of amorous hermaphrodites amusing themselves; while above, suspended against the spacious wainscoting of the wall, a painting of a man, elegantly corseted, with a violet in his moustache, 'Study of a Parisian', and its pendant, 'Portrait of a Lady', signed Van Dongen, were the chief outstanding objects that the room contained.

'One would have thought that at forty she would have given up having babies,' Madame Ruiz mused, choosing a glossy cherry from the basket at her side.

Through the open window a sound of distant music caught her ear.

'Ah! If only he were less weak,' she sighed, her thoughts turning towards the player, who seemed to be enamoured of the opening movement (rapturously repeated) of *L'Après-midi d'un faune*.

The venetorial habits of Vittorio Ruiz had been from his earliest years the source of his mother's constant chagrin and despair. At the age of five he had assaulted his Nurse, and, steadily onward, his passions had grown and grown. . . .

'It's the fault of the wicked climate,' Madame Ruiz reflected, as her companion, Miss Edwards, came in with the post.

'Thanks, Eurydice,' she murmured, smilingly exchanging a butterfly kiss.

'It's going to be oh so hot today!'

'Is it, dear?'

'Intense,' Miss Edwards predicted, fluttering a gay-daubed paper fan.

Sprite-like, with a little strained ghost-face beneath a silver shock of hair, it seemed as if her long blue eyes had absorbed the Cunan sea.

'Do you remember the giant with the beard?' she asked, 'at the Presidency fête?'

'Do I?'

'And we wondered who he could be!'

'Well?'

'He's the painter of Women's Backs, my dear!'

'The painter of women's *what*?'

'An artist.'

'Oh.'

'I wanted to know if you'd advise me to sit.'

'Your back is charming, dear, *c'est un dos d'élite.*'

'I doubt, though, it's classic,' Miss Edwards murmured, pirouetting slowly before the glass.

But Madame Ruiz was perusing her correspondence and seemed to be absorbed.

'They're to be married, in Munich, on the fifth,' she chirruped.

'Who?'

'Elsie and Baron Sitmar.'

'Ah, Ta-ra, dear! In those far worlds ...' Miss Edwards impatiently exclaimed, opening wide a window and leaning out.

Beneath the flame-trees, with their spreading tops a mass of crimson flower, coolly white-garbed gardeners, with naked feet and big bell-shaped hats of straw, were sweeping slowly, as in some rhythmic dance, the flamboyant blossoms that had fallen to the ground.

'Wasn't little Madame Haase, dear, born Kattie von Guggenheim?'

'I really don't know,' Miss Edwards returned, flapping away a fly with her fan.

'This villainous climate! My memory's going. ...'

'I wish I cared for Cuna less, that's all!' Miss Edwards said, her glance following a humming-bird, poised in air, above the sparkling turquoise of a fountain.

'Captain Moonlight ... duty ... (tedious word) ... can't come!'

'Oh?'

'Such a dull post,' Madame Ruiz murmured, pausing to listen to the persuasive tenor voice of her son.

> 'Little mauve nigger boy,
> I t'ink you break my heart!'

'My poor Vitti! Bless him.'

'He was out last night with some Chinese she.'

'I understood him to be going to *Pelléas and Mélisande*.'

'He came to the Opera-house, but only for a minute.'

'Dios!'

'And, oh, dearest.' Miss Edwards dropped her cheek to her hand.

'Was Hatso as ever delicious?' Madame Ruiz asked, changing the topic as her woman returned, followed by a pomeranian of parts, 'Snob'; a dog beautiful as a child.

'We had Gebhardt instead.'

'In Mélisande she's so huge,' Madame Ruiz commented, eyeing severely the legal-looking packet which her maid had brought her.

'Business, Camilla; *how* I pity you!'

Madame Ruiz sighed.

'It seems', she said, 'that for the next nine-and-ninety-years I have let a Villa to a Mr and Mrs Ahmadou Mouth.'

8

FLOOR of copper, floor of gold. . . . Beyond the custom-house door, ajar, the street at sunrise seemed aflame.

'Have you nothing, young man, to declare?'

'. . . Butterflies!'

'Exempt of duty. Pass.'

Floor of silver, floor of pearl. . . .

Trailing a muslin net, and laughing for happiness, Charlie Mouth marched into the town.

Oh, Cuna-Cuna! Little city of Lies and Peril! How many careless young nigger boys have gone thus to seal their Doom!

Although the Sun-god was scarcely risen, already the radiant street teemed with life.

Veiled dames, flirting fans, bent on church or market, were issuing everywhere from their doors, and the air was vibrant with the sweet voice of bells.

To rejoin his parents promptly at their hotel was a promise he was tempted to forget.

Along streets all fresh and blue in the shade of falling awnings, it was fine, indeed, to loiter. Beneath the portico of a church a running fountain drew his steps aside. Too shy to strip and squat in the basin, he was glad to bathe freely his head, feet and chest: then, stirred by curiosity to throw a glance at the building, he lifted the long yellow nets that veiled the door.

It was the fashionable church of La Favavoa, and the extemporary address of the Archbishop of Cuna was in full and impassioned swing.

'Imagine the world, my friends, had Christ been born a girl!' he was saying in tones of tender dismay as Charlie entered.

Subsiding bashfully to a bench, Charlie gazed around.

So many sparkling fans. One, a delicate light mauve one:

147

'Shucks! If only you wa' butterflies!' he breathed, contemplating with avidity the nonchalant throng: then perceiving a richer specimen splashed with silver of the same amative tint: 'Oh, you lil beauty!' And, clutching his itching net to his heart, he regretfully withdrew.

Sauntering leisurely through the cool, mimosa-shaded streets, he approached, as he guessed, the Presidency. A score of shoeblacks lolled at cards or gossip before its gilded pales. Amazed at their audacity (for the President had threatened more than once to 'wring the Public's neck'), Charlie hastened by. Public gardens, brilliant with sarracenias, lay just beyond the palace, where a music-pavilion, surrounded by palms and rocking-chairs, appeared a favourite, and much-frequented, resort; from here he observed the Cunan bay strewn with sloops and white-sailed yachts asleep upon the tide. Strolling on, he found himself in the busy vicinity of the Market. Although larger and more varied, it resembled in other respects the village one at home.

'Say, honey, say' – crouching in the dust before a little pyre of mangoes, a lean-armed woman besought him to buy.

Pursued by a confusion of voices, he threaded his way deftly down an alley dressed with booths. Pomegranates, some open with their crimson seeds displayed, banana-combs, and big, veined water-melons, lay heaped on every side.

'I could do wid a slice ob watteh-million,' he reflected: 'but to lick an ice-cream dat tempt me more!' Nor would the noble fruit of the baobab, the paw-paw, or the pine turn him from his fancy.

But no ice-cream stand met his eye, and presently he resigned himself to sit down upon his heels, in the shade of a potter's stall, and consider the passing crowd.

Missionaries with freckled hands and hairy, careworn faces, followed by pale girls wielding tambourines of the Army of the Soul, foppish nigger bucks in panamas and palm-beach suits so cocky, Chinamen with osier baskets, their nostalgic eyes aswoon, heavily straw-hatted nuns trailing their dust-coloured rags, and suddenly, oh, could it be? – but there was no mistaking that golden waddle: 'Mamma!'

Mamma, Mammee, Mrs Ahmadou Mouth. All in white, with snow-white shoes and hose so fine, he hardly dare.

'Mammee, Mammee, oh, Mammee. . . .'

'Sonny mine! My lil boy!'

'Mammee.'

'Just to say!'

And, oh, honies! Close behind, behold Miami, and Edna too: the Miss Lips, the fair Lips, the smiling Lips. How spry each looked. The elder (grown a trifle thinner), sweet *à ravir* in tomato-red, while her sister, plump as a corn-fattened partridge, and very perceptibly powdered, seemed like the flower of the prairie sugar-cane when it breaks into bloom.

'We've been to a Music-hall an' a pahty, an' Snowball has dropped black kittens.' Forestalling Miami, Edna rapped it out.

'Oh shucks!'

'An' since we go into S'ciety, we keep a boy in buttons!'

Mrs Mouth turned about.

'Where is dat idjit coon?'

'He stay behind to bargain for de pee-wee birds, Mammee, fo' to make de taht.'

'De swindling tortoise.'

'An' dair are no vacancies at de University: not fo' any ob us!' Edna further retailed, going off into a spasm of giggles.

She was swinging a wicker-basket, from which there dangled the silver forked tail of a fish.

'Fo' goodness' sake gib dat sea-porcupine to Ibum, Chile,' Mrs Mouth commanded, as a perspiring niggerling in livery presented himself.

'Ibum, his arms are full already.'

'Just come along all to de Villa now! It dat mignon an' all so nice. An' after de collation,' Mrs Mouth (shocked on the servants' account at her son's nude neck) raised her voice, 'we go to de habadasher in Palmbranch Avenue an' I buy you an Eton colleh!'

9

'PRANCING NIGGER, I t'ink it bery strange dat Madame Ruiz she nebba call.'

'Sh'o.'

'In August-Town, S'ciety less stuck-up dan heah!'

Ensconced in rocking-chairs, in the shade of the ample porch of the Villa Vista Hermosa, Mr and Mrs Mouth had been holding a desultory *tête-à-tête*.

It was a Sabbath evening, and a sound of reedy pipes and bafalons, from a neighbouring café, filled with a feverish sadness the brilliantly lamp-lit street.

'De airs ob de neighbehs, dat dair affair; what matter mo' am de chillen's schoolin'.'

'Prancing Nigger, I hope your Son an' Daughters will yet take dair Degrees, an' if not from de University, den from Home. From heah.'

'Hey-ho-day, an' dat would be a miracle!' Mr Mouth mirthlessly laughed.

'Dose chillens hab learnt quite a lot already.'

' 'Bout de shops an' cinemas!'

Mrs Mouth disdained a reply.

She had taken the girls to the gallery at the Opera one night to hear *Louise*, but they had come out, by tacit agreement, in the middle of it: the plainness of Louise's blouse, and the lack of tunes . . . the suffocation of the gallery . . . Once bit twice shy, they had not gone back again.

'All your fambly need, Prancing Nigger, is social opportunity! But what is de good ob de Babtist parson?'

Mr Mouth sketched a gesture.

'Sh'o, Edna, she some young yet. . . . But Miami dat *distinguée*; an', doh I her mother, b'lieb me dat is one ob de choicest girls I see; an' dat's de trute.'

'It queer,' Mr Mouth abstrusely murmured, 'how many skeeter-bugs dair are 'bout dis ebenin'!'

'De begonias in de window-boxes most lik'ly draw dem. But as I was saying, Prancing Nigger, I t'ink it bery strange dat Madame Ruiz nebba call.'

'P'r'aps she out ob town.'

'Accordin' to de paper, she bin habing her back painted, but what dat fo' I dunno.'

'Ah shouldn't wonder ef she had some trouble ob a dorsal kind; same as me gramma mumma long agone.'

'Dair'd be no harm in sendin' one obe de chillens to inquire. Wha' you t'ink, sah?' Mrs Mouth demanded, plucking from off the porch a pale hanging flower with a languorous scent.

Mr Mouth glanced apprehensively skyward.

The mutters of thunder and intermittent lightning of the finest nights.

'It's a misfortnit we eber left Mediavilla,' he exclaimed uneasily, as a falling star, known as a thief star, sped swiftly down the sky.

'Prancing Nigger,' Mrs Mouth rose, remarking, 'befo' you start to grumble, I leab you alone to your Jereymiads!'

'A misfortnit sho' nuff,' he mused, and regret for the savannah country and the tall palm-trees of his village oppressed his heart. Moreover, his means (derived from the cultivation of the *Musa paradisica*, or Banana) seemed likely to prove ere long inadequate to support the whims of his wife, who after a lifetime of contented nudity appeared to be now almost insatiable for dress.

A discordant noise from above interrupted the trend of his thoughts.

'Sh'o, she plays wid it like a toy,' he sighed, as the sound occurred again.

'Prancing Nigger, de water-supply cut off!'

'It's de Lord's will.'

'Dair's not a drop, my lub, in de privy.'

''Cos it always in use!'

'I b'lieb dat lil half-caste Ibum, 'cos I threaten to gib him notice, do somet'in' out ob malice to de chain.'

'Whom de Lord loveth He chasteneth!' Mr Mouth observed, 'an' dose bery words (ef you look) you will find in de twelfth chapter an' de sixth berse ob de Book ob Hebrews.'

'Prancing Nigger, you datways selfish! Always t'inkin' ob your soul, instead ob your obligations towards de fambly.'

'Why, wha' mo' can I do dan I've done?'

Mrs Mouth faintly shrugged.

'I had hoped', she said, 'dat Nini would hab bin ob use to de girls, but dat seem now impossible!' For Mrs Snagg had been traced to a house of ill-fame, where it appeared, she was an exponent of the Hodeidah – a lascive Cunan dance.

'Understand dat any sort of intimacy 'tween de Villa an' de *Closerie des Lilas* Ah must flatly forbid.'

'Prancing Nigger, as ef I should take your innocent chillens to call on po' Nini; not dat eberyt'ing about her at de *Closerie* is not elegant an' nice. Sh'o, some ob de inmates ob dat establishment possess mo' diamonds dan dair betters do outside! You'd be surprised ef you could see what two ob de girls dair, Dinah an' Lew. . . .'

'Enuf!'

'It isn't always Virtue, Prancing Nigger, dat come off best!' And Mrs Mouth might have offered further observations on the matter of ethics had not her husband left her.

IO

Past the Presidency and the public park, the Theatres
Maxine Bush, Eden-Garden, and Apollo, along the Avenida
and the Jazz Halls by the wharf, past little suburban shops,
and old, deserted churchyards where bloom geraniums,
through streets of squalid houses, and onward skirting pleasure lawns and orchards, bibbitty-bobbitty, beneath the
sovereign brightness of the sky, crawled the Farananka tram.

Surveying the landscape listlessly through the sticks of her
fan, Miss Edna Mouth grew slightly bored – alas, poor child;
couldst thou have guessed the blazing brightness of thy Star,
thou wouldst doubtless have been more alert!

'Sh'o, it dat far an' tejus,' she observed to the conductor,
lifting upon him the sharp-soft eyes of a paroquet.

She was looking bewitching in a frock of silverish *mous-
seline* and a violet tallyho cap, and dangled upon her knees an
intoxicating sheaf of the blossoms known as Marvel of Peru.

'Hab patience, lil Missey, an' we soon be dah.'

*

'He tells me, dear child, he tells me,' Madame Ruiz was
rounding the garden path, upon the arm of her son, 'he tells
me, Vitti, that the systole and diastole of my heart's muscles
are slightly inflamed; and that I ought, darling, to be *very*
careful. . . .'

Followed by a handsome borzoi and the pomeranian Snob,
the pair were taking their usual post-prandial exercise beneath
the trees.

'Let me come, Mother, dear', he murmured without inter-
rupting, 'over the other side of you; I always like to be on
the right side of my profile!'

'And really, since the affair of Madame de Bazvalon, my
health has hardly been what it was.'

'That foolish little woman,' he uncomfortably laughed.

'He tells me my nerves need rest,' she declared, looking pathetically up at him.

He had the nose of an actress, and ink-black hair streaked with gold, his eyes seemed to be covered with the freshest of fresh dark pollen, while nothing could exceed the vivid pallor of his cheeks or the bright sanguine of his mouth.

'You go out so much, Mother.'

'Not so much!'

'So very much.'

'And he forbids me my opera-box for the rest of the week! So last night I sat at home, dear child, reading the Life of Lazarillo de Tormes.'

'I don't give a damn', he said, 'for any of your doctors.'

'So vexing, though; and apparently Lady Bird has been at death's door, and poor Peggy Povey too. It seems she got wet on the way to the Races; and really I was *sorry* for her when I saw her in the paddock; for the oats and the corn, and the wheat and the tares, and the barley and the rye, and all the rest of the reeds and grasses in her pretty Lancret hat, looked like nothing so much as manure.'

'I adore to folly her schoolboy's moustache!'

'My dear, Age is the one disaster,' Madame Ruiz remarked, raising the rosy dome of her sunshade a degree higher above her head.

They were pacing a walk radiant with trees and flowers as some magician's garden, that commanded a sweeping prospect of long, livid sands, against a white green sea.

'There would seem to be several new yachts, darling,' Madame Ruiz observed.

'The Duke of Wellclose with his duchess (on their wedding-tour) arrived with the tide.'

'Poor man; I'm told that he only drove to the church after thirty brandies!'

'And the *Sea-Thistle*, with Lady Violet Valesbridge, and, *oh*, such a crowd.'

'She used to be known as "The Cat of Curzon Street", but I hear she is still quite incredibly pretty,' Madame Ruiz murmured, turning to admire a somnolent peacock, with moping fan, poised upon the curved still arm of a marble maenad.

'How sweet something smells.'

'It's the China lilies.'

'I believe it's my handkerchief . . .' he said.

'Vain wicked boy; ah, if you would but decide, and marry some nice, intelligent girl.'

'I'm too young yet.'

'You're *twenty-six*!'

'And past the age of folly-o,' he made airy answer, drawing from his breast-pocket a flat, jewel-encrusted case, and lighting a cigarette.

'Think of the many men, darling, of twenty-six . . .' Madame Ruiz broke off, focusing the fruit-bearing summit of a slender areca palm.

'Foll-foll-folly-o!' he laughed.

'I think I'm going in.'

'Oh, why?'

'Because,' Madame Ruiz repressed a yawn, 'because, dear, I feel armchairish.'

With a kiss of the finger-tips (decidedly distinguished hands had Vittorio Ruiz), he turned away.

Joying frankly in excess, the fiery noontide hour had a special charm for him.

It was the hour, to be sure, of 'the Faun'!

'Aho, Ahi, Aha!' he carolled, descending half trippingly a few white winding stairs that brought him upon a fountain. Palms, with their floating fronds radiating light, stood all around.

It was here 'the creative mood' would sometimes take him, for he possessed no small measure of talent of his own.

His *Three Hodeidahs*, and *Five Phallic Dances for Pianoforte and Orchestra*, otherwise known as 'Suite in Green', had taken the whole concert world by storm, and, now, growing more audacious, he was engaged upon an opera to be known, by and by, as *Sumaïa*.

'Ah Atthis, it was Sappho who told me – ' tentatively he sought an air.

A touch of banter there.

'*Ah Atthis –* ' One must make the girl feel that her little secret is out . . .; quiz her; but let her know, and pretty plainly, that the Poetess has been talking. . . .

'*Ah Atthis –* '

But somehow or other the lyric mood today was obdurate and not to be persuaded.

'I blame the oysters! After oysters – ' he murmured, turning about to ascertain what was exciting the dogs.

She was coming up the drive with her face to the sun, her body shielded behind a spreading bouquet of circumstance.

'It's all right; they'll not hurt you.'

'Sh'o, I not afraid!'

'Tell me who it is you wish to see.'

'Mammee send me wid dese flowehs. . . .'

'Oh! But how scrumptious.'

'It strange how dey call de bees; honey-bees, sweat-bees, bumble-bees an' all!' she murmured, shaking the blossoms into the air.

'That's only natural,' he returned, his hand falling lightly to her arm.

'Madame Ruiz is in?'

'She is: but she is resting; and something tells me', he suavely added, indicating a grassy bank, 'you might care to repose yourself too.'

And indeed after such a long and rambling course she was glad to accept.

'De groung's as soft as a cushom,' she purred, sinking with nonchalance to the grass.

'You'd find it', he said, 'even softer, if you'll try it nearer me.'

'Dis a mighty pretty place!'

'And you – ' but he checked his tongue.

'Fo' a villa so grand, dair must be mo' dan one privy?'

'Some six or seven!'

'Ours is broke.'

'You should get it mended.'

'De aggervatiness'!' she wriggled.

'Tell me about them.'

And so, not without digressions, she unfolded her life.

'Then you, Charlie, and Mimi are here, dear, to study?'

'As soon as de University is able to receibe us; but dair's a waiting list already dat long.'

'And what do you do with all your spare time?'

'Goin' round de shops takes up some ob it. An' den, ob course, dair's de Cinés. Oh, I do love de Lara. We went last night to see *Souls in Hell*.'

'I've not been.'

'Oh it was his choice.'

'Was it? Why?'

'De scene ob dat story', she told him, 'happen foreign; 'way crost de big watteh, on de odder side ob de world ... an' de principal gal, she married to a man who neglect her (ebery ebenin' he got to pahtys an' biars), while all de time his wife she sit at home wid her lil pickney at her breas'. But dair anodder gemplum (a friend ob de fambly) an' he afiah to woe her; but she only shake de head, slowly, from side to side, an' send dat man away. Den de hubsom lose his fortune, an', oh, she dat 'stracted, she dat crazed ... at last she take to gamblin', but dat only make t'ings worse. Den de friend ob de fambly come back, an' offer to pay all de expenses ef only she unbend: so she cry, an' she cry, 'cos it grieb her to leab her pickney to de neglect ob de serbants (dair was three ob dem, an old buckler, a boy, an' a cook), but, in de end, she do, an' frtt! away she go in de fambly carriage. An' den, bimeby, you see dem in de bedroom doin' a bit ob funning.'

'What?'

'Oh ki; it put me in de gigglements. ...'

'Exquisite kid.'

'Sh'o, de coffee-concerts an' de pictures, I don't nebba tiah ob dem.'

'Bad baby.'

'I turned thirteen.'

'You are?'

'By de Law ob de Island, I a spinster ob age!'

'I might have guessed it was the Bar! These law-students,' he murmured, addressing the birds.

'Sh'o, it's de trute,' she pouted, with a languishing glance through the sticks of her fan.

'I don't doubt it,' he answered, taking lightly her hand.

'Mercy,' she marvelled: 'is dat a watch dah, on your arm?'

'Dark, bright baby!'

'Oh, an' de lil "V.R." all in precious stones so blue.' Her frail fingers caressed his wrist.

'Exquisite kid.' She was in his arms.

'Vitti, Vitti! –' It was the voice of Eurydice Edwards. Her face was strained and quivering. She seemed about to faint.

II

EVER so lovely are the young men of Cuna-Cuna – Juarez, Jotifa, Enid – (these, from many, to distinguish but a few) – but none so delicate, charming, and squeamish as Charlie Mouth.

'Attractive little Rose . . .' 'What a devil of a dream . . .' the avid belles would exclaim when he walked abroad, while impassioned widows would whisper 'Peach!'

One evening, towards sundown, just as the city lifts its awnings, and the deserted streets start seething with delight, he left his home to enjoy the grateful air. It had been a day of singular oppressiveness, and, not expecting overmuch of the vesperal breezes, he had borrowed his mother's small Pompadour fan.

Ah, little did that nigger boy know as he strolled along what novel emotions that promenade held in store!

Disrelishing the dust of the Avenida, he directed his steps towards the Park.

He had formed already an acquaintanceship with several young men, members, it seemed, of the University, and these he would sometimes join, about this hour, beneath the Calabash-trees in the Marcella Gardens.

There was Abe, a lad of fifteen, whose father ran a Jazz Hall on the harbour-beach, and Ramon, who was destined to enter the Church, and the intriguing Esmé, whose dream was the Stage, and who was supposed to be 'in touch' with Miss Maxine Bush, and there was Pedro, Pedro ardent and obese, who seemed to imagine that to be a dress-designer to foreign Princesses would yield his several talents a thrice-blessed harvest.

Brooding on these and other matters, Charlie found himself in Liberty Square.

Here, the Cunan Poet, Samba Marcella's effigy arose – that 'sable singer of Revolt'.

Aloft, on a pedestal, soared the Poet, laurel-crowned, thick-lipped, woolly, a large weeping Genius, with a bold taste for draperies, hovering just beneath; her one eye closed, the other open, giving her an air of winking confidentially at the passers-by.

' "Up, Cŭnans, up! To arms, to arms!"' he quoted, lingering to watch the playful swallows wheeling among the tubs of rose-oleanders that stood around.

And a thirst, less for bloodshed than for a sherbet, seized him.

It was a square noted for the frequency of its bars, and many of their names, in flickering lights, showed palely forth already.

Cuna! City of Moonstones; how faerie art thou in the blue blur of dusk!

Costa Rica. Chile Bar. To the Island of June. . . .

Red roses against tall mirrors, reflecting the falling night.

Seated before a cloudy cocktail, a girl with gold cheeks like the flesh of peaches addressed him softly from behind: 'Listen, lion!'

But he merely smiled on himself in the polished mirrors, displaying moist-gleaming teeth and coral gums.

A fragrance of aromatic cloves . . . a mystic murmur of ice. . . .

A little dazed after a Ron Bacardi, he moved away. 'Shine, sah?' The inveigling squeak of a shoeblack followed him.

Sauntering by the dusty benches along the pavement-side, where white-robed negresses sat communing in twos and threes, he attained the Avenue Messalina with its spreading palms, whose fronds hung nerveless in the windless air.

Tinkling mandolins from restaurant gardens, light laughter, and shifting lights.

Passing before the Café de Cuna, and a people's 'Dancing', he roamed leisurely along. Incipient Cyprians, led by vigilant, blanched-faced queens, youths of a certain life, known as bwam-wam bwam-wams, gaunt pariah dogs with questing eyes, all equally were on the prowl. Beneath the Pharaohic pilasters of the Theatre Maxine Bush a street crowd had formed before a notice described 'Important', which informed the Public that, owing to a 'temporary hoarseness', the role of Miss Maxine Bush would be taken, on that occasion, by Miss Pauline Collier.

The Marcella Gardens lay towards the end of the Avenue, in the animated vicinity of the Opera. Pursuing the glittering thoroughfare, it was interesting to observe the pleasure announcements of the various theatres, picked out in signs of fire: *Aïda: The Jewels of the Madonna: Clara Novotny and Lily Lima's Season.*

Vending bags of roasted peanuts, or sapodillas and avocado pears, insistent small boys were importuning the throng.

'Go away; I can't be bodder,' Charlie was saying, when he seemed to slip; it was as though the pavement were a carpet snatched from under him, and, looking round, he was surprised to see, in a confectioner's window, a couple of marble-topped tables start merrily waltzing together.

Driven onwards by those behind, he began stumblingly to run towards the Park. It was the general goal. Footing it a little ahead, two loose women and a gay young man (pursued by a waiter with a napkin and a bill), together with the horrified, half-crazed crowd; all, helter-skelter, were intent upon the Park.

Above the Calabash-trees, bronze, demoniac, the moon gleamed sourly from a starless sky, and although not a breath of air was stirring, the crests of the loftiest palms were set arustling by the vibration at their roots.

'Oh, will nobody *stop* it?' a terror-struck lady implored.

Feeling quite white and clasping a fetish, Charlie sank all panting to the ground.

Safe from falling chimney-pots and sign-boards (that for 'Pure Vaseline', for instance, had all but caught him), he had much to be thankful for.

'Sh'o nuff, dat was a close shave,' he gasped, gazing dazed about him.

Clustered back to back near by upon the grass, three stolid matrons, matrons of hoary England, evidently not without previous earthquake experience, were ignoring resolutely the repeated shocks.

'I always follow the fashions, dear, at a distance!' one was saying: 'this little gingham gown I'm wearing I had made for me after a design I found in a newspaper at my hotel.'

'It must have been a pretty old one, dear – I mean the paper, of course.'

'New things are only those you know that have been forgotten.'

'Mary ... there's a sharp pin, sweet, at the back of your ... *Oh!*'

Venturing upon his legs, Charlie turned away.

By the Park palings a few 'Salvationists' were holding forth, while, in the sweep before the bandstand, the artists from the Opera, in their costumes of *Aïda*, were causing almost a greater panic among the ignorant than the earthquake itself. A crowd, promiscuous rather than representative, composed variously of chauffeurs (making a wretched pretence, poor chaps, of seeking out their masters), Cyprians, patricians (these in opera cloaks and sparkling diamonds), tourists, for whom the Hodeidah girls would *not* dance that night, and bwam-wam bwam-wams, whose equivocal behaviour, indeed, was perhaps more shocking even than the shocks, set the pent Park ahum. Yet notwithstanding the upheavals of Nature, certain persons there were bravely making new plans.

'How I wish I could, dear! But I shall be having a houseful of women over Sunday – that's to say.'

'Then come the week after.'

'Thanks, then, I *will*.'

Hoping to meet with Abe, Charlie took a pathway flanked with rows of tangled roses, whose leaves shook down at every step.

And it occurred to him with alarming force that perhaps he was an orphan.

Papee, Mammee, Mimi, and lil Edna – the villa drawing-room on the floor. ...

His heart stopped still.

'An' dey in de spirrit world – in heaven hereafter!' He glanced with awe at the moon's dark disk.

'All in dair cotton shrouds. . . .'

What if he should die and go to the Bad Place below?

'I mizzable sinney, Lord. You heah, Sah? you heah me say dat? Oh, Jesus, Jesus, Jesus,' and weeping, he threw himself down among a bed of flowers.

When he raised his face it was towards a sky all primrose and silver pink. Sunk deep in his dew-laved bower, it was sweet to behold the light. Above him great spikes of blossom were stirring in the idle wind, while birds were chanting voluntaries among the palms. And in thanksgiving, too, arose the matin bells. From Our Lady of the Pillar, from the church of La Favavoa in the West, from Saint Sebastian, from Our Lady of the Sea, from Our Lady of Mount Carmel, from Santa Teresa, from St Francis of the Poor.

12

But although by the grace of Providence the city of Cuna-Cuna had been spared, other parts of the island had sustained irremediable loss. In the Province of Casuby, beyond the May Day Mountains, many a fair banana or sugar estate had been pitifully wrecked, yet what caused perhaps the widest regret among the Cunan public was the destruction of the famous convent of Sasabonsam. One of the beauties of the island, one of the gems of tropic architecture, celebrated, made immortal (in *The Picnic*) by the Poet Marcella, had disappeared. A Relief Fund for those afflicted had at once been started, and, as if this were not enough, the doors of the Villa Alba were about to be thrown open for 'An Evening of Song and Gala' in the causes of charity.

'Prancing Nigger, dis an event to take exvantage ob; dis not a lil t'ing, love, to be sneezed at at all,' Mrs Mouth eagerly said upon hearing the news, and she had gone about ever since, reciting the names in the list of Patronesses, including that of the Cunan Archbishop.

It was the auspicious evening.

In their commodious, jointly shared bedroom, the Miss Lips, the fair Lips, the smiling Lips were maiding one another in what they both considered to be the 'Parisian way'; a way, it appeared, that involved much nudging, arch laughter, and, even, some prodding.

'In love? Up to my ankles! Oh, yes.' Edna blithely chuckled.

'Up to your topknot!' her sister returned, making as if to pull it.

But with the butt end of the curling-tongs Edna waved her away.

Since her visit to the Villa Alba 'me, an' Misteh Ruiz' was all her talk, and to be his reigning mistress the summit of her dreams.

'Come on, man, wid dose tongs; 'cos I want 'em myself,' Miami murmured, pinning a knot of the sweet night jasmine deftly above her ear.

Its aroma evoked Bamboo.

Oh, why had he not joined her? Why did he delay? Had he forgotten their delight among the trees, the giant silk-cotton-trees, with the hammer-tree-frogs chanting in the dark: Rig-a-jig-jig, rig-a-jig-jig?

'Which you like de best, man, dis lil necklash or de odder?' Edna asked, essaying a strand of orchid-tinted beads about her throat.

'I'd wear dem both,' her sister advised.

'I t'ink, on de whole, I wear de odder; de one he gib me de time he take exvantage ob my innocence.'

'Since dose imitation pearls, honey – he gib you anyt'ing else?'

'No; but he dat generous! He say he mean to make me a lil pickney gal darter: an', oh, won't dat be a day,' Edna fluted, breaking off at the sound of her mother's voice in the corridor.

'. . . and tell de cabman to take de fly-bonnets off de horses,' she was instructing Ibum as she entered the room.

She had a gown of the new mignonette satin, with 'episcopal' sleeves lined with red.

'Come, girls, de cab is waiting; but perhaps you no savey dat.'

They didn't; and, for some time, dire was the confusion.

In the Peacock drawing-room of the Villa Alba the stirring ballet music from *Isfahan* filled the vast room with its thrilling madness. Upon a raised estrade, a corps of dancing boys, from Sankor, glided amid a murmur of applause.

The combination of charity and amusement had brought together a crowded and cosmopolitan assembly and, early though it was, it was evident already that with many more new advents there would be a shortage of chairs. From their yachts had come several distinguished birds of passage, exhaling an atmosphere of Paris and Park Lane.

Wielding a heavy bouquet of black feathers, Madame Ruiz,

robed in a gown of malmaison cloth-of-silver, watched the dancers from an alcove by the door.

Their swaying torsos, and weaving gliding feet, fettered with chains of orchids and hung with bells, held a fascination for her.

'My dear, they beat the Hodeidahs! I'm sure I never saw anything like it,' the Duchess of Wellclose remarked admiringly: 'that little one, Fred,' she murmured, turning towards the Duke.

A piece of praise a staid small body in a demure lace cap chanced to hear.

This was 'the incomparable' Miss McAdam, the veteran ballet mistress of the Opera-house, and inventrix of the dance. Born in the frigid High Street of Aberdeen, 'Alice', as she was universally known among enthusiastic patrons of the ballet, had come originally to the tropics as companion to a widowed clergyman, when, as she would relate (in her picturesque, native brogue), at the sight of *Nature* her soul had awoke. Self-expression had come with a rush; and, now that she was ballet mistress of the Cunan Opera, some of the daring *ensembles* of the Scottish spinster would embarrass even the good Cunans themselves.

'I've warned the lads', she whispered to Madame Ruiz, 'to cut their final figure on account of the Archbishop. But young boys are so excitable, and I expect they'll forget!'

Gazing on their perfect backs, Madame Ruiz could not but mourn the fate of the Painter, who, like Dalou, had specialized almost exclusively on this aspect of the human form; for, alas, that admirable Artist had been claimed by the Quake; and although his portrait of Madame Ruiz remained unfinished . . . there was still a mole, nevertheless, in gratitude, and as a mark of respect she had sent her Rolls car to the Mass in honour of his obsequies, with the *crêpe* off an old black dinner-dress tied across the lamps.

'I see they're going to,' Miss McAdam murmured, craning a little to focus the Archbishop, then descanting to two ladies with deep purple fans.

'Ah, well! It's what they do in *Isfahan*,' Madame Ruiz commented, turning to greet her neighbour Lady Bird.

'Am I late for Gebhardt?' she asked, as if Life itself hinged upon the reply.

A quietly silly woman, Madam Ruiz was often obliged to lament the absence of intellect at her door: accounting for it as the consequence of a weakness for negroes, combined with a hopeless passion for the Regius Professor of Greek at Oxford.

But the strident cries of the dancers and the increasing volume of the music discouraged all talk, though ladies with collection-boxes (biding their time) were beginning furtively to select their next quarry.

Countess Katty Taosay, *née* Soderini, a little woman and sure of the giants, could feel in her psychic veins which men were most likely to empty their pockets: English Consul ... pale and interesting, he would not refuse to stoop and fumble, nor Follinsbe 'Peters', the slender husband of a fashionable wife, nor Charlie Campfire, a young boy like an injured camel, heir to vast banana estates, the darling, and six foot high if an inch.

'Why do big men like little women?' she wondered, waving a fan powdered with blue *paillettes:* and she was still casting about for a reason when the hectic music stopped.

And now the room echoed briefly with applause, while admiration was divided between the super-excellence of the dancers and the living beauty of the rugs which their feet had trod – rare rugs from Bokhara-i-Shareef, and Kairouan-city-of-Prayer, lent by the mistress of the house.

Entering on the last hand-clap, Mr and Mrs Mouth, followed by their daughters, felt, each in their several ways, they might expect to enjoy themselves.

'Prancing Nigger, what a *furore!*' Mrs Mouth exclaimed. 'You b'lieb, I hope, now, dat our tickets was worth de money.'

Plucking at the swallow-tails of an evening 'West-End', Mr Mouth was disinclined to re-open a threadbare topic.

'It queah how few neegah dair be,' he observed, scanning

the brilliant audience, many of whom, taking advantage of an interval, were flocking towards a buffet in an adjoining conservatory.

'Prancing Nigger, I feel I could do wid a glass ob champagne.'

Passing across a corridor, it would have been interesting to have explored the spacious vistas that loomed beyond. 'Dat must be one ob de priveys,' Edna murmured, pointing to a distant door.

'Seben, Chile, did you say?'

'If not more!'

'She seem fond ob flowehs,' Mr Mouth commented, pausing to notice the various plants that lined the way: from the roof swung showery azure flowers that commingled with the theatrically-hued cañas, set out in crude, bold, colour-schemes below, that looked best at night. But in their malignant splendour the orchids were the thing. Mrs Abanathy, Ronald Firbank (a dingy lilac blossom of rarity untold), Prince Palairet, a heavy blue-spotted flower, and rosy Olive Moon-light, were those that claimed the greatest respect from a few discerning connoisseurs.

'Prancing Nigger, you got a chalk mark on your "West end". Come heah, sah, an' let me brush it.'

Hopeful of glimpsing Vittorio, Miami and Edna sauntered on. With arms loosely entwined about each other's hips they made, in their complete insouciance, a conspicuous couple.

'I'd give sumpin' to see de bedrooms, man, 'cos dair are chapels, an' barf-rooms, beside odder conveniences off dem,' Edna related, returning a virulent glance from Miss Eurydice Edwards with a contemptuous, pitying smile.

Traversing a throng, sampling sorbets and ices, the sisters strolled out upon the lawn.

The big silver stars, how clear they shone – infinitudes, infinitudes.

'Adieu, hydrangeas, adieu, blue, burning South!'

The concert, it seemed, had begun.

'Come chillens, come!'

In the vast drawing-room, the first novelty of the evening –
an aria from *Sumaïa* – had stilled all chatter. Deep-sweet,
poignant, the singer's voice was conjuring Sumaïa's farewell
to the Greek isle of Mitylene, bidding farewell to its gracious
women, and to the trees of white or turquoise in the gardens
of Lesbos.

'Adieu, hydrangeas – '

Hardly a suitable moment, perhaps, to dispute a chair. But
neither the Duchess of Wellclose nor Mrs Mouth were
creatures easily abashed.

'I pay, an' I mean to hab it.'

'You can't; it's taken!' the duchess returned, nodding
meaningly towards the buffet, where the duke could be seen
swizzling whisky at the back of the bar.

'Sh'o! Dese white women seem to t'ink dey can hab ebbery-
t'ing.'

'Taken,' the duchess repeated, who disliked what she called
the *parfum d'Afrique* of the 'sooties', and, as though to
intimidate Mrs Mouth, she gave her a look that would have
made many a Peeress in London quail.

Nevertheless, in the stir that followed the song chairs were
forthcoming.

'From de complexion dat female hab, she look as doh she
bin boiling bananas!' Mrs Mouth commented comfortably,
loud enough for the duchess to hear.

'Such a large congregation should su'tinly assist de fund!'
Mr Mouth resourcefully said, envisaging with interest the
audience; it was not every day that one could feast the gaze on
the noble baldness of the Archbishop, or on the subtle
silhouette of Miss Maxine Bush, swathed like an idol in an
Egyptian tissue woven with magical eyes.

'De woman in de window dah,' Mrs Mouth remarked,
indicating a dowager who had the hard but resigned look of
the mother of six daughters in immediate succession, 'hab a
look, Prancing Nigger, ob your favourite statesman.'

'De immortal Wilberforce!'

'I s'poge it's de whiskers,' Mrs Mouth replied, ruffling
gently her 'Borgia' sleeves for the benefit of the Archbishop.

Rumour had it he was fond of negresses, and that the black
private secretary he employed was his own natural son, while
some suspected indeed a less natural connexion.

But Madame Hatso (of Blue Brazil, the Argentine; those
nights in Venezuela and Buenos Ayres, '*bis*' and '*bravas*'!
How the public had roared) was curtseying right and left, and
Mrs Mouth, glancing round to address her daughters, perceived with vexation that Edna had vanished.

In the garden he caught her to him.

'Flower of the Sugar Cane!'

'Misteh Ruiz. . . .'

'Exquisite kid.'

'I saw you thu de window-glass all de time, an' dair was
I! laughing so silent-ly. . . .'

'My little honey.'

'. . . no; 'cos ob de neighbehs,' she fluted, drawing him
beneath the great flamboyants that stood like temples of
darkness all around.

'Sweetheart.'

'I 'clar to grashis!' she delightedly crooned as he gathered
her up in his arms.

'My little Edna . . . ? . . . ? . . . ?'

'Where you goin' wid me to?'

'There,' and he nodded towards the white sea sand.

A yawning butler, an insolent footman, a snoring coachman, a drooping horse. . . .

The last conveyance had driven away, and only a party of
'b – dy niggers,' supposed to be waiting for a daughter, was
keeping the domestics from their beds.

Ernest, the bepowdered footman, believed them to be
thieves, and could have sworn he saw a tablespoon in the
old coon's pocket.

Hardly able to restrain his tears, Mr Mouth sat gazing
vacuously at the floor.

'Wha' can keep de chile? . . . O Lord . . . I hope dair
noddin' wrong.'

'On such a lovely ebenin' what is time?' Mrs Mouth exclaimed, taking up an attitude of night-enchantment by the open door.

A remark that caused the butler and his subordinate to cough.

'It not often I see de cosmos look so special!'

'Ef she not heah soon, we better go widout her,' Miami murmured, who was examining the visitors' cards on the hall table undismayed by the eye of Ernest.

'It's odd she should so procrastinate; but *la jeunesse, c'est le temps où l'on s'amuse*,' Mrs Mouth blandly declared, seating herself tranquilly by her husband's side.

'Dair noddin', I hope, de matteh. . . .'

'Eh, suz, my deah! Eh, suz.' Reassuringly, she tapped his arm.

'Sir Victor Virtue, Lady Bird, Princess Altamisal,' Miami tossed their cards.

'Sh'o it was a charming ebenin'! Doh I was sorry for de duchess, wid de duke, an' he all nasty drunk wid spirits.'

'I s'poge she use to it.'

'It was a perfect skangle! Howebber, on de whole, it was quite an enjoyable pahty – doh dat music ob Wagner, it gib me de retches.'

'It bore me, too,' Miami confessed, as a couple of under-footmen made their appearance and, joining their fidgeting colleagues by the door, waited for the last guests to depart, in a mocking, whispering group.

'Ef she not here bery soon,' Miami murmured, vexed by the servants' impertinent smiles.

'Sh'o, she be here directly,' Mrs Mouth returned, appraising through her fan-sticks the footmen's calves.

'It daybreak already!' Miami yawned, moved to elfish mirth by the over-emphasis of rouge on her mother's round cheeks.

But under the domestics' mocking stare their talk at length was chilled to silence.

From the garden came the plaintive wheepling of a bird (intermingled with the coachman's spasmodic snores), while above the awning of the door the stars were wanly paling.

'Prancing Nigger, sah, heah de day. Dair no good waitin' any more.'

It was on their return from the Villa Alba that they found a letter signed 'Mamma Luna', announcing the death of Bamboo.

13

HE had gone out, it seemed, upon the sea to avoid the earth-quake (leaving his mother at home to take care of the shop), but the boat had overturned, and the evil sharks . . .

In a room darkened against the sun, Miami, distracted, wept. Crunched by the maw of a great blue shark: 'Oh, honey.'

Face downward, with one limp arm dangling to the floor, she bemoaned her loss: such love-blank, and aching void! Like some desolate, empty cave, filled with clouds, so her heart.

'An' to t'ink dat I eber teased you!' she moaned, reproaching herself for the heedless past; and as day passed over day still she wept.

One mid-afternoon, some two weeks later, she was reclining lifelessly across the bed, gazing at the sun-blots on the floor. There had been a mild disturbance of a seismic nature that morning, and indeed slight though unmistakable shocks had been sensed repeatedly of late.

'Intercession' services, fully choral – the latest craze of society – filled the churches at present, sadly at the expense of other places of amusement, many of which had been obliged to close down. A religious revival was in the air, and in the Parks and streets elegant dames would stop one another in their passing carriages and pour out the stories of their iniquitous lives.

Disturbed by the tolling of a neighbouring bell, Miami reluctantly rose.

'Lord! What a din; it gib a po' soul de grabe-yahd creeps,' she murmured, lifting the jalousie of a sun-shutter and peering idly out.

Standing in the street was a Chinese laundrymaid, chatting with two Chinamen with osier baskets, while a gaunt pariah dog was rummaging among some egg-shells and banana-skins in the dust before the gate.

'Dat lil fool-fool Ibum, he throw ebberyt'ing out ob de window an' nebba t'ink ob de stink,' she commented, as an odour of decay was wafted in on a gust of the hot trade wind. The trade winds! How pleasantly they used to blow in the village of Mediavilla. The blue trade wind, the gold trade wind caressing the bending canes. . . . City life, what had it done for any of them, after all? Edna nothing else than a harlot (since she had left them there was no other word), and Charlie fast going to pieces, having joined the Promenade of a notorious Bar with its bright particular galaxy of boys.

'Sh'o, ebberyt'ing happier back dah,' she mused, following the slow gait across the street of some barefooted nuns; soon they would be returning, with many converts and pilgrims, to Sasabonsam, beyond the May Day Mountains, where remained a miraculous image of Our Lady of the Sorrows still intact. How if she joined them, too? A desire to express her grief, and thereby ease it, possessed her. In the old times there had been many ways: tribal dances and wild austerities. . . .

She was still musing, self-absorbed, when her mother, much later, came in from the street.

There had been a great Intercessional, it seemed, at the Cathedral, with hired singers from the Opera-house and society women as thick as thieves, '*gnats*', she had meant to say (Tee-hee!), about a corpse. Arturo Arrivabene . . . a voice like a bull . . . and she had caught a glimpse of Edna driving on the Avenue Amanda, looking almost Spanish in a bandeau beneath a beautiful grey tilt hat.

But Miami's abstraction discouraged confidences.

'Why you so *triste*, Chile? Dair no good at all in frettin'.'

'Sh'o nuff.'

'Dat death was on de cards, my deah, an' dair is no mistakin' de fac'; an' as de shark is a rapid feeder it all ober sooner dan wid de crocodile, which is some consolation for dose dat remain to mourn.'

'Sh'o, it bring not an atom to me!'

''Cos de process ob de crocodile bein' sloweh dan dat ob de shark – '

'Ah, say no more,' Miami moaned, throwing herself in a

storm of grief across the bed. And as all efforts to appease made matters only worse, Mrs Mouth prudently left her.

'Prancing Nigger, she seem dat sollumcholly an' depressed,' Mrs Mouth remarked at dinner, helping herself to some guava-jelly that had partly dissolved through lack of ice.

'Since de disgrace ob Edna dat scarcely s'prisin',' Mr Mouth made answer, easing a little the napkin at his neck.

'She is her own woman, me deah sah, an' *I* cannot prevent it!'

In the convivial ground-floor dining-room of an imprecise style, it was hard, at times, to endure such second-rate company as that of a querulous husband.

Yes, marriage had its dull side, and its drawbacks; still, where would society be (and where morality!) without the married women?

Mrs Mouth fetched a sigh.

Just at her husband's back, above the ebony sideboard, hung a Biblical engraving, after Rembrandt, of the *Woman Taken in Adultery,* the conception of which seemed to her exaggerated and overdone, knowing full well, from previous experience, that there need not, really, be so much fuss. . . . Indeed, there need not be any: but to be *Taken* like that! A couple of idiots.

'W'en I look at our chillen's chairs, an' all ob dem empty, in my opinion we both betteh deaded,' Mr Mouth brokenly said.

'I dare say dair are dose dat may t'ink so,' Mrs Mouth returned, refilling her glass; 'but, Prancing Nigger, I am not like dat: no, sah!'

'Where's Charlie?'

'I s'poge he choose to dine at de lil Cantonese restaurant on de quay,' she murmured, setting down her glass with a slight grimace: how *ordinaire* this cheap red wine! Doubtless Edna was lapping the wines of paradise! Respectability had its trials. . . .

'Dis jelly mo' like lemon squash,' Mr Mouth commented.

''Cos dat lil liard Ibum, he again forget de ice! Howebber, I hope soon to get rid ob him: for de insolence ob his bombax is more dan I can stand,' Mrs Mouth declared, lifting her voice on account of a piano-organ in the street just outside.

'I s'poge today Chuesd'y? It was a-Chuesd'y – God forgib dat po' frail chile.'

'Prancing Nigger, I allow Edna some young yet for dat position; I allow dat to be de matteh ob de case but, me good sah! bery likely she marry him later.'

'Pah.'

'An' why not?'

'Chooh, nebba!'

'Prancing Nigger, you seem to forget dat your elder daughter was a babe ob four w'en I put on me nuptial arrange blastams to go to de Church.'

'Sh'o, I wonder you care to talk ob it!'

'An', today, honey, as I sat in de Cathedral, lis'nin' to de Archbishop, I seemed to see Edna, an' she all in *dentelles* so *chic,* comin' up de aisle, followed by twelve maids, all ob good blood, holdin' flowehs an' wid hats kimpoged ob feddehs – worn raddeh to de side, an' I heah a stranger say: "Excuse me, sah, but who dis fine marriage?" an' a voice make reply: "Why, dat Mr Ruiz de milliona'r-'r-'r," an' as he speak, one ob dese Italians from de Opera-house commence to sing "De voice dat brieved o'er Eden," an' Edna she blow a kiss at me an' laugh dat arch.'

'Nebba!'

'Prancing Nigger, "wait an' see"!' Mrs Mouth waved prophetically her fan.

'No, nebba,' he repeated, his head sunk low in chagrin.

'How you know, sah?' she queried, rising to throw a crust of loaf to the organ man outside.

The wind with the night had risen, and a cloud of blown dust was circling before the gate.

'See de raindrops, deah; here come at last de big rain.'

'. . .'

'Prancing Nigger!'

'Ah'm thinkin'.'

14

IMPROVISING at the piano, Piltzenhoffer, kiddy-grand, he
was contented, happy. The creative fertility, bursting from
a radiant heart, more than ordinarily surprised him. 'My
most quickening affair since – ' he groped, smiling a little
at several particular wraiths, more or less bizarre, that, in
their time, had especially disturbed him. 'Yes; probably!' he
murmured enigmatically, striking an intricate, virile chord.

'Forgib me, dearest! I was wid de manicu' of de fingeh-
nails.'

'Divine one.'

She stood before him.

Hovering there between self-importance and madcapery,
she was exquisite quite.

'All temperament . . .!' he murmured, capturing her deftly
between his knees.

She was wearing a toilette of white *crêpe de chine,* and a large
favour of bright purple Costa-Rica roses.

'Soon as de sun drop, dey set out, deah: so de manicu' say.'

'What shall we do till then?'

'. . . or, de pistols!' she fluted, encircling an arm about his
neck.

'Destructive kitten,' he murmured, kissing, one by one,
her red, polished nails.

'Honey! Come on.'

He frowned.

It seemed a treason almost to his last mistress, an exotic
English girl, perpetually shivering, even in the sun, this
revolver practice on the empty quinine-bottles she had left
behind. Poor Meraude! It was touching what faith she had in
a dose of quinine! Unquestionably she had been faithful to
that. And dull enough, too, it had made her. With her albums
of photographs, nearly all of midshipmen, how insufferably
had she bored him: – 'This one, darling, tell me, isn't he – I,

really – he makes me – and this one, darling! An Athenian viking, with hair like mimosa, and what ravishing hands! – oh my God! – I declare – he makes me – ' Poor Meraude; she had been extravagant as well!

'Come on, an' break some bokkles!'

'There's not a cartridge left,' he told her, setting her on his knee.

> 'Ha-ha! Oh, hi-hi!
> Not a light:
> Not a bite!
> What a Saturday Night!'

she trilled, taking off a comedian from the Eden Garden.

Like all other negresses she possessed a natural bent for mimicry and a voice of that lisping quality that would find complete expression in songs such as: 'Have you seen my sweet garden ob Flowehs?', 'Sst! Come closer, Listen heah', 'Lead me to the Altar, Dearest', and 'His Little Pink, proud, Spitting-lips are Mine'.

'What is that you're wearing?'

'A souvenir ob today; I buy it fo' luck,' she rippled, displaying a black briar cross pinned to her breast.

'I hope it's blessed?'

'De nun dat sold it, didn't say. Sh'o, it's dreadful to t'ink ob po' Mimi, an' she soon a pilgrim all in blistehs an' rags,' she commented, as a page-boy with bejasmined ears appeared at the door.

'Me excuse. . . .'

'How dare you come in, lil saucebox, widdout knockin'?'

'Excuse, missey, but . . .'

'What?'

Ibum hung his head.

'I only thoughted, it bein' Crucifix day, I would like to follow in de procession thu de town.'

'Bery well: but be back in time fo' dinner.'

'T'ank you, missey.'

'An' mind fo' once you are!'

'Yes, missey,' the niggerling acquiesced, bestowing a slow

smile on Snob and Snowball, who had accompanied him into the room. Easy of habit, as tropical animals are apt to be, it was apparent that the aristocratic pomeranian was paying sentimental court to the skittish mouser, who, since her περιπέτεια of black kittens, looked ready for anything.

'Sh'o, but she hab a way wid her!' Ibum remarked, impressed.

'Lil monster, take dem both, an' den get out ob my sight,' his mistress directed him.

Fingering a battered volume that bore the bookplate of Meraude, Vittorio appeared absorbed.

'Honey.'

'Well?'

'Noddin'.'

In the silence of the room a restless bluebottle, attracted by the wicked leer of a chandelier, tied up incredibly in a bright green net, blended its hum with the awakening murmur of the streets.

'Po' Mimi. I hope she look up as she go by.'

'Yes, by Jove.'

'Doh after de rude t'ings she say to me – ' she broke off, blinking a little at the sunlight through the thrilling shutters.

'If I remember, beloved, you were both equally candid,' he remarked, wandering out upon the balcony.

It was on the palm-grown Messalina, an avenue that comprised a solid portion of the Ruiz estate, that he had installed her, in a many-storied building, let out in offices and flats.

Little gold, blue, lazy, and romantic Cuna, what chastened mood broods over thy life today!

'Have you your crucifix? Won't you buy a cross?' persuasive, feminine voices rose up from the pavement below. Active again with the waning sun, 'workers', with replenished wares, were emerging forth from their respective depots nursing small lugubrious baskets.

'Have you bought your cross?' The demand, when softly cooed by some solicitous patrician, almost compelled an answer; and most of the social world of Cuna appeared to be vending crosses, or 'Pilgrims' medals' in imitation 'bronze', this afternoon, upon the kerb. At the corner of Valdez Street, across the way, Countess Katty Taosay (*née* Soderini), austere in black with Parma violets, was presiding over a depot festooned with nothing but rosaries, that 'professed' themselves, as they hung, to the suave trade wind.

> 'Not a light:
> Not a bite!
> What a – '

Edna softly hummed, shading her eyes with a big feather fan.

It was an evening of cloudless radiance; sweet and mellow as is frequent at the close of summer.

'Oh, ki, honey! It so cleah I can see de lil iluns ob yalleh sand far away b'yond de Point!'

'Dearest!' he inattentively murmured, recognizing on the Avenue the elegant cobweb wheels of his mother's Bolivian buggy.

Accompanied by Eurydice Edwards, she was driving her favourite mules.

'An' de shipwreck off de coral reef, oh, ki!'

'Let me find you the long-glass, dear,' he said, glad for an instant to step inside.

Leaning with one foot thrust nimbly out through the balcony-rails towards the street, she gazed absorbed.

Delegates of agricultural guilds bearing banners, making for the Cathedral square (the pilgrims' starting-point), were advancing along the avenue amidst applause: fruit-growers, rubber-growers, sugar-growers, opium-growers, all doubtless wishful of placating Nature that redoubtable Goddess by showing a little honour to the Church. 'O Lord, *not* as Sodom,' she murmured, deciphering a text attached to the windscreen of a luxurious automobile.

'Divine one, here they are.'

'T'anks, honey, I sée best widdout,' she replied, following the Bacchic progress of two girls in soldiers' forage-caps, who were exciting the gaiety of the throng.

'Be careful, kid; don't lean too far. . . .'

'Oh, ki, if dey don't exchange kisses!'

But the appearance of the Cunan Constabulary, handsome youngsters, looking the apotheosis themselves of earthly lawlessness, in their feathered sunhats and bouncing kilts, created a diversion.

'De way dey stare up; I goin' to put on a tiara!'

'Wait, do, till supper,' he entreated, manipulating the long-glass to suit his eye.

Driving or on foot, were the usual faces.

Seated on a doorstep, Miss Maxine Bush, the famous actress, appeared to be rehearsing a smart society role, as she flapped the air with a sheet of street-foul paper, while, rattling a money-box, her tame monkey, 'Jutland-ho,' came as prompt for a coin as any demned Duchess.

'Ha-ha, Oh, hi-hi!' Edna's blasted catches. 'Bless her,' he exclaimed, re-levelling the glass. Perfect. Good lenses these; one could even read a physician's doorplate across the way: 'Hours 2–4, Agony guaranteed' – obviously, a dentist; and the window-card, too, above, 'Miss – ? Miss – ? Speciality: Men past thirty.'

Four years to wait. Patience.

Ooof! There went 'Alice' and one of her boys. Bad days for the ballet! People afraid of the Operahouse ... that chandelier ... and the pictures on the roof. ... And wasn't that little Lady Bird? running at all the trousers: '*have* you your crucifix! ...? ?'

'Honey. ...'

She had set a crown of moonstones on her head, and had moonstone bracelets on her arms.

'My queen.'

'I hope Mimi look up at me!'

'Vain one.'

Over the glistering city the shadows were falling, staining the white-walled houses here and there as with some purple pigment.

'Accordin' to de lates' 'ticklers, de Procession follow de Paseo only as far as de fountain.'

'Oh. ...'

'Where it turn up thu Carmen Street, into de Avenue Messalina.'

Upon the metallic sheen of the evening sky she sketched the itinerary lightly with her fan.

And smiling down on her uplifted face, he asked himself whimsically how long he would love her. She had not the brains, poor child, of course, to keep a man for ever. Heigho. Life indeed was often hard. . . .

'Honey, here dey come!'

A growing murmur of distant voices, jointly singing, filled liturgically the air, just as the warning salute, fired at sundown from the heights of the fort above the town, reverberated sadly.

'Oh, la, la,' she laughed, following the wheeling flight of some birds that rose startled from the palms.

'The Angelus. . . .'

'Hark, honey: what is dat dey singin'?'

> 'A thousand ages in Thy sight
> Are like an evening gone;
> Short as the watch that ends the night
> Before the rising sun.'

Led by an old negress leaning on her hickory staff, the procession came.

Banners, banners, banners.

'I hope Mimi wave!'

Floating banners against the dusk. . . .

'Oh, honey! See dat lil pilgrim-boy?'

> 'Time like an ever-rolling stream,
> Bears all its sons away;
> They fly forgotten, as a dream
> Dies at the opening day.'

'Mimi, Mimi!' She had flung the roses from her dress. 'Look up, my deah, look up.'

But her cry escaped unheard.

> 'They fly forgotten, as a dream
> Dies – '

The echoing voices of those behind lingered a little.

'Edna.'

She was crying.

'It noddin'; noddin' at all! But it plain she refuse to forgib me!'

'Never.'

'Perspirin', an' her skirt draggin', sh'o, she looked a fright.'

He smiled: for indeed already the world was perceptibly moulding her. . . .

'Enuff to scare ebbery crow off de savannah!'

'And wouldn't the farmers bless her.'

'Oh, honey!' Her glance embraced the long, lamp-lit avenue with suppressed delight.

'Well.'

'Dair's a new dancer at de Apollo tonight. Suppose we go?'

Havana – Bordighera

CONCERNING
THE ECCENTRICITIES OF
CARDINAL PIRELLI

———————————

*

I

HUDDLED up in a cope of gold wrought silk he peered around. Society had rallied in force. A christening – and not a child's.

Rarely had he witnessed, before the font, so many brilliant people. Were it an heir to the DunEden acres (instead of what it *was*) the ceremony could have hardly drawn together a more distinguished throng.

Monsignor Silex moved a finger from forehead to chin, and from ear to ear. The Duquesa DunEden's escapades, if continued, would certainly cost the Cardinal his hat.

'And ease my heart by splashing fountains.'

From the choir-loft a boy's young voice was evoking Heaven.

'His hat!' Monsignor Silex exclaimed aloud, blinking a little at the immemorial font of black Macael marble that had provoked the screams of pale numberless babies.

Here Saints and Kings had been baptized, and royal Infantas, and sweet Poets, whose high names thrilled the heart.

Monsignor Silex crossed his breast. He must gather force to look about him. Frame a close report. The Pontiff, in far-off Italy, would expect precision.

Beneath the state baldequin, or Grand Xaymaca, his Eminence sat enthroned ogled by the wives of a dozen grandees. The Altamissals, the Villarasas (their grandee-ships' approving glances, indeed, almost eclipsed their wives'), and Catherine, Countess of Constantine, the most talked-of beauty in the realm, looking like some wild limb of Astaroth in a little crushed 'toreador' hat round as an athlete's coif with hanging silken balls, while beside her a stout, dumpish dame, of enormous persuasion, was joggling, solicitously, an object that was of the liveliest interest to all.

Head archly bent, her fine arms divined through darkling

laces, the Duquesa stood, clasping closely a week-old police-dog in the ripple of her gown.

'Mother's pet!' she cooed, as the imperious creature passed his tongue across the splendid uncertainty of her chin.

Monsignor Silex's large, livid face grew grim.

What – disquieting doubt – if it were her Grace's offspring after all? Praise heaven, he was ignorant enough regarding the schemes of nature, but in an old lutrin once he had read of a young woman engendering a missel-thrush through the channel of her nose. It had created a good deal of scandal to be sure at the time: the Holy Inquisition, indeed, had condemned the impudent baggage, in consequence, to the stake.

'That was the style to treat them,' he murmured, appraising the assembly with no kindly eye. The presence of Madame San Seymour surprised him; one habitually so set apart and devout! And Madame La Urench, too, gurgling away freely to the fourlegged Father: 'No, my naughty Blessing; no, not now! ... By and by, a *bone*.'

Words which brought the warm saliva to the expectant parent's mouth.

Tail awag, sex apparent (to the affected slight confusion of the Infanta Eulalia-Irene), he crouched, his eyes fixed wistfully upon the nozzle of his son.

Ah, happy delirium of first parenthood! Adoring pride! Since times primeval by what masonry does it knit together those that have succeeded in establishing here, on earth, the vital bonds of a family's claim? Even the modest sacristan, at attention by the font, felt himself to be superior of parts to a certain unproductive chieftain of a princely House, who had lately undergone a course of asses' milk in the surrounding mountains – all in vain!

But, supported by the Prior of the Cartuja, the Cardinal had arisen for the act of Immersion.

Of unusual elegance, and with the remains, moreover, of perfect looks, he was as wooed and run after by the ladies as any *matador*.

'And thus being cleansed and purified, I do call thee "Crack"!' he addressed the Duquesa's captive burden.

Tail sheathed with legs 'in master's drawers,' ears cocked, tongue pendent. . . .

'Mother's mascot!'

'Oh, take care, dear; he's removing all your rouge!'

'*What?*'

'He's spoilt, I fear, your roses.' The Countess of Constantine tittered.

The Duquesa's grasp relaxed. To be seen by all the world at this disadvantage.

'Both?' she asked, distressed, disregarding the culprit, who sprang from her breast with a sharp, sportive bark.

What rapture, what freedom!

'*Misericordia!*' Monsignor Silex exclaimed, staring aghast at a leg poised, inconsequently, against the mural-tablet of the widowed duchess of Charona – a woman who, in her lifetime, had given over thirty million pezos to the poor!

Ave Maria purissima! What challenging snarls and measured mystery marked the elaborate recognition of father and son, and would no one then forbid their incestuous frolics?

In agitation Monsignor Silex sought fortitude from the storied windows overhead, aglow in the ambered light as some radiant missal.

It was St Eufraxia's Eve, she of Egypt, a frail unit numbered above among the train of the Eleven Thousand Virgins: an immaturish schoolgirl of a saint, unskilled, inexperienced in handling a prayer, lacking the vim and native astuteness of the incomparable Theresa.

Yes; divine interference, 'twixt father and son, was hardly to be looked for, and Eufraxia (she of Egypt) had failed too often before. . . .

Monsignor Silex started slightly, as, from the estrade beneath the dome, a choir-boy let fall a little white spit.

Dear child, as though *that* would part them!

'Things must be allowed to take their "natural" course,' he concluded, following the esoteric antics of the reunited pair.

Out into the open, over the Lapis Lazuli of the floor, they flashed, with stifled yelps, like things possessed.

'He'll tear my husband's drawers!' the duquesa lamented.

'The duque's legs. Poor Decima.' The Infanta fell quietly to her knees.

'Fortify . . . asses . . .' the royal lips moved.

'Brave darling,' she murmured, gently rising.

But the duquesa had withdrawn, it seemed, to repair her ravaged roses, and from the obscurity of an adjacent confessional-box was calling to order Crack.

'Come, Crack!'

And to the Mauro-Hispanic rafters the echo rose.

'Crack, Crack, Crack, Crack. . . .'

2

From the Calle de la Pasión, beneath the blue-tiled mirador of the garden wall, came the soft brooding sound of a seguidilla. It was a twilight planned for wooing, unbending, consent; many, before now, had come to grief on an evening such. 'It was the moon.'

Pacing a cloistered walk, laden with the odour of sun-tired flowers, the Cardinal could not but feel the insidious influences astir. The bells of the institutions of the Encarnacion and the Immaculate Conception, joined in confirming Angelus, had put on tones half-bridal, enough to create vague longings, or sudden tears, among the young patrician boarders.

'Their parents' daughters – convent-bred,' the Cardinal sighed.

At the Immaculate Conception, dubbed by the Queen, in irony, once 'The school for harlots', the little Infanta Maria-Paz must be lusting for her Mamma and the Court, and the lilac carnage of the ring, while chafing also in the same loose captivity would be the roguish *niñas* of the pleasure-loving duchess of Sarmento, girls whose Hellenic ethics had given the good Abbess more than one attack of fullness.

Morality. Poise! For without temperance and equilibrium – The Cardinal halted.

But in the shifting underlight about him the flushed camellias and the sweet night-jasmines suggested none; neither did the shape of a garden-Eros pointing radiantly the dusk.

'For unless we have balance – ' the Cardinal murmured, distraught, admiring against the elusive nuances of the after-glow the cupid's voluptuous hams.

It was against these, once, in a tempestuous mood that his mistress had smashed her fan-sticks.

'Would that all liaisons would break as easily!' his Eminence framed the prayer: and musing on the appalling constancy of a certain type, he sauntered leisurely on. Yes, enveloping women like Luna Sainz, with their lachrymose, tactless 'mys', how shake them off? 'My' Saviour, 'my' lover, 'my' parasol – and, even, 'my' virtue. . . .

'Poor dearie.'

The Cardinal smiled.

Yet once in a way, perhaps, he was not averse to being favoured by a glimpse of her: 'A little visit on a night like this.' Don Alvaro Narciso Hernando Pirelli, Cardinal-Archbishop of Clemenza, smiled again.

In the gloom there, among the high thickets of bay and flowering myrtle. . . . For, after all, bless her, one could not well deny she possessed the chief essentials: 'such, poor soul, as they are!' he reflected, turning about at the sound as of the neigh of a horse.

'Monseigneur. . . .'

Bearing a biretta and a silver shawl, Madame Poco, the venerable Superintendent-of-the-palace, looking, in the blue moonlight, like some whiskered skull, emerged, after inconceivable peepings, from among the leafy limbo of the trees.

'Ah, Don Alvaro, sir! Come here.'

'Pest!' His Eminence evinced a touch of asperity.

'Ah, Don, Don . . .' and skimming forward with the grace of a Torero lassooing a bull, she slipped the scintillating fabric about the prelate's neck.

'Such nights breed fever, Don Alvaro, and there is mischief in the air.'

'Mischief?'

'In certain quarters of the city you would take it almost for some sortilege.'

'What next?'

'At the Encarnación there's nothing, of late, but seediness. Sister Engracia with the chicken-pox, and Mother Claridad with the itch, while at the College of Noble Damosels, in the Calle Santa Fé, I hear a daughter of Don José Illescas, in a fit of caprice, has set a match to her coronet.'

'A match to her what?'

'And how explain, Don Alvaro of my heart, these constant shots in the Cortès? Ah, *sangre mio,* in what times we live!'

Ambling a few steps pensively side by side, they moved through the brilliant moonlight. It was the hour when the awakening fireflies are first seen like atoms of rosy flame floating from flower to flower.

'Singular times, sure enough,' the Cardinal answered, pausing to enjoy the transparent beauty of the white dripping water of a flowing fountain.

'And ease my heart by splashing – tum-tiddly-um-tum,' he hummed. 'I trust the choir-boys, Dame, are all in health?'

'Ah, Don Alvaro, no, sir!'

'Eh?'

'No, sir,' Madame Poco murmured, taking up a thousand golden poses.

'Why, how's that?'

'But few now seem keen on Leapfrog, or Bossage, and when a boy shows no wish for a game of Leap, sir, or Bossage – '

'Exactly,' his Eminence nodded.

'I'm told it's some time, young cubs, since they've played pranks on Tourists! Though only this afternoon little Ramón Ragatta came over queazy while demonstrating before foreigners the Dance of the Arc, which should teach him in future not to be so profane: and as to the acolytes, Don Alvaro, at least half of them are absent, confined to their cots, in the wards of the pistache Fathers!'

'Tomorrow, all well, I'll take them some melons.'

'Ah, Don, Don!!'

'And, perhaps, a cucumber,' the Cardinal added, turning valedictionally away.

The tones of the seguidilla had deepened and from the remote recesses of the garden arose a bedlam of nightingales and frogs.

It was certainly incredible how he felt immured.

Yet to forsake the Palace for the Plaza he was obliged to stoop to creep.

With the Pirelli pride, with resourceful intimacy he communed with his heart: deception is a humiliation; but humiliation is a Virtue – a Cardinal, like myself, and one of the delicate violets of our Lady's crown. . . . Incontestably, too – he had a flash of inconsequent insight, many a prod to a discourse, many a sapient thrust, delivered *ex cathedra,* amid the broken sobs of either sex, had been inspired, before now, by what prurient persons might term, perhaps, a 'frolic'. But away with all scruples! Once in the street in mufti, how foolish they became.

The dear street. The adorable Avenidas. The quickening stimulus of the crowd: truly it was exhilarating to mingle freely with the throng!

Disguised as a cabellero from the provinces or as a matron (disliking to forgo altogether the militant bravoura of a skirt), it became possible to combine philosophy, equally, with pleasure.

The promenade at the Trinidades seldom failed to be diverting, especially when the brown Bettita or the Ortiz danced! *Olé,* he swayed his shawl. The Argentina with Blanca Sanchez was amusing too; her ear-tickling little song 'Madrid is on the Manzanares', trailing the ''ares' indefinitely, was sure, in due course, to reach the Cloisters.

Deliberating critically on the numerous actresses of his diocese, he traversed lightly a path all enclosed by pots of bergamot.

And how entrancing to perch on a bar-stool, over a glass of old golden sherry!

'Ah Jesus-Maria,' he addressed the dancing lightning in the sky.

Purring to himself, and frequently pausing, he made his way, by ecstatic degrees, towards the mirador on the garden wall.

Although a mortification, it was imperative to bear in mind the consequences of cutting a too dashing figure. Beware display. Vanity once had proved all but fatal: 'I remember it was the night I wore ringlets and was called "my queen".'

And with a fleeting smile, Don Alvaro Pirelli recalled the persistent officer who had had the effrontery to attempt to molest him: 'Stalked me the whole length of the Avenue

Isadora!' It had been a lesson. 'Better to be on the drab side,' he reflected, turning the key of the garden tower.

Dating from the period of the Reformation of the Nunneries, it commanded the privacy of many a drowsy patio.

'I see the Infanta has begun her Tuesdays!' he serenely noted, sweeping the panorama with a glance.

It was a delightful prospect.

Like some great guitar the city lay engirdled ethereally by the snowy Sierras.

'Foolish featherhead,' he murmured, his glance falling upon a sunshade of sapphire chiffon, left by Luna: '"my" parasol!' he twirled the crystal hilt.

'Everything she forgets, bless her,' he breathed, lifting his gaze towards the magnolia blossom cups that overtopped the tower, stained by the eternal treachery of the night to the azure of the St Virgin. Suspended in the miracle of the moonlight their elfin globes were at their zenith.

'Madrid is on the Manzan-ares,' he intoned.

But 'Clemenza', of course, is in white Andalucia.

3

AFTER the tobacco-factory and the railway-station, quite the liveliest spot in all the city was the cathedral-sacristia. In the interim of an Office it would be besieged by the laity, often to the point of scrimmage: aristocrats and mendicants, relatives of acolytes – each had some truck or other in the long lofty room. Here the secretary of the chapter, a burly little man, a sound judge of women and bulls, might be consulted gratis, preferably before the supreme heat of day. Seated beneath a sombre study of the Magdalen waylaying our Lord (a work of wistful interest ascribed to Valdés Leal), he was, with tactful courtesy, at the disposal of anyone soliciting information as to 'vacant dates', or 'hours available', for some impromptu function. Indulgences, novenas, terms for special masses – with flowers and music? Or, just plain; the expense, it varied! Bookings for baptisms, it was certainly advisable to book well ahead; some mothers booked before the birth – ; ah-hah, the little Juans and Juanas; the angelic babies! And arrangements for a corpse's lying-in-state: 'Leave it to me.' These, and such things, were in his province.

But the secretarial bureau was but merely a speck in the vast shuttered room. As a rule, it was by the old pagan sarcophaguses, outside the vestry-door, 'waiting for Father', that *aficionados* of the cult liked best to foregather.

It was the morning of the Feast of San Antolin of Panticosa, a morning so sweet, and blue and luminous, and many were waiting.

'It's queer the time a man takes to slip on a frilly!' the laundress of the Basilica, Doña Consolacion, observed, through her fansticks, to Tomás the beadle.

'Got up as you get them. . . .'

'It's true, indeed, I've a knack with a rochet!'

'Temperament will out, Doña Consolacion; it cannot be hid.'

The laundress beamed.

'Mine's the French.'

'It's God will *whatever* it is.'

'It's the French,' she lisped, considering the silver rings on her honey-brown hands. Of distinguished presence, with dark matted curls at either ear, she was the apotheosis of flesh triumphant.

But the entry from the vestry of a file of monsignore imposed a transient silence – a silence which was broken only by the murmur of passing mule bells along the street.

Tingaling, tingaling: evocative of grain and harvest the sylvan sound of mule bells came and went.

Doña Consolacion flapped her fan.

There was to be question directly of a Maiden Mass.

With his family all about him, the celebrant, a youth of the People, looking childishly happy in his first broidered cope, had bent, more than once, his good-natured head, to allow some small brothers and sisters to inspect his tonsure.

'Like a little, little star!'

'No. Like a *perra gorda*.'

'No, like a little star,' they fluted, while an irrepressible grandmother, moved to tears and laughter, insisted on planting a kiss on the old 'Christian' symbol. 'He'll be a Pope some day, if he's spared!' she sobbed, transported.

'Not he, the big burly bull.' Mother Garcia of the Company of Jesus addressed Doña Consolacion with a mellifluent chuckle.

Holding a bouquet of sunflowers and a basket of eggs she had just looked in from Market.

'Who knows, my dear?' Doña Consolacion returned, fixing her gaze upon an Epitaph on a vault beneath her feet. '"He was a boy and she dazzled him." Heigh-ho! Heysey-ho . . .! Yes, as I was saying.'

'Pho: I'd like to see him in a Papal tiara.'

'It's mostly luck. I well recall his Eminence when he was nothing but a trumpery curate,' Doña Consolacion declared, turning to admire the jewelled studs in the ears of the President of the College of Noble Damosels.

'Faugh!' Mother Garcia spat.

'It's all luck.'

'There's luck and luck,' the beadle put in. Once he had confined by accident a lady in the souterrains of the cathedral, and only many days later had her bones and a diary, a diary documenting the most delicate phases of solitude and loneliness, *a woman's contribution to Science,* come to light; a piece of carelessness that had gone against the old man in his preferment.

'Some careers are less fortunate than others,' Mother Garcia exclaimed, appraising the sleek silhouette of Monsignor Silex, then precipitantly issuing from the Muniment-Room.

It was known he was not averse to a little stimulant in the bright middle of the morning.

'He has the evil Eye, dear, he has the evil Eye,' Doña Consolacion murmured, averting her head. Above her hung a sombre Ribera, in a frame of elaborate blackened gilding.

'Ah, well, I do not fear it,' the Companion of Jesus answered, making way for a dark, heavy belle in a handkerchief and shawl.

'Has anyone seen Josito, my little José?'

Mother Garcia waved with her bouquet towards an adjacent portal, surmounted, with cool sobriety, by a long, lavender marble cross. 'I expect he's through there.'

'In the cathedral?'

'How pretty you look, dear, and what a very gay shawl!'

'Pure silk.'

'I don't *doubt* it!'

Few women, however, are indifferent to the seduction of a Maiden Mass, and all in a second there was scarcely one to be found in the whole sacristia.

The secretary at his bureau looked about him: without the presence of *las mujeres* the atmosphere seemed to weigh a little; still, being a Holiday of Obligation, a fair sprinkling of boys, youthful chapter hands whom he would sometimes designate as the 'lesser delights', relieved the place of its austerity.

Through the heraldic windows, swathed in straw-mats to

shut out the heat, the sun-rays entered, tattooing with piquant freckles the pampered faces of the choir.

A request for a permit to view the fabled Orangery in the cloisters interrupted his siestose fancies.

Like luxurious cygnets in their cloudy lawn, a score of young singing-boys were awaiting their cue: Low-masses, cheapness, and economy, how they despised them, and how they would laugh at 'Old Ends' who snuffed out the candles.

'Why should the Church charge *higher* for a short *Magnificat* than for a long *Miserere*?'

The question had just been put by the owner of a dawning moustache and a snub, though expressive, nose.

'Because happiness makes people generous, stupid, and often as not they'll squander, boom, but unhappiness makes them calculate. People grudge spending much on a snivel – even if it lasts an hour.'

'It's the choir that suffers.'

'This profiteering ... The Chapter ...' there was a confusion of voices.

'Order?' A slim lad, of an ambered paleness, raised a protesting hand. Indulged, and made-much-of by the hierarchy, he was Felix Ganay, known as Chief-dancing-choir-boy to the cathedral of Clemenza.

'Aren't they awful?' he addressed a child with a very finished small head. Fingering a score of music he had been taking lead in a mass of Palestrina, and had the vaguely distraught air of a kitten that had seen visions.

'After that, I've not a dry stitch on me,' he murmured, with a glance towards the secretary, who was making lost grimaces at the Magdalen's portrait.

A lively controversy (becoming increasingly more shrill) was dividing the acolytes and choir.

'Tiny and Tibi! Enough.' The intervention came from the full-voiced Christobal, a youngster of fifteen, with soft, peach-textured cheeks, and a tongue never far away. Considered an opportunist, he was one of the privileged six dancing-boys of the cathedral.

'Order!' Felix enjoined anew. Finely sensitive as to his

prerogatives, the interference of his colleague was apt to vex him. He would be trying to clip an altar pose next. Indeed, it was a matter of scandal already, how he was attempting to attract attention, in influential places, by the unnecessary undulation of his loins, and by affecting strong scents and attars, such as Egyptian Tahetant, or Long Flirt through the violet Hours. Himself, Felix, he was faithful to Royal Florida, or even to plain *eau-de-Cologne*, and to those slow Mozarabic movements which alone are seemly to the Church.

'You may mind your business, young Christobal,' Felix murmured, turning towards a big, serious, melancholy boy, who was describing a cigarette-case he had received as fee for singing 'Say it with Edelweiss' at a society wedding.

'Say it with what?' the cry came from an oncoming-looking child, with caressing liquid eyes, and a little tongue the colour of raspberry-cream – *so bright*. Friend of all sweets and dainties, he held San Antolin's day chiefly notable for the Saint's sweet biscuits, made of sugar and white-of-egg.

'And you, too, Chicklet. Mind your business, can't you?' Felix exclaimed, appraising in some dismay a big, bland woman, then descending upon the secretary at his desk, with a slow, but determined, waddle.

Amalia Bermudez, the fashionable Actress-manageress of the Teatro Victoria Eugenia, was becoming a source of terror to the chapter of Clemenza. Every morning, with fatal persistence, she would aboard the half-hypnotized secretary with the request that the Church should make 'a little christian' of her blue chow, for unless it could be done it seemed the poor thing wasn't *chic*. To be *chic* and among the foremost vanward; this, apart from the Theatre, meant all to her in life, and since the unorthodox affair of 'the DunEdens', she had been quite upset by the chapter's evasive refusals.

'If a police-dog, then why not a chow?' she would ask. 'Why not my little Whisky? Little devil. Ah, believe me, Father, she has need of it; for she's supposed to have had a snake by my old dog Conqueror! ... And yet you won't receive her? Oh, it's heartless. Men are cruel. ....'

'There she is! Amalia – the Bermudez': the whisper spread,

arresting the story of the black Bishop of Bechuanaland, just begun by the roguish Ramón.

And in the passing silence the treble voice of Tiny was left talking all alone.

'. . . frightened me like Father did, when he kissed me in the dark like a lion': – a remark that was greeted by an explosion of coughs.

But this morning the clear, light laugh of the comedienne rang out merrily. 'No, no, *hombre*,' she exclaimed (tapping the secretary upon the cheek archly with her fan), 'now don't, don't stare at me, and intimidate me like that! I desire only to offer "a Mass of Intention", fully choral, *that the Church may change her mind.*'

And when the cannon that told of Noon was fired from the white fortress by the river far away she was still considering programmes of music by Rossini and Cimarosa, and the colour of the chasubles which the clergy should wear.

4

At the season when the oleanders are in their full perfection, their choicest bloom, it was the Pontiff's innovation to install his American type-writing apparatus in the long Loggie of the Apostolic Palace that had been in disuse since the demise of Innocent XVI. Out-of-doorish, as Neapolitans usually are, Pope Tertius II was no exception to the rule, preferring blue skies to golden ceilings – a taste for which indeed many were inclined to blame him. A compromise between the state-saloons and the modest suite occupied by his Holiness from choice, these open Loggie, adorned with the radiant frescoes of Luca Signorelli, would be frequently the scene of some particular Audience, granted after the exacting press of official routine.

Late one afternoon the Pontiff after an eventful and arduous day was walking thoughtfully here alone. Participating no longer in the joys of the world, it was, however, charming to catch, from time to time, the distant sound of Rome – the fitful clamour of trams and cabs, and the plash of the great twin-fountains in the court of St Damascus.

Wrapped in grave absorption, with level gaze, the lips slightly pinched, Pope Tertius II paced to and fro, occasionally raising a well-formed (though hairy) hand, as though to dismiss his thoughts with a benediction. The nomination of two Vacant Hats, the marriage annulment of an ex-hereditary Grand Duchess, and the 'scandals of Clemenza', were equally claiming his attention and ruffling his serenity.

He had the head of an elderly lady's-maid, and an expression concealed by layers of tactful caution.

'Why can't they all behave?' he asked himself plaintively, descrying Lucrezia, his prized white squirrel, sidling shyly towards him.

She was the gift of the Archbishop of Trebizond, who had found her in the region of the Coelian hill.

'Slyboots, slyboots,' Pope Tertius exclaimed, as she skipped from reach. It was incredible with what playful zest she would spring from statue to statue; and it would have amused the Vicar of Christ to watch her slip and slide, had it not suggested many a profound moral metaphor applicable to the Church. 'Gently, gently,' he enjoined; for once, in her struggles, she had robbed a fig-leaf off a 'Moses'.

'Yes, why can't they all behave?' he murmured, gazing up into the far pale-blueness.

He stood a brief moment transfixed, as if in prayer, oblivious of two whispering chamberlains.

It was the turn-in-waiting of Baron Oschatz, a man of engaging exquisite manners, and of Count Cuenca, an individual who seemed to be in perpetual consternation.

Depositing a few of the most recent camera portraits of the Pontiff requiring autograph in a spot where he could not fail but see them, they formally withdrew.

It had been a day distinguished by innumerable Audiences, several not uninteresting to recall. . . .

Certainly the increasing numbers of English were decidedly promising, and bore out the sibylline predictions of their late great and sagacious ruler – Queen Victoria.

'The dear *santissima* woman,' the Pontiff sighed, for he entertained a sincere, if brackish, enthusiasm for the lady who for so many years had corresponded with the Holy See under the signature of *the Countess of Lost-waters.*

'Anglicans . . . ? Heliolatries and sun-worshippers,' she had written in her most masterful hand, 'and your Holiness may believe us', she had added, 'when we say especially our beloved Scotch.'

'I shouldn't wonder enormously if it were true,' the Pope exclaimed, catching through a half-shut door a glimpse of violet stockings.

Such a display of old, out-at-heel hose could but belong to Cardinal Robin.

There had been a meeting of the Board for Extraordinary Ecclesiastical Affairs, and when, shortly afterwards, the

Cardinal was admitted he bore still about him some remote trace of faction.

He had the air of a cuttle-fish, and an inquiring voice. Inclined to gesture, how many miles must his hands have moved in the course of the sermons that he had preached!

Saluting the sovereign Pontiff with a deep obeisance, the Cardinal came directly to the point.

'These schisms in Spain . . . '

'They are ever before me,' His Holiness confessed.

'With priests like Pirelli, the Church is in peril!' the Cardinal declared, with a short, abysmal laugh.

'Does he suppose we are in the times of Baal and Moloch?' the Pope asked, pressing a harassed hand to his head. A Neapolitan of Naples (O Bay of Napoli. See Vesuvius, *and die*), he had curly hair that seemed to grow visibly; every few hours his tonsure would threaten to disappear.

The Cardinal sent up his brows a little.

'If I may tender the advice of the secret Consistory', he said, 'your Holiness should Listen-in.'

'To what end?'

'A snarl, a growl, a bark, a yelp, coming from the font, would be quite enough to condemn . . .'

'*Per Bacco.* I should take it for a baby.'

'. . . condemn', the Cardinal pursued, 'this Pirelli for a *maleficus pastor*. In which case, the earlier, the better, the unfrocking. . . .'

The Pontiff sighed.

The excellent Cardinal was as fatiguing as a mission from Salt Lake City.

'Evidently,' he murmured, detecting traces of rats among the papyrus plants in the long walk below.

'They come up from the Tiber!' he exclaimed, piloting the Cardinal dexterously towards a flight of footworn steps leading to the Court of Bramante.

'It's a bore there being no lift!' he commented (the remark was a Vatican cliché), dismissing the Cardinal with a benediction.

'A painful interview,' the Holy Father reflected, regarding

the Western sky. An evening rose and radiant altogether. . . .

Turning sadly, he perceived Count Cuenca.

A nephew of the Dean of the Sacred College, it was rumoured that he was addicted, in his 'home' above Frascati, to the last excesses of the pre-Adamite Sultans.

'A dozen blessings, for a dozen Hymens – but only eleven were sent,' he was babbling distractedly to himself. He had been unstrung all day, 'just a mass of foolish nerves', owing to a woman, an American, it seemed, coming for her Audience in a hat edged with white and yellow water-lilies. She had been repulsed successfully by the Papal Guard, but it had left an unpleasant impression.

'How's that?' the Vicar of Christ exclaimed: he enjoyed to tease his Chamberlains – especially Count Cuenca.

The Count turned pale.

' — ' he replied inaudibly, rolling eyes at Lucrezia.

Baron Oschatz had 'deserted' him; and what is one Chamberlain, alas, without another?

'The photographs of your Holiness are beside the bust of Bernini!' he stammered out, beating a diplomatic retreat.

Pope Tertius II addressed his squirrel.

'Little slyboots,' he said, 'I often laugh when I'm alone.'

5

BEFORE the white façade of the DunEden Palace, commanding the long, palm-shaded Paseo del Violôn, an array of carriages and limousines was waiting; while, passing in brisk
succession beneath the portico, like a swarm of brilliant
butterflies, each instant was bringing more. Dating from the
period of Don Pedro *el cruel*, the palace had been once the
residence of the famous Princesse des Ursins, who had left
behind something of her conviviality and glamour. But it is
unlikely that the soirées of the exuberant and fanciful Princesse
eclipsed those of the no less exuberant Duquesa DunEden.
It was to be an evening (flavoured with rich heroics) in honour
of the convalescence of several great ladies, from an attack of
'Boheara', the new and fashionable epidemic, diagnosed by
the medical faculty as 'hyperaesthesia with complications'; a
welcoming back to the world in fact of several despotic
dowagers, not one perhaps of whom, had she departed this
life, would have been really much missed or mourned! And
thus, in deference to the intimate nature of the occasion, it
was felt by the solicitous hostess that a Tertulia (that mutual
exchange of familiar or intellectual ideas) would make less
demand on arms and legs than would a ball: just the mind
and lips ... a skilful rounding-off here, developing there,
chiselling, and putting-out feelers; an evening dedicated to
the furtherance of intrigue, scandal, love, beneath the eager
eyes of a few young girls, still at school, to whom a quiet party
was permitted now and then.

Fingering a knotted scapular beneath a windy arch Mother
St-Mary-of-the-Angels was asking God His will. Should she
wait for Gloria and Clyte (they might be some time) or return
to the convent and come back again at twelve? 'The dear
girls are with their mother,' she informed her Maker, inclining
respectfully before the Princess Aurora of the Asturias, who had
just arrived attended by two bearded gentlemen with tummies.

Hopeful of glimpsing perhaps a colleague, Mother St-Mary moved a few steps impulsively in their wake. It was known that Monseigneur the Cardinal-Archbishop himself was expected, and not infrequently one ecclesiastic will beget another.

The crimson saloon, with its scattered group of chairs, was waxing cheery.

Being the day it was, and the social round never but slightly varying, most of the guests had flocked earlier in the evening to the self-same place, i.e. the Circus, or *Arena Amanda*, where it was subscription night, and where, at present, there was an irresistibly comic clown.

'One has only to think of him to –!' the wife of the Minister of Public Instruction exclaimed, going off into a fit of wheezy laughter.

'What power, what genius, what – !' The young wife of the Inspector of Rivers and Forests was at a loss. Wedded to one of the handsomest though dullest of men, Marvilla de Las Espinafre's perfervid and exalted nature kept her little circle in constant awe, and she would be often jealous of the Forests (chiefly scrub) which her husband, in his official capacity, was called upon to survey. 'Don't lie to me. I know it! You've been to the woods.' And after his inspection of the aromatic groves of Lograno, Phaedra in full fury tearing her pillow with her teeth was nothing to Marvilla. 'Why, dear? Because you've been *among the Myrtles*,' was the explanation she chose to give for severing conjugal relations.

'Vittorio forbids the circus on account of germs,' the wife of the President of the National Society of Public Morals murmured momentously.

'Really, with this ghastly Boheara, I shall not be grieved when the time comes to set out for dear Santander!' a woman with dog-rose cheeks, and puffed, wrinkled eyes, exclaimed, focusing languishingly the Cardinal.

'He is delicious in handsomeness tonight!'

'A shade battered. But a lover's none the worse in my opinion for acquiring technique,' the Duchess of Sarmento declared.

'A lover; what? His Eminence . . . ? ?'

The duchess tittered.

'Why not? I expect he has a little woman to whom he takes off his clothes,' she murmured, turning to admire the wondrous Madonna of the Mule-mill attributed to Murillo.

On a wall-sofa just beneath, crowned with flowers and aigrettes, sat Conca, Marchioness of Macarnudo.

'*Qué tal?*'

'My *joi de vivre* is finished; still, it's amazing how I go on!' the Marchioness answered, making a corner for the duchess. She had known her 'dearest Luiza' since the summer the sun melted church bells and their rakish, pleasure-loving, affectionate hearts had dissolved together. But this had not been yesterday; no; for the Marchioness was a *grandmother* now.

'Conca, Conca: one sees you're in love.'

'He's from *Avila*, dear – the footman.'

'What!'

'Nothing *classic* – but, *oh*!'

'Fresh and blonde? I've seen him.'

'Such sep . . .'

'Santiago be praised!'

The Marchioness of Macarnudo plied her fan.

'Our hands first met at table . . . yes, dear; but what I always say is, one spark explodes the mine!' And with a sigh she glanced rhapsodically at her fingers, powdered and manicured and encrusted with rings. 'Our hands met first at table,' she repeated.

'And . . . and the rest?' the duchess gasped.

'I sometimes wish, though, I resembled my sister more, who cares only for amorous, "delicate" men – the Claudes, so to speak. But there it is! And, anyway, dear,' the Marchioness dropped her voice, 'he keeps me from thinking (ah perhaps more than I should) of my little grandson. Imagine, Luiza . . . Fifteen, white, and vivid rose, and ink-black hair. . . .' And the Marchioness cast a long, pencilled eye towards the world-famous Pietà above her head. 'Queen of Heaven, defend a weak woman from *that*!' she besought.

Surprised, and considerably edified, by the sight of the dowager in prayer, Mother St-Mary-of-the-Angels was emboldened to advance: The lovely, self-willed donkey (or was it a mule?) that Our Lady was prodding, one could almost stroke it, hear it bray. . . .

Mother St-Mary-of-the-Angels could have almost laughed. But the recollection of the presence of royalty steadied her.

Behind pink lowered portières it had retired, escorted by the mistress of the house. She wore a gown of ivory-black with heavy golden roses and a few of her large diamonds of ceremony.

'I love your Englishy-Moorishy cosy comfort, Decima, and I love – ' the Princess Aurora had started to rave.

'An hyperaesthesia injection? . . . a beaten egg?' her hostess solicitously asked.

'*Per caritad!*' the Princess fluted, stooping to examine a voluptuous small *terre cuite*, depicting a pair of hermaphrodites amusing themselves.

She was looking like the ghost in the Ballet of Ghislaine, after an unusually sharp touch of Boheara; eight-and-forty hours in bed, and, scandal declared, not alone.

'A Cognac? . . . a crême de Chile? . . .'

'Nothing, nothing,' the Princess negligently answered, sweeping her long, primrose trailing skirts across the floor.

It was the boudoir of the Winterhalters and Isabeys, once the bright glory of the Radziwollowna collection, which, after several decades of disesteem, were returning to fashion and favour.

'And I love – ' she broke off, nearly stumbling over an old blind spaniel, that resided in a basket behind the 'supposed original' of the Lesbia of Lysippus.

'Clapsey, Clapsey!' her mistress admonished. The gift of a dear and once intimate friend, the dog seemed inclined to outlive itself and become a nuisance.

Alas, poor, fawning Clapsey! Fond, toothless bitch. Return to your broken doze, and dream again of leafy days in leaf Parks, and comfy drives and escapades long ago. What sights you saw when you could see; fountains, and kneeling kings, and grim beggars at Church doors (those at San Eusebio were the worst). And sheltered spas by glittering seas: Santander! And dark adulteries and dim woods at night.

'And I love your Winterhalters!'

Beneath one of these, like a red geranium, was Cardinal Pirelli.

'Oh, your Eminence, the utter forlornness of Society! ... Besides, (oh, my God!) to be the *one* Intellectual of a Town ...' a wizened little woman, mistaken, not infrequently, for 'Bob Foy', the jockey, was exclaiming plaintively.

'I suppose?' Monseigneur nodded. He was looking rather Richelieu, draped in ermines and some old lace of a beautiful fineness.

'It's pathetic how entertaining is done now. Each year meaner. There was a time when the DunEdens gave balls, and one could count, as a rule, on supper. Tonight, there's nothing but a miserable Buffet, with flies trimming themselves on the food; and the champagne that I tasted, well, I can assure your Eminence it was more like foul flower-water than Mumm.'

'Disgraceful,' the Cardinal murmured, surrendering with suave dignity his hand to the lips of a pale youth all mouchoir and waist.

These kisses of young men, ravished from greedy Royalty, had a delicate savour.

The One Intellectual smiled obliquely.

'Your Eminence I notice has several devout salve-stains already,' she murmured, defending her face with her fan.

'Believe me, not all these imprints were left by men!'

The One Intellectual glanced away.

'The Poor Princess! I ask you, has one the right to look *so* dying?'

'Probably not,' the Cardinal answered, following her ethereal transit.

It was the turn of the tide, and soon admittance to the boudoir had ceased causing 'heartburnings'.

Nevertheless some few late sirens were only arriving.

Conspicuous among these was Catherine (the ideal-questing, God-groping, and insouciant), Countess of Constantine, the aristocratic heroine of the capital, looking half-charmed to be naked and alive. Possessing but indifferent powers of conversation – at Tertulias and dinners she seldom shone – it was yet she who had coined that felicitous phrase: *Some men's eyes are sweet to rest in.*

Limping a little, since she had sprained her foot, alas, while turning backward somersaults to a negro band in the black ballroom of the Infanta Eulalia-Irene, her reappearance after the misadventure was a triumph.

'Poor Kitty: it's a shame to ask her, if it's not a ball!' the Inspector of Rivers and Forests exclaimed, fondling the silvery branches of his moustache.

But, at least, a Muse, if not musicians, was at hand.

Clasping a large bouquet of American Beauty-roses, the Poetess Diana Beira Baixa was being besieged by admirers, to 'give them something; just something! *Anything* of her own.' Wedded, and proclaiming (in *vers libres*) her lawful love, it was whispered she had written a paean to her husband's '. . .' beginning *Thou glorious wonder!* which was altogether too conjugal and intimate for recitation in society.

'They say I utter the cry of sex throughout the Ages,' she murmured, resting her free hand idly on the table of gold and lilac lacquer beside her.

The Duchess-Dowager of Vizeu spread prudishly her fan.

'Since me maid set me muskito net afire, I'm just a bunch, me dear, of hysterics,' she declared.

But requests for 'something; just something!' were becoming insistent, and indeed the Muse seemed about to comply when, overtaken by the first alarming symptoms of 'Boheara', she fell with a long-drawn sigh to the floor.

6

REPAIRING the vast armholes of a chasuble, Madame Poco, the venerable Superintendent-of-the-palace, considered, as she worked, the social status of a Spy. It was not without a fleeting qualm that she had crossed the borderland that divides mere curiosity from professional vigilance, but having succumbed to the profitable proposals of certain monsignori, she had grown as keen on her quarry as a tigress on the track.

'It's a wearing life you're leading me, Don Alvaro; but I'll have you,' she murmured, singling out a thread.

For indeed the Higher-curiosity is inexorably exacting, encroaching, all too often, on the hours of slumber and rest.

'It's not the door-listening', she decided, 'so much as the garden, and, when he goes awenching, the Calle Nabuchodonosor.'

She was seated by an open window, commanding the patio and the gate.

'*Vamos, vamos!*' Madame Poco sighed, her thoughts straying to the pontifical supremacy of Tertius II, for already she was the Pope's Poco, his devoted Phoebe, his own true girl: 'I'm true blue, dear. True blue.'

Forgetful of her needle, she peered interestedly on her image in a mirror on the neighbouring wall. It was a sensation of pleasant novelty to feel between her skull and her mantilla the notes of the first instalment of her bribe.

'Earned, every *perra gorda*, earned!' she exclaimed, rising and pirouetting in elation before the glass.

Since becoming the courted favourite of the chapter, she had taken to strutting-and-languishing in private before her mirror, improvising occult dance-steps, semi-sacred in character, modelled on those of Felix Ganay at White Easter, all in the flowery Spring. Ceremonial poses such as may be observed in storied-windows and olden *pietàs* in churches

(Dalilaesque, or Shulamitish, as the case might be) were her especial delight, and from these had been evolved an eerie 'Dance of Indictment'.

Finger rigid, she would advance ominously with slow, Salomé-like liftings of the knees upon a phantom Cardinal: 'And thus I accuse thee!' or 'I denounce thee, Don Alvaro, for,' etc.

'*Dalila!* You old sly gooseberry,' she chuckled, gloating on herself in the greenish-spotted depth of a tall, time-corroded glass.

Punch and late hours had left their mark.

'All this Porto and stuff to keep awake make a woman liverish,' she commented, examining critically her tongue.

It was a Sunday evening of *corrida*, towards the Feast of Corpus, and through the wide-open window came the near sound of bells.

Madame Poco crossed and recrossed her breast.

They were ringing 'Paula', a bell which, tradition said, had fused into its metal one of the thirty pieces of silver received by the Iscariot for the betrayal of Christ.

'They seem to have asked small fees in those days,' she reflected, continuing her work.

It was her resolution to divide her reward between masses for herself and the repose and 'release' (from Purgatory) of her husband's soul, while anything over should be laid out on finery for a favourite niece, the little Leonora, away in the far Americas.

Madame Poco plied pensively her needle.

She was growing increasingly conscious of the physical demands made by the Higher-curiosity upon a constitution already considerably far-through, and the need of an auxiliary caused her to regret her niece. More than once, indeed, she had been near the point of asking Charlotte Chiemsee, the maid of the Duchess of Vizeu to assist her. It was Charlotte who had set the duchess's bed-veils on fire while attempting to nip a romance.

But alone and unaided it was astonishing the evidence

Madame Poco had gained, and she smiled, as she sewed, at the recollection of her latest capture – the handkerchief of Luna Sainz.

'These hennaed heifers that come to confess! ...' she scoffed sceptically. For Madame Poco had some experience of men – those brown humbugs (so delicious in tenderness) – in her time. 'Poor soul! He had the prettiest teeth ...' she murmured, visualizing forlornly her husband's face. He had been coachman for many years to the sainted Countess of Triana, and he would tell the story of the pious countess and the vermin she had turned to flowers of flame while foraging one day among some sacks before a second-hand-clothes shop. It was she, too, who, on another occasion, had changed a handful of marsh-slush into fine slabs of chocolate, each slab engraved with the insignia of a Countess and the sign of the Cross.

'Still, she didn't change *him*, though!' Madame Poco reflected dryly, lifting the lid to her work-box.

Concealed among its contents was a copy of the gay and curious *Memoirs of Mlle Emma Crunch*, so famous as 'Cora Pearl'; – a confiscated bedside-book once belonging to the Cardinal-Archbishop.

'Ps, ps!' she purred, feeling amorously for her scissors beneath the sumptuous oddments of old church velvet and brocade that she loved to ruffle and ruck.

'Ps.'

She had been freshening a little the chasuble worn last by his Eminence at the baptism of the blue-eyed police-pup of the Duquesa DunEden, which bore still the primrose trace of an innocent insult.

'A disgraceful business altogether,' Madame Poco sighed.

Not everyone knew the dog was christened in *white menthe*. ...

'Sticky stuff,' she brooded: 'and a liqueur I never cared for! It takes a lot to beat aniseed brandy; when it's old. Manzanilla runs it close; but it's odd how a glass or two turns me muzzy.'

She remained a moment lost in idle reverie before the

brilliant embroideries in her basket. Bits of choice beflowered brocade, multi-tinted, inimitably faded silks of the epoca of Theresa de Ahumada, exquisite tatters, telling of the Basilica's noble past, it gladdened the eyes to gaze on. What garden of Granada could show a pink to match that rose, or what sky show a blue as tenderly serene as that azure of the St Virgin?

'*Vamos,*' she exclaimed, rising: 'it's time I took a toddle to know what he's about.'

She had last seen the Cardinal coming from the orange orchard with a dancing-boy and Father Fadrique, who had a mark on his cheek left by a woman's fan.

Her mind still dwelling on men (those divine humbugs), Madame Poco stepped outside.

Traversing a white-walled corridor, with the chasuble on her arm, her silhouette, illumined by the splendour of the evening sun, all but caused her to start.

It was in a wing built in the troublous reign of Alfonso the Androgyne that the vestments were kept. Whisking by a decayed and ancient painting, representing 'Beelzebub' at Home, she passed slowly through a little closet supposed to be frequented by the ghosts of evil persons long since dead. Just off it was the vestry, gay with blue azulejos tiles of an admirable lustre.

They were sounding Matteo now, a little bell with a passionate voice.

'The pet!' Madame Poco paused to listen. She had her 'favourites' among the bells, and Matteo was one of them. Passiaflora, too – but Anna, a light slithery bell, 'like a housemaid in hysterics', offended her ear by lack of tone; Sebastian, a complaining, excitable bell, was scarcely better – 'a fretful lover!' She preferred old 'Wanda' the Death-bell, a trifle monotonous, and fanatical perhaps, but 'interesting', and opening up vistas to varied thought and speculation.

Lifting a rosary from a linen-chest, Madame Poco laid the chasuble within. It was towards this season she would usually renew the bags of bergamot among the Primate's robes.

'This espionage sets a woman all behindhand,' she commented to Tobit, the vestry cat.

Black as the Evil One, perched upon a Confessional's ledge, cleansing its belly, the sleek thing sat.

It was the 'ledge of forgotten fans', where privileged Penitents would bring their tales of vanity, infidelity, and uncharitableness to the Cardinal once a week.

'Directing half a dozen duchesses must be frequently a strain!' Madame Poco deliberated, picking up a discarded mitre and trying it absently on.

With a plume at the side or a cluster of balls, it would make quite a striking toque, she decided, casting a fluttered glance on the male effigy of a pale-faced member of the Quesada family, hewn in marble by the door.

'*Caramba!* I thought it was the Cardinal; it gave me quite a turn,' she murmured, pursuing lightly her way.

Being a Sunday evening of corrida, it was probable the Cardinal had mounted to his aerie, to enjoy the glimpse of Beauty returning from the fight.

Oh, mandolines of the South, warm throats, and winged songs, winging . . .

Following a darkened corridor with lofty windows closely barred, Madame Poco gained an ambulatory, terminated by a fresco of Our Lady, ascending to heaven in a fury of paint.

'These damp flags'll be the death of me,' she complained, talking with herself, turning towards the garden.

Already the blue pushing shadows were beguiling from the shelter of the cloister eaves the rueful owls. A few flittermice, too, were revolving around the long apricot chimneys of the Palace, that, towards sunset, looked like the enchanted castle of some sleeping Princess.

'Bits of pests,' she crooned, taking a neglected alley of old bay-tree laurels, presided over by a plashing fountain comprised of a Cupid sneezing. Wary of mole-hills and treacherous roots, she roamed along, preceded by the floating whiteness of a Persian peacock, mistrustful of the intentions of a Goat-sucker owl. Rounding a sequestered garden seat beneath an aged cypress, the bark all scented knots, Madame Poco halted.

Kneeling before an altar raised to the cult of Our Lady of Dew, Cardinal Pirelli was plunged in prayer.

'*Salve. Salve Regina.* ...' Above the tree-tops a bird was singing.

7

THE College of Noble Damosels in the Calle Santa Fé was in a whirl. It was 'Foundation' day, an event annually celebrated with considerable fanfaronade and social éclat. Founded during the internecine wars of the Middle Age, the College, according to early records, had suffered rapine on the first day of term. Hardly, it seemed, had the last scholar's box been carried upstairs than a troop of military had made its appearance at the Pension gate demanding, with 'male peremptoriness', a billet. 'I alone,' the Abbess ingeniously states, in relating the poignant affair in her unpublished diary: 'I alone did all I was able to keep them from them, for which they (the scholars) called me "greedy".' Adding, not without a touch of modern socialism in disdain for titles, that she had prefered 'the staff-officers to the Field-Marshal,' while as to ensigns, in her estimation, why, 'one was worth the lot.'

Polishing urbanely her delicate nails, the actual President, a staid, pale woman with a peacock nose, recalled the chequered past. She hoped his Eminence when he addressed the girls, on handing them their prizes, would refer to the occasion with all the tactfulness required.

'When I think of the horrid jokes the old Marqués of Illescas made last year,' she murmured, bestowing a harrowed smile on a passing pupil.

She was ensconced in a ponderous fauteuil of figured velvet (intended for the plump posterior of Royalty) beneath the incomparable '*azulejos*' ceiling of the Concert-room, awaiting the return of Madame Always Alemtejo, the English governess, from the printers, in the Plaza de Jesus, with the little silver-printed programmes (so like the paste-board cards of brides!), which, as usual, were late.

'Another year we'll type them,' she determined, awed by the ardent tones of a young girl rehearsing an aria from the new opera, *Leda* – 'Gaze not on Swans.'

'Ah, gaze not so on Swan-zzz! . . .'

'Crisper, child. Distinction. Don't exaggerate,' the President enjoined, raising a hand to the diamonds on her heavy, lead-white cheeks.

Née an Arroyolo, and allied by marriage with the noble house of Salvaterra, the headmistress in private life was the Dowager-Marchioness of Pennisflores.

'*Nosotros,* you know, are not candidates for the stage! Bear in mind your moral,' she begged, with a lingering glance at her robe of grey georgette.

The word 'moral', never long from the President's lips, seemed, with her, to take on an intimate tinge, a sensitiveness of its own. She would invest the word at times with an organic significance, a mysterious dignity, that resembled an avowal made usually only in solemn confidence to a doctor or a priest.

The severity of my moral. The prestige of my moral. The perfection of my moral. She has no dignity of moral. I fear a person of no positive moral. Nothing to injure the freshness of her moral. A difficulty of moral. The etiquette of my moral. The majesty of my moral, etc., etc. – as uttered by the President, became, psychologically, interesting *dicta*.

'Beware of a facile moral!' she added, for the benefit of the singer's accompanist, a young nun with a face like some strange white rock, who was inclined to give herself married airs, since she had been debauched, one otiose noon, by a demon.

'Ah, Madame Always.' The President swam to meet her.

British born, hailing from fairy Lisbon, Madame Always Alemtejo seemed resigned to live and die in a land of hitches.

'The delay is owing to the Printers' strike,' she announced. 'The Plaza's thronged: the Cigar factory girls, and all the rag-tag and bobtail, from the Alcazaba to the Puerta del Mar, are going out in sympathy, and – '

'The tarts?'

'The t's from Chamont are on the way.'

It was the President's custom to lay all vexations before

Nostra Señora de los Remedios, the college's divine Protectress, with whose gracious image she was on the closest footing.

Consulting her now as to the concert-programmes, the President recalled that no remedy yet had been found for Señorita Violeta de las Cubas, who had thrown her engagement ring into a place of less dignity than convenience and refused to draw it out.

'Sapphires, my favourite stones,' the President reflected, wondering if she should ask 'la Inglese' to recover it with the asparagus-tongs.

But already a few *novios*, eager to behold their *novias* again, were in the Patio beneath the 'Heiresses' Wing', exciting the connoisseurship of a bevy of early freshness.

'You can tell *that* by his eyebrows!' a girl of thirteen, and just beginning as a woman, remarked.

'*Que barbaridad.*'

'Last summer at Santander Maria-Manuela and I bathed with him, and one morning there was a tremendous sea, with *terrific* waves, and we noticed unmistakably.'

'I can't explain; but I adore all that mauvishness about him!'

'I prefer Manolito to Gonzalito, though neither thrill me like the Toreador Tancos.'

Assisted by Fräulein Pappenheim and Muley, the President's negress maid, they were putting the final touches to their vestal frocks.

'Men are my raging disgust,' a florid girl of stupendous beauty declared, saturating with a flacon of *Parfum cruel* her prematurely formed silhouette.

'Nsa, nsa, señorita,' Muley mumbled. 'Some know better dan dat!'

'To hell with them!'

'*Adios*, Carlo. *Adios*, Juan. Join you down dah in one minute.' The negress chuckled jauntily.

'Muley, Muley,' Fräulein chided.

'What wonder next I 'bout to hear?'

Delighting in the tender ferocities of Aphrodite, she was

ever ready to unite the *novio* to the *novia*. For window-vigils (where all is hand play) few could contrive more ingeniously than she those fans of fresh decapitated flowers, tuberose punctuated with inebriating jasmine, so beloved in the East by the dark children of the sun. Beyond Cadiz the blue, the beautiful, in palm-girt Marrakesh, across the sea, she had learnt other arts besides. . . .

'Since seeing Peter Prettylips on the screen the Spanish type means nothing to me.' Señorita Soledad, a daughter of the first Marqués of Belluga, the greatest orange-king in the Peninsula, remarked.

'How low. She is not noble.'

'I *am* noble.'

'Oh no; you're not.'

'Cease wrangling,' Fräulein exclaimed, 'and enough of that,' she added sharply, addressing a *novio*-less little girl looking altogether bewitching of naughtiness as she tried her ablest to seduce by her crude manoeuvres the fiancé of a friend. Endowed with the lively temperament of her grandmother, Conca, Marchioness of Macarnudo, the impressionable, highly amative nature of the little Obdulia gave her governesses some grounds for alarm. At the Post Office one day she had watched a young man lick a stamp. His rosy tongue had vanquished her. In fact, at present, she and a class-chum, Milagros, were 'collecting petals' together – and much to the bewilderment of those about them, they might be heard on occasion to exclaim, at Mass, or in the street: 'Quick, did you see it?' 'No.' 'Santissima! *I* did!'

'Shrimp. As if Gerardo would look at her!' his *novia* scoffed. 'But let me tell you, young woman,' she turned upon the shrinking Obdulia, 'that social ostracism, and even, in certain cases', (she slapped and pinched her), '*assassination* attends those that thieve or tamper with another's lover! And Fräulein will correct me if I exaggerate.'

Fräulein Pappenheim was a little woman already drifting towards the sad far shores of forty, with no experience of the pains of Aphrodite caused by men; only at times she would complain of stomach aches in the head.

'Dat is so,' Muley struck in sententiously for her. 'Dair was once a young lady ob Fez – '

But from the Patio the college chaplain, Father Damien Forment, known as 'Shiny-nose', was beckoning to the heiresses to join their relatives in the reception-hall below.

Since that sanguinary period of Christianity, synchronizing with the foundation of the institution of learning in the Calle Santa Fé, what changes in skirts and trousers the world has seen. Alone unchanging are women's ambitions and men's desires.

'Dear child. . . . She accepts him . . . but a little *à contre-cœur*,' the President was saying to the Marchioness of las Cubas, an impoverished society belle, who often went without bread in order to buy lip-sticks and rouge.

'With Violeta off my hands . . . Ah, President, if only Cecilio could be suitably *casada*.'

'In my little garden I sometimes work a brother. The heiresses' windows are all opening to the flowers and trees. . . . The boy should be in polo kit. A uniform interests girls,' the President murmured, turning with an urbane smile to welcome the Duquesa DunEden.

She had a frock of black kasha, signed Paul Orna, with a cluster of brown-and-pink orchids, like sheep's-kidneys, and a huge feather hat.

'I'm here for my God-girl, Gloria,' she murmured, glancing mildly round.

Incongruous that this robust, rich woman should have brought to the light of heaven no heir, while the unfortunate Marchioness, needy, and frail of physique, a wraith, did not know what to do with them!

The President dropped a sigh.

She was prepared to take a dog of the daughterless Duquesa. A bitch, of course. . . . But let it be Police, or Poodle! It would lodge with the girls. A cubicle to itself in the heiresses' wing; and since there would be no extra class-charge for dancing or drawing, no course *in belli arti*, some reduction of fees might be arranged. . . . 'We would turn her out a creature of breeding. . . . An eloquent tail-wave, a disciplined moral,

and with a reverence moreover for house-mats and carpets.'
The President decided to draw up the particulars of the pro-
spectus by and by.

'Your Goddaughter is quite one of our most promising
exhibitioners,' she exclaimed, indicating with her fan some
water-colour studies exposed upon the walls.

'She comes of a mother with a mania for painting,' the
Duquesa declared, raising a lorgnon, critically, before the
portrait of a Lesbian, with dying, fabulous eyes.

'Really?'

'A positive passion,' the Duquesa answered, with a swift,
discerning glance at an evasive 'nude', showing the posterior
poudrederizé of a Saint.

'I had no idea,' the President purred, drawing attention to
a silvery streetscape.

'It's the Rambla from the back of Our Lady of the Pillar!
It was rare fun doing it, on account of the *pirropos* of the
passers-by,' the artist, joining them, explained.

'Dear child, I predict for her a great deal of admiration
very soon,' the President murmured, with a look of reproach
at a youthful pupil as she plied her boy-Father with embar-
rassing questions: 'Who are the chief society women in the
moon? What are their names? Have they got motor-cars
there? Is there an Opera-House? Are there bulls?'

The leering aspect of a lady in a costume of blonde Guadalmedina lace and a hat wreathed with clipped black cocks'
feathers arrested her.

Illusion-proof, with long and undismayed service in Love's
House (sorry brutes, all the same, though, these men, with
their selfishness, fickleness, and lies!) the Marchioness of
Macarnudo with her mysterious 'legend' (unscrupulous
minxes, all the same, though, these women, with their pet-
tiness, vanity and ...!), was too temperamentally intriguing
a type to be ignored.

'Isn't that little Marie Dorothy with the rosebuds stuck all
over her?' she asked her granddaughter, who was teasing her
brother on his moustache.

'To improve the growth, the massage of a *novia*'s hand,'

she fluted, provoking the marchioness to an involuntary nervous gesture. Exasperated by resistance, struggling against an impossible infatuation, her Spanish ladyship was becoming increasingly subject to passing starts. Indeed only in excitement and dissipation could her unsatisfied longings find relief. Sometimes she would run out in her car to where the men bathe at Ponte Delgado, and one morning, after a ball, she had been seen standing on the main road to Cadiz in a cabuchon tiara, watching the antics of some nude muleteers: *Black as young Indians* – she had described them later.

'My sweet butterfly! What next?' she exclaimed, ogling Obdulia, whose elusive resemblance to her brother was really curiously disturbing.

Averting a filmy eye, she recognized Marvilla de las Espinafres, airing anti-patriotic views on birth control, her arms about an adopted daughter. 'Certainly not; most decidedly *no*! I should scream!' she was saying as from the Concert-room the overture began thinning the crowd.

'It's nothing else than a national disaster', the marchioness declared to her grandson, 'how many women nowadays seem to shirk their duty!'

'Well, the de las Cubas hasn't, anyway,' he demurred.

'Poor thing. They say she jobs her mules,' the marchioness murmured, exchanging a nod with the passing President.

Something, manifestly, had occurred to disturb the equilibrium of her moral.

'Such a disappointment, Nostra Señora!' she exclaimed. 'Monseigneur, it seems, has thrown me over.'

'Indeed; how awkward!'

'I fear though even more so for his chapter.'

'He is not ill?'

'*Cardinal Pirelli has fled the capital!*'

8

STANDING amid gardens made for suffering and delight is the disestablished and, *sic transit*, slowly decaying monastery of the Desierto. Lovely as Paradise, oppressive perhaps as Eden, it had been since the days of the mystic Luigi of Granada a site well suited to meditation and retreat. Here, in the stilly cypress-court, beneath the snowy sierras of Santa Maria la Blanca, Theresa of Avila, worn and ill, though sublime in laughter, exquisite in beatitude, had composed a part of the *Way of Perfection*, and, here, in these same realms of peace, dominating the distant city of Clemenza and the fertile plains of Andalucia, Cardinal Pirelli, one blue midday towards the close of summer, was idly considering his Defence. '*Apologia*, no; merely a defence,' he mused: 'merely', he flicked the ash-tip of a cigar, 'a defence! I defend myself, that's all! . . .'

A sigh escaped him.

Divided by tranquil vineyards and orange-gardens from the malice and vindictiveness of men it was difficult to experience emotions other than of forgiveness and love.

'Come, dears, and kiss me,' he murmured, closing consentingly his eyes.

It was the forgetful hour of noon, when Hesperus from his heavens confers on his pet Peninsula the boon of sleep.

'A nice nap he's having, poor old gentleman.' Madame Poco surveyed her master.

Ill at ease and lonely in the austere dismantled house, she would keep an eye on him at present almost as much for company as for gain.

As handsome and as elegant as ever, his physiognomy in repose revealed a thousand strange fine lines, suggestive subtleties, intermingled with less ambiguous signs, denoting stress and care.

'He's growing almost huntedish,' she observed, casting a

brief glance at the literature beside him – *The Trial of Don Fernando de la Cerde*, Bishop of Barcelona, defrocked for putting young men to improper uses; a treatise on *The Value of Smiles*; an old volume of *Songs*, by Sà de Miranda; *The Lives of Five Negro Saints*, from which escaped a bookmark of a dancer in a manton.

'Everything but his Breviary,' she commented, perceiving a soutané form through the old flowered ironwork of the courtyard gateway.

Regretting her better gown of hooped watered-silk, set aside while in retreat (for economy's sake), Madame Poco fled to put it on, leaving the visitor to announce himself.

The padre of Our Lady of the Valley, the poor padre of Our Lady, would the Primate know? Oh, every bird, every rose could have told him that: the padre of Our Lady bringing a blue trout for his Eminence's supper from the limpid waters of Lake Orense.

Respecting the Primate's rest Father Felicitas, for so, also, was he named, sat down discreetly to await his awakening.

It was a rare sweetness to have the Cardinal to himself thus intimately. Mostly, in the city, he would be closely surrounded. Not that Father Felicitas went very much to town; no; he disliked the confusion of the streets, and even the glories of the blessed basilicas made him scarcely amends for the quiet shelter of his hills.

The blessed basilicas, you could see them well from here. The giralda of St Xarifa, and the august twin towers of the cathedral, and the azulejos dome of St Eusebio, that was once a pagan mosque; while of Santissima Marias, Maria del Carmen, Maria del Rosario, Maria de la Soledad, Maria del Dolores, Maria de las Nieves, few cities in all the wide world could show as many.

'To be sure, to be sure,' he exclaimed absently, lifting his eyes to a cloudlet leisurely pointing above the lofty spur of the Pico del Mediodia. 'To be sure,' he added, seeking to descry the flower-like bellcot of Our Lady of the Valley just beneath.

But before he had discovered it, half concealed by trees, he was reminded by the sound of a long-drawn, love-sick wail, issuing out of the very entrails of the singer, of the lad left in charge of his rod by the gate.

'On the Bridge to Alcantara.'

With its protracted cadences and doleful, vain-yearning reaches, the voice, submerged in all the anguish of a *malagueña*, troubled, nostalgically, the stillness.

God's will be done. It was enough to awaken the Primate. Not everyone relished a *malagueña*, a dirgeful form of melody introduced, tradition said, and made popular in the land, long, long ago, beneath the occupation of the Moors.

Father Felicitas could almost feel the sin of envy as he thought of the flawless choir and noble triumphal organ of the cathedral yonder.

Possessed of no other instrument, Our Lady of the Valley depended at present on a humble guitar. Not that the blessed guitar, with its capacity for emotion, is unworthy to please God's listening ear, but Pepe, the lad appointed to play it, would fall all too easily into those Jotas, Tangos, and Cuban Habaneiras, learnt in wayside *fondas* and fairs. Some day, Father Felicitas did not doubt, Our Lady would have an organ, an organ with pipes. He had prayed for it so often; oh, so often; and once, quite in the late of twilight while coming through the church, he had seen her, it seemed, standing just where it should be. It had been as though a blinding whiteness.

'A blinding whiteness,' he murmured, trembling a little at the recollection of the radiant vision.

Across the tranquil court a rose-red butterfly pursued a blue. 'I believe the world is all love, only no one understands,' he meditated, contemplating the resplendent harvest plains steeped in the warm sweet sunlight.

'My infinite contrition!' The Cardinal spoke.

A rare occurrence in these days was a visitor, and now with authority ebbing, or in the balance at least, it was singular how he felt a new interest in the concerns of the diocese. The birth-rate and the death-rate and the super-rate, which it was to be feared that the Cortès –

Sailing down the courtyard in her watered-silken gown, Madame Poco approached with Xeres and Manzanilla, fresh from the shuttered snowery or nieveria.

'And I've just buried a bottle of champagne, in case your Eminence should want it,' she announced as she inviolably withdrew.

'As devoted a soul as ever there was, and loyal to all my interests,' the Primate exclaimed, touched.

'God be praised!'

'An excellent creature,' the Cardinal added, focusing on the grey high road beyond the gate two youths on ass back, seated close.

'Andalucians, though of another parish.'

'I should like much to visit my diocese again; it's some while since I did,' the Cardinal observed, filling the Padre's glass.

'You'd find up at Sodré a good many changes.'

'Have they still the same little maid at the Posada de la Melodia?'

'Carmencita?'

'A dainty thing.'

'She went Therewards about the month of Mary.'

'America? It's where they all go.'

'She made a ravishing corpse.'

'Ahi.'

And Doña Beatriz too had died; either in March or May. It was she who would bake the old Greek Sun-bread, and although her heirs had sought high and low no one could find the receipt.

The Cardinal expressed satisfaction.

'*Bestemmia*,' he breathed; 'and I trust they never may; for on the Feast of the Circumcision she invariably caused to be laid before the high-altar of the cathedral a peculiarly shaped loaf to the confusion of all who saw it.'

And the Alcalde of Ayamonte, Don Deniz, had died on

the eve of the bachelor's party he usually gave when he took off his winter beard.

'Ahi; this death . . .'

Ah, yes, and since the delicacies ordered by the corpse could not well be countermanded they had been divided among Christ's poor.

Left to himself once more Cardinal Pirelli returned reluctantly to his Defence.

Half the diocese it seemed had gone 'Therewards,' while the rest were at Biarritz or Santander. . . .

'A nice cheery time this is!' he murmured, oppressed by the silent cypress-court. Among the blue, pointing shadows, a few frail oleanders in their blood-rose ruby invoked warm brief life and earth's desires.

'A nice cheery time,' he repeated, rising and going within.

The forsaken splendour of the vast closed cloisters seemed almost to augur the waning of a cult. Likewise the decline of Apollo, Diana, Isis, with the gradual downfall of their Temples, had been heralded, in past times, by the dispersal of their priests. It looked as though Mother Church, like Venus or Diana, was making way in due turn for the beliefs that should follow: 'and we shall begin again with intolerance, martyrdom, and converts,' the Cardinal ruminated, pausing before an ancient fresco depicting the Eleven Thousand Virgins, or as many as there was room for.

Playing a lonely ball game against them was the disrespectful Chicklet.

'Young vandal,' the Cardinal chided, caressing the little acolyte's lustrous locks.

'Monseigneur? . . .'

'There: run along; and say a fragrant prayer for me, Child.'

Flinging back a shutter drawn fast against the sun, the boundless prospect from the balcony of his cell recalled the royal Escorial. The white scattered terraces of villas set in dark deeps of trees, tall palms, and parasol-pines so shady, and, almost indistinguishable, the white outline of the sea, made insensibly for company.

Changing into a creation of dull scarlet *crêpe*, a cobweb

dubbed 'summer-exile', Cardinal Pirelli felt decidedly less oppressed. 'Madrid is on the Manzanares,' he vociferated, catching sight of the diligence from Sodré. Frequently it would bring Frasquito, the postman – a big tawny boy, overgiven to passing the day in the woods with his gun and his guitar.

'The mail bag is most irregular,' he complained, fastening a few dark red, almost black, roses to his cincture. It was Cardinal Pirelli's fancy while in retreat to assume his triple-Abraham, or mitre, and with staff in hand to roam abroad as in the militant Springtide of the Church.

'When kings were cardinals,' he murmured quietly as he left the room.

It was around the Moorish water-garden towards shut of day he liked most to wander, seeking like some Adept to interpret in the still deep pools the mirrored music of the sky.

All, was it vanity? These pointing stars and spectral leaning towers, this mitre, this jewelled ring, these trembling hands, these sweet reflected colours, white of daffodil and golden rose. All, was it vanity?

Circling the tortuous paths like some hectic wingless bird, he was called to the refectory by the tintinnabulation of a bell.

In the deep gloominous room despoiled of all splendour but for a dozen old Zurbarians flapping in their frames, a board, set out with manifest care, was prepared for the evening meal.

Serving both at Mass and table, it was the impish Chicklet who, with a zealous napkin-flick (modelled on the *mozos* of the little café-cum-restaurant 'As in Ancient Andalucia' patronized by rising toreadors and *aficionados* of the Ring), showed the Primate to his chair.

Having promised José the chef a handsome indulgence, absolved him from bigamy, and raised his wages, Cardinal Pirelli, in gastronomy nothing if not fastidious, had succeeded in inducing him to brave the ghostly basements of the monastery on the mount.

Perhaps of the many charges brought against the Primate

by his traducers, that of making the sign of the cross with his left foot at meals was the most utterly unfounded – looking for a foot-cushion would have been nearer the truth.

Addressing the table briefly in the harmonious Latin tongue, his Eminence sat down with an impenetrable sigh.

With vine-sprays clinging languorously to the candle-stands, rising from a bed of nespoles, tulips, and a species of wild orchid known as Devil's-balls, the Chicklet, to judge from his floral caprices, possessed a little brain of some ambition, not incapable of excess.

'I thought you were tired of jasmine, sir, and th'orange bloom's getting on,' he chirruped, coming forward with a cup of cold, clear consommé, containing hearts, coronets, and most of the alphabet in vermicelli.

'I'm tired, true, child; but not of jasmine,' the Primate returned, following a little contretemps of a marqués' crown, sinking amid a frolicsome bevy of *O's*.

'I hope it's right, sir?'

'Particularly excellent, child – tell José so.'

'Will I bring the trout, sir?'

'Go, boy,' the Cardinal bade him, opening a volume by the menu-stand formed of a satyr sentimentalizing over a wood-nymph's breasts.

While in retreat it was his fancy, while supping, to pursue some standard work of devotion, such as Orthodoxy so often encourages or allows: it was with just such a golden fairy-tale as this that he had once won a convert: Poor woman. What had become of her? Her enthusiasm, had it lasted? She had been very ardent. Perfervid! 'Instruction' would quite wear it out of them. St Xarifa's at fall of day; . . . an Autumn affair! Chrysanthemums; big bronze frizzlies. A Mrs Mandarin Dove. American. Ninety million sterling. Social pride and religious humility, how can I reconcile? The women in Chicago. My God! ! ! My little step-daughter. . . . Her Father, fortunately. . . . Yes, your Eminence, he's dead. And, oh, I'm *glad*. Is it naughty? And then her photograph *à la* Mary of Magdala, her hair unbound, décolletée, with a dozen long strands of pearls. 'Ever penitently yours, Stella Mandarin Dove.'

'I'd rather have had the blonde Ambassadress to the Court of St James,' he reflected, toying with the fine table-glass of an old rich glamour. A fluted bell cup sadly chipped provoked a criticism and a citation from Cassiodorus on the 'rude' ways of boys.

Revolving around an austere piece of furniture that resembled a Coffin-upon-six-legs, the Chicklet appeared absorbed.

'I hear it's the Hebrew in heaven, sir. Spanish is seldom spoken,' he exclaimed seraphically.

'Tut, dear child. Who says so?' the Primate wondered, his eyes wandering in melancholy towards the whitest of moons illumining elusively the room – illumining a long, sexless face with large, mauve, heroic lips in a falling frame, and an 'apachey', blue-cheeked Christ, the Cardinal noticed.

'Who, sir? Why, a gentlemen I was guide to once!'

The Cardinal chuckled comprehensively.

'I should surmise, dear child, there was little to show.'

'What, not the crypt, sir? Or the tomb of the beautiful Princess Eboli, the beloved of Philip the Second, sir?'

'Jewel boy. Yum-yum.' The Cardinal raised his glass.

'And the bells, sir? Last night, I'll tell you, sir, I thought I heard old "Wanda" on the wind.'

'Old Wanda, boy?'

'She rings for deaths, sir.'

'Nonsense, child; your little ears could never hear as far,' the Cardinal answered, deliberating if a lad of such alertness and perception might be entrusted to give him a henna shampoo: it was easy enough to remove the towels before it got too red. The difficulty was to apply the henna; evenly everywhere; fair play all round; no favouring the right side more than the left, but golden Justice for each grey hair. Impartiality: proportion! 'Fatal, otherwise,' the Primate reasoned.

'Are you ready for your Quail, sir?'

'Quail, quail? Bring on the *dulces*, boy,' his Eminence murmured, regarding absently through the window the flickering arc-lights of Clemenza far away. Dear beckoning lamps, dear calling lamps; lamps of theatres, cinemas, cabarets, bars, and dancings; lamps of railway-termini, and excessively lit hotels, *olé* to you, enchantress lights!

'And after all, dears, if I did,' the Cardinal breathed, tracing a caricature of his Holiness upon the table-cloth lightly with a dessert-fork. ('Which I certainly deny' . . .), he brooded, disregarding the dissolving Orange ice *à la* Marchioness of Macarnudo.

'Had you anything in the Lottery, sir?'

'Mind your business, boy, and remove this ballroom nastiness,' the Primate snapped.

It was while lingering, after dinner, over some choice vintage, that he oftenest would develop the outline of his Defence. To escape the irate horns of the Pontiff's bull (Die, dull beast) he proposed pressing the 'Pauline Privilege', unassailable, and confirmed *A.D. 1590* by Pope Sixtus V, home to the battered beauty of the Renaissance hilt. 'With the elegance and science', he murmured, 'of a *matador*.'

'I have the honour to wish you, sir, a good and pleasant night.'

'Thanks, boy.'

'And if you should want me, sir' . . . the youthful acolyte possessed the power to convey the unuttered.

'If?? . . . And say a fragrant prayer for me, child,' the Cardinal enjoined.

Resting an elbow among the nespoles and tulips (dawn-pink and scarlet, awakening sensitively in the candle-glow), he refilled reflectively his glass.

'God's providence is over all,' he told himself, considering dreamfully a cornucopia heaped with fruit. Being just then the gracious Autumn, a sweet golden-plum called 'Don Jaime of Castile' was in great perfection. It had been for the Southern orchards a singularly fertile year. Never were seen such gaily rouged peaches, such sleek violet cherries, such immensest white grapes. Nestling delectably amid its long, deeply-lobed leaves, a pomegranate (fruit of joy) attracted the Cardinal's hand.

Its seeds, round and firm as castanets, evoked the Ortiz. 'Ah, Jesus-Maria. The evening she waved her breasts at me!' he sighed, attempting to locate the distant lights of the Teatro Trinidades. Interpreting God's world, with her roguish limbs and voice, how witching the child had been but lately in *The Cistus of Venus*. Her valse-refrain 'Green Fairy Absinthe' (with a full chorus in tights) had been certainly, theatrically (if, perhaps, not socially), the hit of the season.

'The oleanders come between us,' he deliberated, oppressed by the amative complaint of some sweet-throated, summer night-bird.

'It's queer, dears, how I'm lonely!' he exclaimed, addressing the ancient Zurbarans flapping austerely in their frames.

The Archbishop of Archidona, for all his air of pomposity, looked not unsympathetic, neither, indeed, did a little lady with a nimbus, casting melting glances through the spokes of a mystic wheel.

'It's queer − ; you'd be surprised!' he murmured, rising and setting an oval moon-backed chair beside his own.

As usual the fanciful watch-dogs in the hills had begun their disquieting barking.

'The evenings are suicide,' he ruminated, idly replenishing his glass.

Sometimes, after the fifth or sixth bumper, the great Theresa herself would flit in from the garden. Long had her radiant spirit 'walked' the Desierto, seeking, it was supposed, a lost sheet of the manuscript of her *Way of Perfection*. It may have been following on the seventh or even the eighth bumper that the Primate remarked he was not alone.

She was standing by the window in the fluttered moonshine, holding a knot of whitish heliotropes.

'Mother?'

St John of the Cross could scarcely have pronounced the name with more wistful ecstasy.

Worn and ill, though sublime in laughter, exquisite in tenderness she came towards him.

'. . . Child?'

'Teach me, oh, teach me, dear Mother, the Way of Perfection.'

9

VERIFYING private dates, revising here and there the cathedral list of charges, Don Moscosco, the secretary of the chapter, seated before his usual bureau, was at the disposal of the public. A ministerial crisis had brought scattered Fashion home to town with a rush, and the pressure of work was enormous. 'Business' indeed had seldom been livelier, and chapels for Masses of special intention were being booked in advance as eagerly as opera-boxes for a première, or seaside-villas in the season.

'If the boys are brisk we might work in Joseph,' he mused, consulting with closely buttoned lips his Tarifa and plan; 'although I'd rather not risk a clash.'

Unknown to double-let like his compères on occasion outside, the swarthy little man was a master organizer, never forgetting that the chapter's welfare and prestige were inseparable from his own. Before allotting a chapel for a mass of Intent, it was his rule to analyse and classify the 'purity' of the intention (adding five per cent where it seemed not altogether to be chaste, or where the purpose was 'obscure').

'I see no inconvenience,' he murmured, gauging delicately the motif of a couple of great ladies of the bluest blood in Spain who were commissioning masses for the safety of a favourite toreador in an approaching *corrida*.

'Five hundred flambeaux, at least, between them,' the secretary, negligently, spat.

It was the twenty-first day of September (which is the Feast of St Firmin), and the sacristia, thronged with mantons and monsignori, resembled some vast shifting parterre of garden-flowers. Having a little altercation together, Mother Mary of the Holy Face and Mother Garcia of the Company of Jesus, alone, seemed stable. In honour of St Firmin the door of Pardon (closed half the year) had just been thrown open,

bringing from the basilica an odour of burning incense and
the strains of a nuptial march.

How many of the bridal guests knew of the coffin installed
in the next chapel but one? the little man wondered, rising
gallantly to receive a client.

She wore no hat, but a loose veil of gold and purple
enveloped her hair and face.

'I fear for him!'

'There, there. What is it?'

'I fear for him' – a man and the stars, nights of sweet love,
oleander flowers were in her voice.

By her immense hooped earrings, as large as armlets,
he knew her for the Adonira, the mistress of the toreador
Tancos.

'Come to me after the Friday *miserere*,' the official objected:
'let me entreat an appointment.'

'No. Now.'

'Well.'

'I want a Mass.'

'The intention being . . .?' The secretary sent up his brows
a little.

'His safety.'

'Whose?'

'My lover's.'

'But, señorita, it's all done! It's all *done*, dear lady,' the
words were on Don Moscosco's lips. Still, being the pink
of chivalry with *las mujeres* and a man of business, he murmured: 'With what quantity of lights?'

'Two. Just for him and me.'

'Tell me how you would prefer them,' he exclaimed,
glancing whimsically towards the canvas of the Magdalen
waylaying our Lord.

'How I would –' she stammered, opening and closing the
fansticks in her painted, love-tired hands.

'You would like them long and, I dare say, gross?'

'The best,' she breathed, almost fainting as though from
some fleeting delicious vision in the air.

'Leave it to me,' Don Moscosco said, and dropping

expressively his voice he added: 'Come, senorita; won't you make a date with me?'

'A date with you?'

'Ah-hah, the little Juans and Juanas; the charming cherubs!' the secretary archly laughed.

Returning however no answer she moved distractedly away.

'Two tapers! *Two*. As many only as the animal's horns. It's amazing how some women stint,' he reflected, faintly nettled.

The marriage ceremony was over. From the summit of the *giralda*, volley on volley, the vibrant bells proclaimed the consummation.

'It was all so quick; I hope it's valid?' Madame la Horra, the mother of the 'Bride', looked in to say. With a rose mole here and a strawberry mole there, men (those adorable monsters) accounted her entirely attractive.

'As *though* we should hurry, as *though* we should clip!'

'Eh?'

'As though we were San Eusebio, or the Pilar!'

'Forgive me, I came only to – I, ... I, ... I, ... I think I cried. The first spring flowers looked so beautiful.'

A mother's love, and contrition, perhaps, for her own shortcomings, the secretary brooded. 'I shall knock her off five per cent.'

Lost in bland speculation Don Moscosco considered the assembly collected outside the curtained *camarin* of the Virgin, where the gowns of the Image were dusted and changed.

For Firmin she usually wore an osprey or two and perfumed ball-gloves of Cordoba, and carried a spread fan of gold Guadalmedina lace. Among devotees of the sacristia it was a perpetual wonder to observe how her costumes altered her. Sometimes she would appear quite small, dainty, and French, at others she would recall the sumptuous women of the Argentine and the New World, and *aficionados* would lament their fairy isle of Cuba in the far-off Caribbean Sea.

Traversing imperiously the throng, Don Moscosco beheld the Duquesa DunEden.

Despite the optimism of the gazettes it looked as though

the Government must indeed be tottering, since the Duquesa
too was up from her country *quinta*.

'I have a request to make,' she began, sinking gratefully
to a chair.

'And charmed, in advance, to grant it.'

'I suppose you will have forgotten my old spaniel, Clapsey?'

'Ah, no more dogs!'

'She is passing-out, poor darling; and if the Church could
spare her some trifling favour – '

'Impossible.'

'She is the first toy tail for my little cemetery!'

'Quite impossible.'

'Poor pet,' the Duquesa exclaimed undaunted: 'she has
shared in her time my most intimate secrets: she stands for
early memories; what rambles we'd go together, she and I,
at Santander long ago! I remember Santander, Don Moscosco
(imagine), when there was not even an hotel! A little fishing-
village, so quiet, so quiet; ah, it was nicer, far, and more
exclusive then. . . .'

'I dare say.'

'You know my old, blind, and devoted friend was a gift
from the king; and this morning I said to her: "Clapsey!
Clapsey!" I said: "where's Carlos? Car-los . . . ?" And I'll
take my oath she rallied.'

Don Moscosco unbent a shade: 'A token, is she, of
royalty?'

'He also gave me "Flirt"!'

'Perhaps a brief mass . . .'

'Poor dearest: you'll keep it quiet and black?'

'We say all but the Black.'

'Oh?'

'One must draw the line somewhere!' Don Moscosco
declared, his eye roving towards a sacristan piloting a party
of travel-stained tourists, anxious to inspect the casket containing a feather from the Archangel Gabriel's wing.

'I know your creative taste! I rely on you,' the Duquesa
rose remarking.

Nevertheless, beneath the routine of the sacristia the air

was surcharged with tension. Rival groups, pro- or anti-Pirellian, formed almost irreconcilable camps, and partisanship ran high. Not a few among the cathedral staff had remained true to his Eminence, and Mother Sunlight, a charwoman (who sometimes performed odd jobs at the Palace), had taught her infant in arms to cry: 'Long live Spain and Cardinal Pirelli!'

Enough, according to some extreme anti-Pirellians, to be detrimental to her milk.

'I'm told the Pope has sent for him at last,' the laundress of the Basilica, Doña Consolacion, remarked to Sister June of the Way Dolorous.

'Indeed, indeed; it scarcely does to think!'

'Does anyone call to mind a bit of a girl (from Bilbao she was) that came once to stop as his niece?'

'Inclined to a moustache! Perfectly.'

'Phoebe Poco protests she wasn't.'

'Ah, well; a little *Don Juanism* is good,' the laundress said, and sighed.

'She declares . . .'

'She tells the truest lies, dear, of anyone I know!'

'Be that as it may it's certain he's getting increasingly eccentric. But Sunday last, entertaining his solicitor, it seems he ordered coffee after the *merienda* to be served in two chamber-pots.'

'Shameful – and he in his sunset years!' Mother Mary of the Holy Face commented, coming up with Tomás the beadle.

'It wouldn't surprise me', he declared, drowsily shaking a heavy bouquet of keys, 'if the thread of his life was about to break.'

'*Hombre* . . .' The laundress expressed alarm.

'Often now, towards Angelus, as I climb the tower, I hear the bell Herod talking with old Wanda in the loft. Eeeeeeee! Eeeeeeee! Horrible things they keep saying. Horrible things they keep saying.'

'Nonsense,' Doña Consolacion exclaimed, bestowing a smile on Monsignor Cuxa. Old, and did-did-doddery, how frail he seemed beside Father Fadrique, the splendid swagger of whose chasuble every woman must admire.

'Sent for to Rome: ah, *sangre mio*, I wish someone would send for me,' a girl, with a rose in the hair beautifully placed, sighed romantically.

'Be satisfied with Spain, my dear, and remember that no other country can compare with it!' Doña Generosa, an Aunt of one of the cathedral dancing-boys (who drew a small pension as the widow of the late Leader of applause at the Opera-house), remonstrated.

'I've never travelled', Doña Consolacion blandly confessed: 'but I dare say, dear, you can't judge of Egypt by *Aïda*.'

'Oh, can't I, though?' Doña Generosa sniffed, as the Father of an acolyte raised his voice.

'Spain!' he exclaimed, exalted, throwing a lover's kiss to the air, 'Spain! The most glorious country in God's universe, His admitted masterpiece, His gem, His – ' He broke off, his eloquence dashed by the sad music of Monsignor Cuxa's haemorrhage.

An office in the Chapel of the Crucifix was about to begin, recalling to their duties the scattered employees of the staff.

Hovering by the collection-box for the Souls in Hades, the Moorish maid from the College of Noble Damosels, bound on an errand of trust as ancient as the world, was growing weary of watching the people come and go.

'I must have missed him beneath the trees of the Market Place,' she ruminated, straightening on her head a turban wreathed in blossoms.

It was the matter of a message from Obdulia and Milagros to the radiant youth whose lips they were so idyllically (if perhaps somewhat licentiously) sharing.

'Fo' sh'o dis goin' to put dose heiresses in a quandry,' she deliberated, oppressed by her surroundings.

Eastern in origin like the Mesquita of Cordoba, it was impossible to forget that the great basilica of Clemenza was a Mosque profaned.

Designed for the cult of Islam, it made her African's warm heart bleed to behold it now. Would it were reconverted to its virginal state, and the cry of the muezzin be heard again summoning men to Muhammad's house! Yes, the restitution of the cathedral to Allah was Muley's cherished dream, and it consoled her, on certain days when she was homesick, to stand before the desecrated mihrab in worship, her face turned towards Africa, and palm-girt Marrakesh across the sea.

'I almost inclined to slip across to de Café Goya,' she breathed, moving aside for a shuffling acolyte, bearing a crucifix on a salver.

Led by the pious sisters of the noble order of the Flaming-Hood, the Virgin was returning to her niche.

She was arrayed as though bound for the Bull-ring, in a robe of peacock silk, and a mantilla of black lace.

'*Santissima!* . . .'

'*Elegantissima!*' Devotees dropped adoring to the floor.

Alone, the African remained erect.

'Muhammad mine, how long?' she sighed, turning entreating eyes to the cabbalistic letters and Saracenic tracings of the azulejos arabesques.

IO

MIDNIGHT had ceased chiming from the Belfry tower, and the last seguidilla had died away. Looking fresh as a rose, and incredibly juvenile in his pyjamas of silver-grey and scarlet (the racing-colours of Vittoria, Duchess of Vizeu), the Cardinal seemed disinclined for bed.

Surveying in detachment the preparatives for his journey (set out beneath an El Greco Christ, with outspread, delicate hands), he was in the mood to dawdle.

'These for the Frontier. Those for the train,' he exclaimed aloud, addressing a phantom porter.

Among the personalia was a passport, the likeness of identity showing him in a mitre, cute to tears, though, essentially, orthodox; a flask of Napoleon brandy, to be 'declared' if not consumed before leaving the Peninsula; and a novel, *Self Essence*, on the Index, or about to be.

'A coin, child, and put them for me on the rack,' he enjoined the wraith, regarding through the window the large and radiant stars.

The rhythmic murmur of a weeping fountain filled momentously the night.

Its lament evoked the Chicklet's sobs.

'Did I so wrong, my God, to punish him? Was I too hasty?' the Primate asked, repairing towards an ivory crucifix by Cano; 'yet, Thou knowest, I adore the boy!'

He paused a moment astonished by the revelation of his heart.

'It must have been love that made me do it,' he smiled, considering the incident in his mind. Assuredly the rebuff was unpremeditated, springing directly from the boy's behaviour, spoiling what might have been a ceremony of something more than ordinary poignance.

It had come about so.

There had been held previously during the evening, after

the Basilica's scheduled closing hour, a service of 'Departure', fastidiously private, in the presence only of the little Ostensoir-swinger 'Chicklet', who, missing all the responses, had rushed about the cathedral after mice; for which the Cardinal, his sensitiveness hurt by the lad's disdain and frivolity, had afterwards confined him alone with them in the dark.

'Had it been Miguilito or Joaquin, I should not have cared a straw for their interest in the mice! But somehow this one – ' the Cardinal sighed.

Adjusting in capricious abstraction his cincture, he turned towards the window.

It was a night like most.

Uranus, Venus, Saturn showed overhead their wonted lights, while in the sun-weary cloisters, brightly blue-drenched by the moon, the oleanders in all their wonder – (how swiftly fleeting is terrestrial life) – were over, and the bougainvillaeas reigned instead.

'It must have been that,' he murmured, smiling up at the cathedral towers.

Poor little Don Wilful. The chapter-mice, were they something so amusing to pursue? 'I've a mind, do you know, to join you, boy; I declare I feel quite rompish!' he told himself, gathering up, with a jocund pounce, a heavy mantle of violet cloth-of-gold.

'Tu-whit, tu-whoo.'

Two ominous owls answered one another across the troubled garden.

'I declare I feel –' his hand sought vaguely his heart: it went pit-a-pat for almost nothing now! 'The strain of the diocese,' he breathed, consulting a pierglass of the period of Queen Isabella 'the Ironical'.

'The Court may favour Paul Orna, but in my opinion no one can rival Joey Paquin's "line"; I should like to see him "tailor" our Madonna; one of the worst and most expensively dressed little saints in the world,' his Eminence commented, folding toga-wise the obedient tissues about his slender form.

An aspect so correctly classic evoked the golden Rome of the Imperial Caesars rather than the so tedious Popes.

Repeating a sonorous line from Macrobius, the Cardinal measured himself a liqueur-glass of brandy.

Poor little Don Bright-eyes, alone in the obscurity. It was said a black dervish 'walked' the Coro – one of the old habitués of the Mosque.

'Jewel boy. Yum-yum,' he murmured, setting a mitre like a wondrous mustard-pot upon his head. *Omnia vanitas*; it was intended for Saint Peter's.

'Tu-whit, tu-whoo!'

Grasping a Bishop's stave, remotely shepherdessy, his Eminence opened softly the door.

Olé, the Styx!

Lit by Uranus, Venus, and Saturn only, the consummate tapestries on the stairs recording the Annunciation, Conception, Nativity, Presentation, Visitation, Purification, and Ascension of the Virgin made welcome milestones.

'. . . Visitation, Purification.' The Primate paused on the penultimate step.

On a turn of the stair by the 'Conception', a sensitive panel, chiefly white, he had the impression of a wavering shadow, as of someone following close behind.

Continuing, preoccupied, his descent, he gained a postern door. A few deal cases, stoutly corded for departure, were heaped about it. 'His Holiness, I venture to predict, will appreciate the excellence of our home-grown oranges, not to be surpassed by those of any land,' the Primate purred, sailing forth into the garden.

Oh, the lovely night! Oh, the lovely night! He stood, leaning on his wand, lost in contemplation of the miracle of it.

'Kek, kek, kex.'

In the old lead aqua-butt, by the Chapter-house, the gossiping bull-frogs were discussing their great horned and hoofed relations. . . .

'There was never yet one that didn't bellow!'

'Kek, kek, kex.'

'*Los toros*, forsooth!'

'A blessed climate. . . .' The Primate pursued his way.

It was in the face of a little door like the door of a tomb

in the cathedral's bare façade (troubled only by the fanciful shadows of the trees) that he presently slipped his key.

Olé, the Styx!

He could distinguish nothing clearly at first beyond the pale forked fugitive lightning through the triple titanic windows of the chancel.

'Sunny-locks, Don Sunny-locks?' the Cardinal cooed, advancing diffidently, as though mistrustful of meeting some charwoman's pail.

Life had prepared him for these surprises.

Traversing on his crozier a spectral aisle, he emerged upon the nave.

Flanked by the chapels of the Crucifix, of the Virgin, of the Eldest Son of God, and of divers others, it was here as bright as day.

Presumably Don April-showers was too self-abashed to answer, perhaps too much afraid. ... 'If I recollect, the last time I preached was on the theme of Flagellation,' the Primate mused, considering where it caught the moon the face of a fakir in ecstasy carved amid the corbels.

'A sermon I propose to publish,' he resolved, peering into the chapel of Santa Lucia. It was prepared, it seemed, in anticipation of a wedding, for stately palms and branches of waxen peach-bloom stood all about. 'Making circulation perilous,' the Primate mused, arrested by the determined sound of a tenacious mouse gnawing at a taper-box.

'An admirable example in perseverance!' he mentally told himself, blinking at the flickering mauve flowers of light in the sanctuary lamps.

Philosophizing, he penetrated the engrailed silver doors connecting the chapel of the Magdalen.

The chapel was but seldom without a coffin, and it was not without one now.

Since the obsequies of the brilliant Princess Eboli it had enjoyed an unbroken vogue.

Besides the triumphal monument of the beloved of Philip II, the happy (though, perhaps, not the happiest) achievement of Jacinto Bisquert, there were also mural tablets to the

Duchesses of Pampeluna (*née* Mattosinhos), Polonio (*née* Charona), and Sarmento (*née* Tizzi-Azza), while the urn and ashes of the Marchioness of Orcasitas (*née* Ivy Harris) were to be found here too, far from the race and turmoil of her native New York.

'*Misericordia!* Are you there, boy?' the Cardinal asked, eyeing abstractedly the twin-hooded caryatides that bore the fragile casket white as frozen snow containing the remains of the all-amiable princess.

Folded in dainty sleep below, he perceived the lad.

Witching as Eros, in his loose-flowing alb, it seemed profane to wake him!

'... And lead us not into temptation,' the Primate murmured, stooping to gaze on him.

Age of bloom and fleeting folly: Don Apple-cheeks!

Hovering in benison he had almost a mind to adopt the boy, to enter him for Salamanca or, remoter, Oxford, and perhaps (by some bombshell codicil) even make him his heir.

'How would you like my Velasquez, boy? ...' His Eminence's hand framed an airy caress. 'Eh, child? Or my Cano Crucifix? ... I know of more than one bottle-nosed dowager who thinks she'll get it! ... You know my Venetian-glass, Don Endymion, is among the choicest in Spain. ...'

There was a spell of singing silence, while the dove-grey mystic lightning waxed and waned.

Aroused as much by it as the Primate's hand, the boy started up with a scream of terror.

'Ouch, sir!'

'*Olé*, boy?'

The panic appeared to be mutual.

'*Oufarella!* ...' With the bound of a young faun the lad was enskied amid the urns and friezes.

The heart in painful riot, the Primate dropped to a chair.

Ouching, Oléing and Oufarelling it, would they never have done? Paternostering Phoebe Poco (shadowing her master) believed they never would. 'Old ogre: why can't he be brisk about it and let a woman back to bed?' she wondered.

Thus will egotism, upon occasion, eclipse morality outright.

'And always be obedient, dear child,' the Cardinal was saying; 'it is one of the five things in Life that matter most.'

'Which are the others, sir?'

'What others, boy?'

'Why, the other four!'

'Never mind now. Come here.'

'Oh, tral-a-la, sir.' Laughing like some wild spirit, the lad leapt (Don Venturesome, Don Venturesome, his Eminence trembled) from the ledge of A Virtuous Wife and Mother (Sarmento, *née* Tizzi-Azza) to the urn of Ivy, the American marchioness.

'You'd not do that if you were fond of me, boy!' The Cardinal's cheek had paled.

'But I *am* fond of you, sir! Very. Caring without caring: don't you know?'

'So you do care something, child?'

'I care a lot! . . .'

Astride the urn of Ivy – poised in air – the Chicklet pellucidly laughed.

'Tell me so again,' the Cardinal begged, as some convent-bell near by commenced sounding for office before aurora.

For behind the big windows the stars were fading.

'It's today they draw the Lottery, sir.'

'Ah; well, I had nothing in it. . . .'

'00050 – that's me!'

The Cardinal fetched a breath.

'Whose is it, boy?' He pointed towards the bier.

'A Poet, sir.'

'A Poet?'

'The name though he had escapes me. . . .'

'No matter then.'

'Where would his soul be now, sir?'

'Never mind, boy; come here.'

'In the next world I should like to meet the Cid, and Christopher Columbus!'

'Break your neck, lad, and so you will.'

'Pablo Pedraza too. . . .'

'Who's that, boy?'

'He was once the flower of the ring, sir; superior even to Tancos; you may recollect he was tossed and ruptured at Ronda; the press at the time was full of it.'

'Our press, dear youth, our press! ! ! . . .' the Primate was about to lament, but an apologetic sneeze from a chapel somewhere in the neighbourhood of the Eldest Son of God arrested him.

It seemed almost to confirm the legend of old, Mosque-sick 'Suliman', said to stalk the temple aisles.

The Cardinal twirled challengingly his stave – *Bible* v. *Koran*; a family case; cousins; Eastern, equally, each; hardy old perennials, no less equivocal and extravagant, often, than the ever-adorable *Arabian Nights*! 'If only Oriental literature *sprawled* less, was more concise! It should concentrate its roses,' he told himself, glancing out, inquiringly, into the nave.

Profoundly soft and effaced, it was a place full of strange suggestion. Intersecting avenues of pillared arches, upbearing waving banners, seemed to beckon towards the Infinite.

'Will you be obliged to change, sir; or shall you go straight through?'

'Straight through, boy.'

'I suppose, as you cross the border, they'll want to know what you have to declare.'

'I have nothing, child, but myself.'

'If 00050 is fortunate, sir, I hope to travel, too – India, Persia, Peru! ! . . . Ah, it's El Dorado, then.'

'El Dorado, boy?' The Cardinal risked an incautious gesture.

'Oh, tral-a-la, sir.' Quick as Cupid the lad eluded him on the evasive wings of a laugh; an unsparing little laugh, sharp and mocking, that aroused the Primate like the thong of a lash.

Of a long warrior line, he had always regarded disobedience (in others) as an inexcusable offence. What would have happened before the ramparts of Zaragoza, Valladolid, Leon, Burgos, had the men commanded by Ipolito Pirelli in the

Peninsular War refused to obey? To be set at defiance by a youngster, a mere cock-robin, kindled elementary ancestral instincts in the Primate's veins.

'Don't provoke me, child, again.'

From pillared ambush Don Prudent saw well, however, to effect a bargain.

'You'd do the handsome by me, sir; you'd not be mean?'

'Eh? . . .'

'The Fathers only give us texts; you'd be surprised, your Greatness, at the stinginess of some!'

'. . .?'

'You'd run to something better, sir; you'd give me something more substantial?'

'I'll give you my slipper, child, if you don't come here!' his Eminence warned him.

'*Oufarella*. . . .'

Sarabandish and semi-mythic was the dance that ensued. Leading by a dozen derisive steps Don Light-of-Limb took the nave. In the dusk of the dawn it seemed to await the quickening blush of day like a white-veiled negress.

'*Olé*, your Purpleship!'

Men (eternal hunters, novelty seekers, insatiable beings) men in their natural lives, pursue the concrete no less than the ideal – qualities not inseldom found combined in fairy childhood.

'*Olé*.'

Oblivious of sliding mantle the Primate swooped.

Up and down, in and out, round and round 'the Virgin' over the worn tombed paving, through St Joseph, beneath the cobweb banners from Barocco to purest Moorish, by early Philip, back to Turân-Shâh – 'Don't exasperate me, boy – along the raised tribunes of the choristers and the echoing coro – the great fane (after all) was nothing but a cage; God' cage; the cage of God! . . .

Through the chancel windows the day was newly breaking as the oleanders will in the spring.

Dispossessed of everything but his fabulous mitre, the Primate was nude and elementary now as Adam himself.

'As you can perfectly see, I have nothing but myself to declare,' he addressed some phantom image in the air.

With advancing day Don Skylark *alias* Bright-eyes *alias* Don Temptation it seemed had contrived an exit, for the cathedral was become a place of tranquillity and stillness.

'Only myself.' He had dropped before a painting of old Dominic Theotocópuli, the Greek, showing the splendour of Christ's martyrdom.

Peering expectantly from the silken parted curtains of a confessional, paternostering Phoebe Poco caught her breath.

Confused not a little at the sight before her, her equilibrium was only maintained by the recollection of her status: 'I'm an honest widow; so I know what men are, bless them!' And stirred to romantic memories she added: 'Poor soul, he had the prettiest teeth. . . .'

Fired by fundamental curiosity, the dame, by degrees, was emboldened to advance. All over was it, with him, then? It looked as though his Eminence was far beyond Rome already.

'May God show His pity on you, Don Alvaro of my heart.'

She remained a short while lost in mingled conjecture. It was certain no morning bell would wake him.

'So.' She stopped to coil her brier-wood chaplet about him in order that he might be less uncovered. 'It's wonderful what us bits of women do with a string of beads, but they don't go far with a gentleman.'

Now that the ache of life, with its fevers, passions, doubts, its routine, vulgarity, and boredom, was over, his serene, unclouded face was a marvelment to behold. Very great distinction and sweetness was visible there, together with much nobility, and love, all magnified and commingled.

'*Adios*, Don Alvaro of my heart,' she sighed, turning away towards the little garden door ajar.

Through the triple windows of the chancel the sky was clear and blue – a blue like the blue of lupins. Above him stirred the wind-blown banners in the Nave.

*Some more books published by Penguins
are described on the
following pages*

COLETTE

'I know of few works which have today offered me such an amused and perfect joy' – *André Gide*
'There is nothing to explain, nothing to criticize, one has only to admire' – *Henri de Montherlant*

Four more titles have been published simultaneously, adding to the considerable number of Colette's novels now available in Penguins. They are:

Claudine at School

The intimate secrets of a sixteen-year-old make a novel which is more daring than *Bonjour Tristesse*, more scandalous than *Lolita*.

Claudine Married

Compared to this story of a young married woman's lesbian affair, encouraged by her husband, '*The Well of Loneliness* looks reassuringly English' – *Daily Telegraph*

Claudine and Annie

Her fourth novel describes precisely and amusingly a woman's emancipation from a tedious marriage.

Claudine in Paris

At seventeen Claudine begins to explore Paris and its vices, and gets more and more involved with a remote cousin old enough to be her father.

Other titles by Colette:

CHANCE ACQUAINTANCES and JULIE DE CARNEILHAN
CHÉRI and THE LAST OF CHÉRI
GIGI and THE CAT
RIPENING SEED
THE VAGABOND

F. SCOTT FITZGERALD

Tender is the Night

Fitzgerald's most complete novel; a penetrating indictment of the twenties.

The Last Tycoon

His unfinished novel is a description of the Hollywood of the 1930s.

The Diamond as Big as the Ritz

AND OTHER STORIES

A collection of his best short work. The title story is a symbolic fairy tale about unlimited wealth.

This Side of Paradise

His first novel concerns the bright young things of the Jazz Age.

The Great Gatsby

This tragic story of a mysterious, fabulously wealthy man is perhaps his most famous work.

For a complete list of books available please write to Penguin Books whose address can be found on the back of the title page